JOE HAYES

Always Above Lava

DEDICATION

This book was written when I was a younger man, then shelved for a decade. I finally came back to finish my story.

It is dedicated to my River Tribe, my mentors, my wild kayak brothers and sisters, to AO, to boatmen of all genders, fireside storytellers, safety boating, beer-hoarding, boulder scouting, groover lugging, family. See you in an eddy soon, I hope.

To Robin for all the love.

And to Jerry Weber and Sue Holt, for taking me, and many others, down there in the first place.

Keep it Straight in the Big Stuff, Stay
out of the Bad Stuff.
- Classic Boatman Advice

You cannot see Grand Canyon in one
view, as if it were a changeless spec-
tacle from which a curtain might be
lifted, but to truly see it you must
toil from month to month through its
labyrinths.

-Major John Wesley Powell,
boatman.

Contents

1

Always Above Lava

Tracer let out a rebel yell, and beat a tattoo on his boat, then reached to high-five both Harper and AJ, bobbing next to him in the eddy. They howled and giggled, fumbling their paddles with wet hands and alternated foolish grins with quick searching glances upstream. Encased in their three kayaks, their spray skirts sealing them in, their battered helmets leaned together in a seething river eddy just yards below the huge madness of Lava Falls.

They had just run Lava, the defining monster rapid of the Grand Canyon, after weeks of inexorably approaching it. Many river miles and moments had passed to reach this day, and now they felt relief. But they were not done with Lava Falls yet. The kayakers watched for the four rafts of their party, still scouting, still adjusting their raft rigs and their personal mojo before pulling away from shore to find their fate in this pass through one of the greatest hydraulic displays in North America. The kayakers in the eddy were the scouts, point men and safety boaters for the rafts above, but their symbiotic group dynamic had become strained in recent miles.

The kayakers were in a rush of spirits, giddy with leftover adrenaline, joy, and relief. They tried to reconstruct what had actually happened to them and their crafts in the powerful water just moments ago. Like a pack of hounds, they talked over each other without caring, contradicted and affirmed each others account, leaned onto each others boats to pass a celebratory joint, and formed a linked floating kayak pod in the swirling eddy.

"My entry was way off the bubble line, but my patented fear-crazed correction stroke saved me."

"I followed your line, but I should have known better."

"That second wave buried me so deep, it got dark and the stars came out."

"You have to move left before Cheesegrater, or the black hole overcomes the downstream gravity, and the Kahuna wave eats you."

"Still, not bad, boys. We're Below Lava and still breathing," said AJ, exhaling and passing the joint.

Tracer grinned his wolf smile. "No way. Not really below. Once you're committed to boating Grand Canyon, you are never really below Lava Falls again. You are either in Lava, or Above Lava. We are all still Above Lava, but now starting on our next cycle."

"Always Above Lava" said Harper softly, and he directed their attention upstream with a nod as the first raft of their group floated into view on the horizon line.

Simultaneously, the three clicked to attention. One pinched out the joint, then quickly zipped away the lighter. Adjusting paddle grips and shoulder muscles, they silently released their grips on each other's cockpits. They focused on the raft and the wild water above them. After so many river miles together, they had formed a mind-melded water organism, able to communicate strategy with nods, eyebrows and intuition. Surfing river waves was still their reason for being, but safety boating for the rafts at big rapids was the one responsibility of the trip they took seriously. They all knew too well what it was like to be near drowning in a big rapid. Besides, there was always the potential for their second favorite river activity: swimmer chase-and-rescue.

Lava Falls was serious. With complex, variable hydraulics and abundant power, it was the Grand Canyon river trip's exclamation point and the boatman's final exam, taken after 179 miles of steadily escalating preliminaries. Lava created more adrenaline than Heinz created ketchup. Water was high this spring, and today Lava was rather huge, roaring with 23,000 cubic feet per second of water, making the central Ledge Hole a sick pit large enough to hold a school bus. It was also forming a flipper wave of certain disaster off the cheesegrater-surfaced Black Rock on the right side, where the kayakers had just made their run. That standard right run was closed to rafts at this high flow level. The rafts would have to run left of the Ledge Hole, close to the left rocks, a first for all the boatmen.

The lead raft was entering the left side, trying to slip between the hazards of the center Ledge Hole and the left bank hydraulics formed by shoreline boulders. It was a tricky entry, because the sharp drop at the head of the rapid kept all but the spray invisible from the river above. You simply scouted from the shore, trying not to become hypnotized and cowed by the deep pulsing roar of the Ledge Hole. Then you climbed in your boat and pulled out on memory, following the mythical, semi-visible line of bubbles which formed on the smooth water at the top of the rapid. Legend had it, the bubble line led to the ideal entry over the lip. Follow the bubbles, they know where they're going, boatmen told each other.

Unexpectedly, it was Goat's raft running first, with the Goat Boatman promoted from his trip-long place as last raft/sweeper, to be the Lava Probe. The Goat, who was the kayakers sole remaining ally among the rafts, was the right choice, for beneath his sleepy drawl he had an unerring sense of river hydraulics and raft trajectory. The other boatmen and passengers watched anxiously from the scout rocks above, trying to memorize his series of oar strokes and his approach angle. The Ledge Hole looked like it would tear off your arms and legs if you went in it today. The Goat Boat crested the first ripple and for an instant Goat gazed benignly down upon the glory of Lava Falls, looking like a farmer trying to decide if it may rain. His boat bucked once and disappeared from the view of the kayakers below behind a white standing wave.

Ugly When It Happens

In truth, the three-man kayak squad in the eddy and the Goat Boatman had become virtual outcasts in camp in the last few days before Lava, as a virus of social recrimination had swept the group. Their long, sunny, laughter-filled trip had entered a state of tension. Differences between the rowdy single males and the kitchen monitor group of wives had ballooned into a rift. In the last few days the group had drifted into a twilight zone of dissension. Differences in scouting and rigging pace, preferred food, sugar and alcohol intake, and camp work/shirk ethics all took on expanded importance in the absence of any real disasters. Like every river trip, their group was a tribal microcosm, and their tribe had become ill below Olo camp.

Dr. Dukie, Christian and Terry rowed rafts, and all had their wives with them. Terry had his 18-year old daughter Sasha, as well. Since Goat was the only bachelor boatman, he tended to eat and drink with the kayakers in camp. AJ and Natalie were newlyweds, married on Day 4 at Nankoweap Camp, and they still had a shine to them, loved by all and lost in each other. Therefore, AJ existed as a kind of social bridge between the increasingly unkept kayakers and the boatmen's wives.

But, the kayakers were inept at making the crossing. Several of the boatman's wives on the trip were childless women of a certain age, and they normally formed a mature, cheerful and resourceful feminine cabinet. Now it seemed to Team Goat they had undergone a gradual transformation into a cabal of Kitchen Ladies, who united in a synchronized pre-menopausal rage against the freeloading males of the group, in a display that had erupted after 14 days at Olo camp. So, it came to pass that the wrath of the Kitchen Ladies was visited upon the unworthy male element, the self-christened Team Goat.

Team Goat was composed of Tracer, Harper, and Goat, with AJ as a sort of volunteer member and group liaison officer. The Goat Boatman and Tracer were former guides, river pros, and their abilities underpinned the entire group safety when the shit came down, or looked like it might. But they had not been called on recently, as the group's ability had improved with the miles of practice. Meanwhile, Team Goat had concentrated on researching and solving the multi-variant Grand Canyon Fun Maximization equation. Their research included seeking hidden side canyon places of outstanding beauty, catching trout on a dry fly, and climbing to likely Anasazi shelter ledges to smoke and visit with their ancestors. The team members were veterans of so many river campaigns, youthful excesses, and personal experience that they needed strong medicine to feel good. They were all in their element down here, free of their accumulated worries and responsibilities, and they reveled in their river escape. Together they sipped whiskey and cackled by the evening fire, drifted far behind the group and took extended backcountry climbs up side canyons that brought them into camp late after the kitchen box was already carried up. In their gravest transgression, they had paid too much attention, with no real intent on seduction, to Sasha, the nubile high school female in the group, daughter of Terry the boatman. The kitchen ladies had their husbands along, and felt that an example must be set regarding flirting with younger women. Sharp words had been exchanged in recent days, on topics ranging from beer hoarding and candy bar hogging to more hurtful accusations. Team Goat withdrew from social interaction, sulked among themselves, and crafted Anasazi split twig figurines twisted into mountain goat shapes. In an inspired retaliation, Harper began to rig the group toilet in ever more distant, hidden and precarious billy goat locations. The tribe members had all become overly in touch with their inner child.

Of course, the kayakers had reinforced common prejudices against their kind by shamelessly surfing to exhaustion on river hydraulics, fly fishing, sponging beers and candy bars from rafts all day, power-shirking camp chores, and generally striving to exceed the daily fun ration.

The kayak squad harmony was still enviable. Tracer was the leader and Chaos Agent, a coyote wave master stirring the pot with Kokopelli spirit. AJ was calm, friendly, blue-eyed devilry, and Harper was in the middle, with a bold line, huge surfing wrecks, a big appetite, and a spirit of no holding back. The kayaks would arrive at a rapid, or better, a surfing wave with a return eddy, and assess the situation's fun potential like trained shepherd dogs. They cruised into independent stations around a desirable surf wave, popping in and out of eddies, crisscrossing each other's tracks and timing one's charge onto the wave face with another's stylish endo off of it. They could communicate without set signals or speech, operating in the roar of spray. Led on by the deft wave touch, howl, and insane laughter of Tracer, they had formed a three-headed pack of river dolphins. AJ's and Harper's boating skill levels had risen like spring runoff, and brought them great satisfaction. Early in the trip after Christian's raft flip, the kayaks had set the Z-drag, caught the swimmers, and directed the rescue of the wrapped raft. That boosted their stock for days, but since then they had neglected their group politics, ogled the young girl, overshirked and understroked the Kitchen Ladies management team. Their natural allies, the trip leader Dr. Dukie and the Boatmen-With-Wives Along, could not protect them now without sacrificing themselves, and could only exchange sympathetic glances after episodes of petty bickering or recrimination in camp. They had rested too long on their laurels, and had earned their status as Team Goat as the river miles eroded away the veneer of polite behavior.

Lava Washes Away All Sins

The Goat Boatman nailed the entry to Lava Falls. His raft fit just between the bad neighborhoods at the top of the rapid, edged past the Ledge Hole, and crashed straight on through the middle and lower waves. Goat's raft swept by the kayaks, and he worked with his oars to catch the lower left eddy at the hot spring, a quarter mile downstream. He made it and waved a salute to the safety boating kayakers as they clustered behind their rock.

Waiting again in the eddy, the kayakers began to shiver. Their chatter dropped off, as the adrenaline of their own runs faded from their systems. The remaining rafters continued to scout, distantly visible on prominent rocks upstream.

"They've officially gone beyond power scouting now. They have fallen under the spell of the Ledge Hole," said Tracer.

"Please do not eat me, O great and terrible river god," intoned Harper, a former Catholic altar boy.

"Remember, if these rafts flip, save the beer first" stated AJ.

Finally, the power scouters waved a signal to the kayakers, and disappeared back to their rafts. After a long absence, a raft suddenly appeared at the river horizon moving to them, and dropped off the end of the world into the rapid. It was Terry and Sasha, the father-daughter team, and they almost hit it perfect. Their boat was perhaps one-half boat width too far to the center. It caught just the edge of the Ledge Hole, the outside envelope of the great depression in the river surface that was the most fearful liquid real estate in the Colorado Plateau. The lip of the powerful backwards hydraulic stopped their forward momentum, and they hung poised in mid-rapid for an instant. Their raft was on the cusp between two downhill surfaces, one leading downriver and one leading sideways into a snarling pit. As Terry threw himself forward against both oars, still planted deep in the river, the raft bounced in place one time, skipping on the speeding water surfaces beneath it. The kayakers were alarmed and all emerged into the current, out from the protection of the eddy rock. They quickly arrayed into downstream tailwaters in chase position, waiting for the outcome. Another second and the raft burst free, shooting away from the Ledge Hole, riding on the downriver velocity, and slamming through a series of overhead standing waves. The shock of the waves threw the boatman out of his seat sideways, but he clung to his oar handles like handrails in a train wreck, and he stayed in the raft. His daughter disappeared beneath green water in the front of the boat, and then her dripping head and hands clutching the safety lines reappeared with a huge smile as the raft swept passed the kayaks, past the lower eddy and quickly around the bend downriver.

The Goat Boatman in the eddy below gave the second raft a double thumbs up as they swept by, and rowed his raft back into position a potato gun shot distance below the rapid. The kayakers struggled a hundred yards back upstream on the river's margin, and finally regained their position behind the boulder at the top of the eddy. The eddy was bubbling like a soup pot, and simply bracing and waiting in the water of the eddy required constant adjustment. The kayaks had been waiting for rafts in the eddy for over an hour now, and their buzz, body temperature, and blood sugar levels were all below optimum. As they waited for the last rafts and shivered, self-righteous attitudes about overscouting rookies, a kayaker's cellular-level need for constant candy bars, and of course the elevated physical and mental commitment required to survive in a kayak versus a raft began to surface in their minds. Finally, the remaining two rafts of their group appeared on the river above, close together and moving in quick succession toward the brink at the top of the rapid.

The first raft held Della, head of the Kitchen Ladies, with her husband Christian rowing. Their raft was well away from the Ledge Hole, but too far away. They dropped over the lip and immediately hit the lead wave on river left formed by a submerged boulder. Their raft was wrenched sideways and jumped as if cuffed from below by a dragon's tail. Both of them were launched out of the boat and disappeared in the river.

"Two swimmers!" cried Harper, as the kayakers' eyes popped and their boats began to scramble out of the eddy. The kayakers had been clustered together and their paddles clashed for a moment in haste, one bonking another's helmet, as they went into full ignition. Three strokes brought the kayaks streaming out of the eddy and into the racing water in chase formation, banking downstream turns as the velocity jumped and the direction of water beneath them reversed. The final raft was now entering the rapid above, the swimmers had not yet surfaced anywhere, and the empty raft was charging down on them, upright and rudderless.

The kayakers burst out of their eddy and into this fluid, ecstatically uncertain scene in fierce chase, tracking multiple converging and diverging objects and assuming separate responsibilities. In a few seconds, the two swimmers had bobbed to the surface in the maelstrom, each on opposite sides of the empty raft and moving swiftly downstream. The raft was upon them, splitting the group and riding down Harper's kayak like a bright yellow freight train. Harper braced with his paddle, trying to block and capture the oncoming raft with his kayak bow. His upstream paddle blade was pinned against the side of the raft, and then he was pushed over, flipped downstream by the blunt nose of the raft.

Automatically, he set up in roll position underwater, swept with his paddle, and rolled towards the surface on the upstream side. Instead of surfacing as he had a hundred other times, he struggled upside down for a long nasty moment, unable to complete his Eskimo roll and reach air, trapped under the bottom of the raft. The front of the raft had ridden over his kayak and was preventing his head from surfacing. Shit! Stuck under a raft in the middle of Lava Falls. But there was still plenty of breath in him. The current pushed him against the raft and fought him when he tried to move. He probed at the raft belly with his paddle from underwater. He fought back a sudden urge to spear and stab at the smooth rubber underside of the raft, to force it aside, to shred it with his fingernails. It sat anchored above, between him and the atmosphere he sought, rushing downstream with a placid uncaring weight. Still underwater, Harper struggled against the current back to the starting position for a roll and retucked his head. Like a switch-hitter changing batting sides in baseball, he mentally reversed his muscle movements, gathered his confidence, and reversed his paddle position for an offside roll. He felt the first surge in his chest of involuntary lung contractions, as his brain cortex tried to command him to take a breath. Suppressing a mounting sense of urgency, he made one calm smooth paddle sweep guided from deep muscle memory. He rolled up downstream, against the current but out from under the raft roof, slowly emerging with his kayak T-boned like a hood ornament across the front of an empty raft still sweeping through Lower Lava Falls. He sucked in a lovely breath of Arizona air. Though he felt he had been gone a long time, they had only raced on 50 yards downstream.

In the river next to him, the other two kayaks had both caught up with swimming Della and corralled her between their boats. Her bobbing head was barely visible at the water surface but her hand was gamely clutching the front end loop of Tracer's boat.

AJ and Tracer looked over from their kayaks, openly relieved to see Harper surface from beneath the raft. Harper grasped the bowline of the raft that had bulldozed him, and swiveled his head searching for Christian, the other swimmer. He saw him just downstream, being pulled into the Goat's raft, which had popped out of the lower eddy as the swimmer floated past. And Dr. Dukie was now coming towards Lower Lava with a boat full of passengers in the last raft, after a clean run past the Ledge Hole. Although the whole group was still sweeping through the lower rapids, everyone was accounted for. Harper took another wonderfully deep breath of air and held the empty raft at a safe distance on its bowline leash.

Tequila Beach Party

Harper pushed free of the raft, and paddled over to Goat's raft as the whole group swung around the bend to Tequila Beach, the big slow eddy below Lower Lava. He handed the bowline off to Goat, and saw the final raft coming down to join them in the eddy.

"Not Baaaaaad!" bleated the Goat, in his trademark line.

"I found this raft floating unattended. Any idea who it belongs to?" said Harper, with his heartbeat still pounding in his helmet and water draining from his sinuses.

"It looked like you were trying to mate with it underwater there, amigo. Don't you know the drain hole is in the back of the boat?" smiled Goat.

"A periodic inspection of the raft floor is good practice." answered Harp with a weak smile, "Nice job on the swimmer rescue, Goat. "

"Well, nice job throwing yourself in front of a runaway train, man! It could have been a long chase down to Lake Mead after an empty raft."

All four rafts and three kayaks now regrouped and pulled into Tequila Beach together, with much backslapping, catcalling and hullaballoo. The tribe poured out of their boats, as Della released her grip on the kayak end-loop and emerged dripping from the river. As her husband hugged her tight at the water's edge and the boats were tied off, an earnest search for all the remaining beer supply was begun on the rafts. After a noisy round of toasts and cheers, lunch was broken out and the people began to wolf down sandwiches. A great bubble of euphoria and joyful noise radiated upward from their beach. The three kayakers and the Goat sat sprawled amid the group, their spray jackets peeled off and their fleece underlayers drying. Harper looked around at the cast of happy characters, and felt the undercurrents of tension dissolving, replaced by relief, buoyant good will and shared celebration. He realized that he had a profound affection for all these people, that each of them was part of what had made the trip work. He felt deeply tired, aware of his blessings, serene and happy to be alive. He took a bite of salami and bagel, the sharp taste of mustard on his tongue like a blessing, with a sip of beer as Amen.

Della approached them, carrying an ammo can marked "Spices". She opened it and ceremoniously poured it in front of them, spilling out a bounty of hidden chocolate candy bars, in fresh unsullied wrappers. Recognizing the honor of the peace offering, the team whooped, pawed the candy, then joyfully bowed in rough unison in the sand at her feet like demented Muslims, crying "We are not worthy!"

She shook her head and looked at them tolerantly. "That's true enough."

Della was vulnerable, still wet and disoriented from her swim.

She looked at Tracer and AJ and took a deep breath. She hesitated and then said with a shy smile, "You guys made a big difference today. I was so glad to see your boats coming after me when I finally surfaced. Your beautiful kayaks. Hey, why did you both come after me, and not after Christian?"

"Yeah, good question!" hollered Christian good-naturedly from his raft with his arm in the beer bag.

They glanced at each other and smiled. AJ reached for his beer and said nothing. Tracer released his full lopsided grin. "Aw, that guy is never gonna drown. Besides, you know where the candy bars are hidden," he replied, but his grin said different.

Somebody yelled, "Let's carry back up and run it again!"

Someone else reached for the river guidebook, "Where are we camping?" Team Goat clinked their beer cans together with a howl, and cried out to the Anasazi ghosts of the Colorado Plateau,

"Always Above Lava!"

2

Nankoweap Wedding

Back before their Lava Falls runs, way back on Day 4, the Dukie Grand Canyon river trip had paused for a layover day to celebrate a wedding. They camped at main Nankoweap Beach, the glorious amphitheater downstream from where the sparkling thread of Nankoweap Creek emerged to the main stem. Ancient Indian granaries were tucked in a shaded pocket of the cliff face, coyote and mule deer tracks followed the shore, sun and shade played a medley of tunes above on the ultimate big screen. Their rafts were tied together in the eddy, a colorful cluster of rubber shapes and metal boxes that seemed impossibly tiny on the heroic scale of the landscape. From a distance they looked more like pocket toys than 18-foot cargo barges.

This river trip had then been in the early stages of a happy, exhausting voyage. As theirs was a private trip, operating under a coveted launch permit issued by Grand Canyon National Park, no paid guides were allowed. Their crew mix of seasoned experience and raw enthusiasm was gelling. They were moving under oar, paddle and muscle power down the Colorado River, through over a hundred named whitewater rapids and hundreds of miles of dreamy flat water. There were equally complex group dynamics and personal waters to navigate, and wide range of motivations and abilities. In all of North America, few outings of this magnitude remain available to free humans without paid guides or government participation. The unique exposure and privileges of a long wilderness river trip suppressed their stock identities. No resumes, degrees, and working or shirking histories mattered. Instead, they were reborn and self-organized (disorganized at times) with new identities as raft boatmen, kayakers, and passengers in an interdependent small society, a river tribe that woke each morning to renewed surprise and joy to be in the bottom of the Grand Canyon, and stretched itself each day to complete the rigging, scouting, paddling, and cooking. The trip was working out the kinks as the miles flowed by, and so far, they found it good.

Each river trip is a mosaic of personalities. This pack included off-duty river guides with thousands of river miles, eager first-timers with eyes and hearts wide open, couples, and kayakers seeking the perfect river wave and perhaps a reprieve from their careers. A core group of paddling buddies, who had met in geology grad school, now made room in their lives for their secret identities as river bums.

Nankoweap was known among river folks for the remote hiking up the side canyon to Nankoweap Mesa, the wild trout in the creek, the migrating bald eagles that fed on the trout, and for memorable parties on rest days in the comfortable camp.

This trip was fairly frothing with layover day excitement now. There was broad satisfaction in completing the first challenges of the trip, including the vexing complexity of the preparation, approach and put-in rigging, and their first raft flip, wrap and recovery, which occurred in the Roaring Twenties. Now the imminent wedding of AJ, an elongate laconic kayaker built like a muscular stork, and his gal, Natalie, who had recently completed her doctorate, was the reason for celebration.

An hour before the sundown wedding, the paddlers had sudsed and rinsed their bodies, donned dresses and fancy cowboy shirts from the bottom of their dry bags and collected wildflowers. Gifts were wrapped, and piled in the sand and cards were signed. The gifts were all the same due to a pre-trip conspiracy: a fleet of used electric toasters, being every last toaster that could be found in the Salvation Army and thrift shops of Flagstaff. The bride and groom were hidden in separate tents preparing. A mood of happy purposefulness reigned in camp, with a guitar player practicing under a Tamarisk tree, people bustling from tents to the rafts and back for items, and a moderate sampling of rum drinks and cocktails underway.

Two sun-browned men were still busy on the beach, where the remaining sunlight hit the Colorado River water and made it bright green. In their arms was a river version of the traditional Jewish wedding hoopah they were creating, the fabric canopy under which the ceremony would take place. They worked efficiently together, lashing flowers, ribbons, four wooden oars and a lace tablecloth into a hoopah that a Yeshiva rabbi would approve of.

Harper, the taller one, wild-haired with a middleweight's build and a baby face, smiled at his work and stood up. He held two oars upright in the sand, and spread a corner of the canopy to the sky as a test. Harper Purcell, almost 34 years old, was free of any thoughts of marriage himself, but was pleased for his kayak buddy AJ. Across the river, the far wall of the canyon ended at the water in cliff of Muav Limestone, with a dusky olive color beginning to glow in the sinking sun. He looked at his partner, who was intently lashing another bundle of flowers to an oar with an intricate woven knot, and spoke.

"Hey, Tracer, I think we can call it good. This hoopah would do an Anasazi Princess proud. And the sun is below the rim. It's wedding time".

Tracer, the second man, was a similar vintage, but more grizzled, dark as a walnut, compact, and muscular. He was Charlie Trace, known as Tracer, 38 years old and on his 12th Grand Canyon trip and umpteenth river trip. He had worked as a guide and kayak safety boater on rivers all over the western states and Alaska, but mostly did his personal, non-paying gigs in Grand Canyon. He listed Phantom Ranch, Colorado River Mile 88, as his home address on his Arizona Driver's License, in a little joke he was having with the Arizona DMV. He had bushy brown hair, eyelashes, and a river beard, and an intense focus on his task. He did not look up for a moment, then said, " I learned this lashing from a surgeon at a first aid seminar for wounds. We can leave a loop tied in it and then stake it out with guy wires. It will hold in a wind. "

Harper said, " No guy wires on a hoopah, Trace. You're over rigging again. The hoopah corners are supported during the ceremony by hand, by four friends or relatives who, you know, symbolically support the union. Then it all folds down for the after party, and you wander in the desert for forty years with your tribe. It's Jewish tradition. I told you, I'm dating a Jewish Goddess back in the real world, and I have to know these things.

And I gotta go wash and shave."

Tracer finished his knot carefully, looked up and squinted at the sun on canyon walls, gauging time.

"This is the real world down here, Harper, not up there. And there is no such thing as over-rigging. When you learn that, you will be ready to come out of your play kayak and rig a raft like a grown-up boatman. And you got no beard to shave." Tracer said. "Tell me this: for a wandering desert tribe, why do the Jews pick such funny hats. Those little round kippas they wear give no shade, and they fall off your head if a prophet farts. Unless they had a hairpin, they all blew away into the Red Sea when Moses busted that Passover surfing wave down on Pharaoh. But, yeah, this looks OK. Let's go get ready. "

They furled the hoopah, brushed sand off a smooth rock and carefully placed it atop the canopy for wind protection, and scampered off to get ready to party.

Glory, Glory Hallelujah

The sun was well below the rim when the group was assembled on the sand. A boatman with a guitar played church chords, and voices were lifted, more or less together, in a spirited version of Amazing Grace. The sunset complied with the spirit of the day, and a glory of soft pink spread across the sky. The cliff opposite the river camp was red and scarlet, vermilion, rose, tawny brown, and olive, with black streaks wandering down the face. An upriver breeze came through the canopy, ruffled the ribbons and kept the bugs down. The river riffles made gentle background music. All eyes turned to where the bride and groom waited for their processional cue.

The groom was elegant in river shorts and sandals, wire-rimmed glasses, many bead necklaces, a pinstriped shirt and a red bow tie. He abandoned all pretense of cool and grinned like a fool as he took a deep breath, reached out for his bride's hand, and walked with her towards their friends. The bride was lovely, a head shorter, delicate in a simple embroidered cotton dress, barefoot and elfin, with her honey blond hair tied back with a ribbon. A bouquet of canyon flowers was in her hand. She seemed too light footed to leave footprints. She smiled the eternal heartbreaking happiness of a bride on the brink. In another life, they were both scientists with advanced degrees (geologists, naturally), but for the moment they looked like Nankoweap locals, come down from canyon dwellings to the river granaries to celebrate their intentions for a shared life.

Harper and Tracer stood tall holding their oars at two corners of the hoopah, dressed in their cleanest long pants, dashing bandanas, thrift-shop cowboy shirts, and sandals. Cookie and Angie, wives of two raft boatmen, held opposite corners, with garlands of tiny daisies in their hair. Dr. Dukie, the trip leader stood beaming and smelling of good rum under the hoopah in a tuxedo T-shirt, with his finger holding a place in a sacred text, as he watched the bride and groom walk across the sand to them. The remaining motley crew all drew close, and the feelings of good will and love in the circle were as strong as the sunset colors across the canyon walls.

From a raven's nest above the Redwall, the tiny group of humans on the sand were miniscule. The human scales of distance, lifespan, and desire all shrank before the endless wall of time exposed around them. But of course, this immense setting only enhanced the need for community and their appreciation of the moment. The wedding crowd was small, but their spirit was grand. They felt the moment strongly, each drinking in the sky colors and the faces around them, to place upon an honored page in their personal histories. They reached the end of the second verse of Amazing Grace at different times, but regrouped for a rousing " I once was lost, but now I'm found, was blind, but now, I see" and faded to a respectful quiet.

Blessing From The Book

The couple reached the canopy, and the guitar stopped. Calm descended. A pair of fast-moving Pintail ducks flew past low, moving upriver so close their wing beats were heard. Dr. Dukie watched the birds, nodded approvingly, and looked out over his reading glasses. All present knew he was a cynical, profane, twice-divorced, thrice-married veteran of the marriage ceremony. In the past, he had been known to say, "If we need to keep the beer cold, just put it next to my ex-wife's heart". But he had recently remarried, to a professor of Economics, and his younger bride had brought him great cheer and some stability. Like outwardly cynical men everywhere, he was vulnerable to deeply romantic moods and he was proud to be leading the ceremony. Now he lifted the text. It was from the ammo can library on his raft, *First Through the Grand Canyon*, by Major John Wesley Powell, *being the record of the Pioneer exploration of the Colorado River, 1869-70, Chapter VIII*". As the crowd held their breath, Dukie said,

"As AJ and Natalie launch on their marriage run, let us help them scout by reading from The Major's book".

He held the book at arms length and read out in his best expert witness testimony voice,

"We are now ready to start on our way down the Great Unknown. Our boats, tied to a common stake, are chafing against each other as they are tossed by a fretful river. "

A wave of appreciation and grins at these familiar words ran through the crowd. They increased to giggles as the bride and groom snuggled against each other suggestively, chafing at their common stake. Dukie continued the passage in a ringing voice,

We are three-quarters of a mile in depths of the earth and the great river shrinks to insignificance, as it dashes its angry waves against the walls and cliffs that rise to the world above.

They are but puny ripples and we, but pygmies, running up and down the sand or lost among the boulders.

We have an unknown distance yet to run; an unknown river yet to explore.

What falls there are, we know not;

What rocks beset the channel, we know not ;

What walls rise over the river, we know not.

Ah, well, we may conjecture many things. The men talk as cheerfully as ever, jests are bandied about freely this morning, but to me the cheer is somber, and the jests are ghastly.

Here Dukie paused, with a faraway look and the word *ghastly* still on his lips, seeming to ponder his own marital history, before sensing impatience in the crowd (or more specifically, in the face of the bride before him). Recollecting himself, he plunged back in to finish with,

With some eagerness, and some anxiety, and some misgiving, we enter the canyon below. We are carried along by the swift water, through walls which rise from its very edge.

He closed the book to ribald cheering. Goat started to chant, "We are….Butt Pygmies!". The canopy swayed alarmingly as the four attendants holding the oars became animated with clapping and the ladies pulled out their cameras and took photos. Dukie held his hands up for calm.

"Now, since AJ and Natalie will exchange their rings and vows in a separate service next month in Chicago, we will close for now with this blessing." Dukie paused dramatically and rose up on his toes to declaim:

"Al and Natalie, May you keep your boats straight in running the Big Stuff, and may you stay out of the Bad Stuff. May you help each other rig, lighten each other's load, bail together when swamped, and rub each other's backs! Visualize Positive Outcomes! Careful with that Tequila, get help lifting the Kitchen Box, and when the going gets rough, remember, as we say when we're scouting Lava, … If It was Easy, Anyone Could Do It!"

He paused for breath.

"I now pronounce you man and wife. Let the Wild Rumpus Begin!"

<u>Let the Wild Rumpus Begin</u>

Joyous celebration broke out immediately. The guitar player broke into the loud, primitive ascending and descending power chords of Cinnamon Girl. The group cheered and beat on dish pots brought up from the kitchen, sounding like a drunken convention hall full of Democrats. A large cooler that had been waiting in the river eddy was brought forth to reveal cans of Guinness, Rolling Rock, and actual glass bottles (not cardboard boxes) of chilled wine. The hoopah holders began to boogie with their canopy supports, dancing to several different beats, all while thrusting the oars up and down like spears to get a parachute action in the canopy, grinning at each other and bumping into folks. Other hands reached for the oars to join in the fun. The canopy ballooned vigorously. The bride and groom kissed long and hard in the middle of it all, then broke to link arms and swirl in a tight fast circle dance. The spinning dance accelerated and their feet flew into a blur, as the drums and cheering surrounding them built. The bride suddenly released A.J.'s arm, spun alone off course, staggered dizzily, overcorrected, and collapsed laughing on her butt in the sand in her wedding gown, her brain spinning.

The cheerful bubble of noise and celebration lifted up from the riverside beach, ascending up past the raven nests, past the ring-tailed cat's lair, past the vast Redwall limestone cliffs that had once been ocean ooze in forgotten seas of mystery. It expanded and soared past the rocks of Supai, the Coconino, the Toroweap, the Kaibab Plateau, and on past the rim. Their joy sailed out to the night sky, twinkling faintly in time with the stars just beginning to shine. The Butt Pygmies danced, and the earth turned, and the crescent moon made a dramatic appearance above the rim, like a guest arriving late to find the party in full swing.

Eventually, after a conga line with the bride and groom at the head had paraded through camp, around the tents and returned to the epicenter, torches were lit, a dinner fire was started and the group relaxed into general laughter, happy babble, steady drinking, and dinner preparation. AJ and Natalie were wed, and all was well.

3

Diamond Morning

Two days after running Lava Falls was the final morning on the river. Everyone awoke feeling a sense of loss mixed with acceptance. It felt good, the completion of something hard and special. The group was dreamy, lost in internal dialogues, as they broke down camp for the last time. After the kitchen box was loaded, they grinned and threw the duffel gear in reckless loose mounds on the rafts, scandalously disorganized and unstrapped. Even normally obsessive boatmen joined in, pushing dry bags they were accustomed to arranging like favorite furniture into a careless pyramid behind their seats (after they had strapped down the kitchen box, of course). Folks piled in and sprawled on the pile. Kayaks were trailed behind on tethers, empty. Harper sat on top of dunnage on Goat's raft with his guitar and played a mournful round of *"Knocking on Heavens Door"*.

The Goat Boatman was the most experienced raft boatman on the trip. Goat was a hardscrabble Texas ranch kid who moved to the Front Range, became a river prodigy, a natural at the oars, but never fit in elsewhere. He had ricocheted around whitewater towns of the western states since leaving college, never accumulating relationships or property. He had lived hand-to-mouth in a raft company warehouse for years, guiding paddleboats full of rowdy Denver customers on the dangerous Class IV Royal Gorge run of the Arkansas River. After a famous disaster there, Goat had come to California a decade ago to try marriage, an engineering degree, and steady work. It had not been a success. Now he lived alone in the mountains above Santa Cruz, a hyperactive, pony-tailed redneck recluse in the redwoods. His cabin was off the grid, deep up a narrow road out of Boulder Creek. A loner by choice, he liked it that little contact was required with the Silicon Valley commuters and back to the land types who lived around him. His income was rumored to involve growing sensimilla on State Forest Land, together with seasonal raft guiding, and obsessive tree felling, log splitting, and firewood sales.

A crazy river stunt in his early days had shaped him as an outcast and given him his nickname and his hatred for authority. When he was a twenty-five year old river guide, high on mushrooms, he had paddled extreme high spring runoff water through the entire set of Arkansas River whitewater in Colorado state, from Granite Gorge to Royal Gorge, almost one hundred miles, in under eight hours, on almost 10,000 cfs, alone in a 16-foot oar raft. He had survived the river-wide holes, drowned cattle and barbed wire fences, the swamped low head dams, and miles of rocky gorges with continuous whitewater. Rangers had officially closed the Arkansas River the day before and had shut down all commercial rafting operations in the state after two drownings. Word got out about his illegal put-in and high water run, and after he passed an attempted capture point, people cheered him from bridges as he roared passed on the flood, tripping on shrooms, and screaming Frank Zappa songs. The river authorities were incensed by his nerve, and the excitement it had caused. They made an example of him to discourage disrespect for river regulations. At the take out he was arrested, handcuffed in front of cameras, fined and stripped of his guide license. Bitter and resentful of rangers forever, he had left the state of Colorado, now known as The Goat Boatman. Now, he sang the dirge along with Harper as they pushed out into the eddy, trying to ignore the imminent departure from where he most belonged.

"Launch the fleet!" cried Dr. Dukie in his best Trip Leader voice.

"So let it be written, so let it be done!" cried Christian from the next raft.

The group shoved off one last time. It was day 18, the end, with their take-out at Diamond Creek a few miles downstream. The outfitter would be waiting with a trailer for the rafts, and a van for them, and a rattling two-hour drive up the Diamond Creek trail (up the creek-bed, mostly). They would be back at the rim before lunch, weirded out by seeing strangers, cars, and stop lights.

There was a sweet sadness. No hostility. The social rifts that had formed late in the trip were erased, washed away in Lava Falls, and in mutual unspoken agreement afterwards to forget petty misunderstandings. The last nights in camp had been marked by small kindnesses. Tales of the trip, of the ring-tailed cat in the kitchen box, the flips and swims, were polished and retold. The kayakers washed all the dishes two nights in a row, and were polite gentlemen. The teen-aged Sasha hinted she liked them better as libidinous rogues, and asked if they would they teach her to kayak on a trip in California this summer. They received the requisite teasing from her Mom about hell freezing over first in good humor.

Consideration of one another's feelings reigned, with poems and sing-alongs at night, as the guitar was passed around the circle. It was the close of grown-up's summer camp. The couples nuzzled each other affectionately and retired to tents early. The weather got better and better, with wildflowers bursting out each day and a string of warm starry nights. The beer supply was exhausted soon after Lava Falls, the cooking sherry gone the same night. The lack of alcohol provided at least some comfort about the impending return to civilization. AJ told a true legend from years past of his famous beer-bag find, the largest eddy-shopping beer haul ever recorded: he had discovered two full cases of beer in a single burlap sack floating in an eddy below Whitmore Wash. They all listened raptly to the tale around the fire, their hands itching for a cold aluminum can. They did have extra coffee, and so they buried it in a secret cache with a note, on the island below Mile 209. They made a pirate map with an X, and swore each other to secrecy about the location. It was a commitment to come back and drink that coffee together, someday, Si Dios Quiere. An excellent greasebomb made of hoarded bacon grease topped the evening off and put a light coating of lard on their dry skin.

They had floated 225 miles, down a great river in one of the most majestic and remote areas of North America. They had been able to forget their income tax bracket, the Bill Clinton and Monica saga underway in D.C., their fax numbers, or why they had ever been intimidated by that mean guy in the accounting department at their last job. They had left the calendar behind, until today. There is no better metaphor for life's journey than a flowing river, and they had been on a corker.

It was not the famous rapids with fearsome reputations that stood out now. For each of them, for the boatmen and the raft passengers and the kayakers, even for Tracer who had made a dozen Colorado trips, and Goat who expressed so little, there was some inexpressible thing that the trip had given them.

For Harper, an unnamed surf wave above Kwagunt Rapid stood out. It was a beauty queen of a wave, with a feathering lip at least six feet tall, stable and twice as wide as a raft. It was poised dramatically at the top of thunderous Kwagunt rapid, like a pretty green gate to the disorderly world of spray and chaos behind it. It was also a one-shot wonder wave, with no hope of paddling back in to surf again from a side-eddy, if you missed it or washed over the top. To an observer, the surfing kayak on a river wave appears to be mostly stationary, as the river flows past. But inside the boat, the perception is speed and breathtakingly quick changes atop a living hydraulic. The river flies past inches from your hands. A delicate balance is constantly amended and preserved. Hip shifts, and instinctive paddle work are vital to remain, carving and probing the wave surfaces to stay atop it. A singularity of focus descends, and time stops.

There at Kwagunt, Harper had reached a balance of speed and gravity, riding his kayak back and forth across the green wall until the entire trip washed out of sight downstream. The peaceful intensity of that ride released the brain chemicals that make old kayakers go out to their sheds and sit in battered plastic kayaks during cold winter days, remembering. Everyone on the trip had some personal version of that heightened life.

So, they paddled out. They were passed in the last river mile by a motor-driven giant blue commercial raft, driving hard to the takeout after dropping passengers at Whitmore Wash for a helicopter trip to the rim. There was a guide driving and a swamper hunkered down amidships. The Dukie party all waved to the almost empty boat and got a friendly nod in return from the guide at the motor. Grand Canyon River Guides were a separate caste in the river community; they were a hard-to-join, confident, elitist, gossipy, guild of committed professionals. They discriminate little on the basis of gender, but they were broadly skeptical of the river abilities of lesser beings. That meant basically everyone, including all guides from other rivers, kayakers, paddleboat guides, or private boaters, in roughly descending order. Like river boatmen everywhere, guides were still out-going fun hogs, opportunistic breeders and feeders, but as Grand Canyon boatmen they saw themselves, (legitimately), as a cadre of trained professionals, keepers of a faith, and the point of the spear in any battle to preserve and protect Grand Canyon. They looked at private boaters much as a working cowboy might look at a kid with a pony; supportive and protective, friendly, not much impressed.

The Dukie trip all put on a brave face when they reached the takeout at Diamond Creek, and saw the unmistakable outline of their outfitter Donnie, a happy beer-keg shaped man with powerful arms, standing on the ramp. With his guidance, the raft were unloaded and came apart quickly, doused with water and deflated. They were rolled and loaded in less time than it had taken most of them to roll up and pack away a sleeping bag at the start of the trip.

"Take–outs are a bummer." said Harper, standing on the ramp

and watching the rafts disappear and their group fabric begin to evaporate.

Tracer stood near him, calmly coiling a line. He looked over at Harper and spoke. "The trick is, to take all the competence and joy we have developed here and carry them over into the rest of your life. " he said quietly. "If I have learned anything in twenty years of river trips, it is this. A trip to the DMV to renew your license can be as full as the day hike to Thunder River. When I rotate my tires, I spin the lug nuts like I'm fly-casting to a wild trout. Getting hired for your next gas station tank pull can be as rewarding as getting the Park Service to give you permit for a river trip. Each morning, wherever I am, I try to rise and greet the day, make coffee, rig for flip, then row twenty miles, and make the camp eddy. Remember, we are still Always Above Lava, just on the next cycle. "

Tracer kept looking at Harper, who was staring up the Diamond Creek road towards the rim. Finally Harper nodded and said softly "OK, I'll give it a try. Always Above Lava, amigo. " He looked at Tracer forlornly. "But what about when I have to go to the mall, Trace?"

" You better wait a little while before you try that, brother. " Tracer laughed. "I haven't been inside a mall in years."

"Hey, let's all go into Vegas and see some strippers and make fun of fat tourists with sunburns." said Dr. Dukie. His wife Colleen was walking past and hit him on the head kindly with a plastic bucket. "Let's get home and see if the cat is still alive" she said and walked to the van. Dukie sighed, and said, "She Who Must Be Obeyed has spoken. I gotta make some money to pay for all this, anyway. " He followed her to the van.

AJ and Natalie were collecting everyone's e-mail addresses, and promising to send their Boulder address out as soon as they had one. Christian and Della were happy sunburned veterans, in love with each other all over again, and ready to buy a raft, go back up to the put-in and start over. Christian asked the outfitter about used raft sales and quizzed Tracer on the Park Service rules for claiming cancellation dates for private river trip permits. Terry the boatman was with his wife and daughter in the van in an intimate family cluster. It was remarkable how much more Sasha looked like her Mom since the start of the trip. The outfitter, respectful of their group moment and sensitive to the tricky dynamics of take-outs, was quietly pleased to see the pain they shared at coming to the end. This was a good one, he thought with satisfaction. It was not always thus at the take out.

"Well, you have not missed much in the world." Donnie told the group. "Clinton is going on trial for Monica, the stock market went above 10,000 for the first time, and everyone is starting to freak out about the Year 2000 is gonna break their computers in 6 months. "

"Worse things could happen, " muttered the Goat as he walked back down to the water edge.

The gear was sorted and loaded on the trailer, the ramp became clear, the kayaks were tied on top. The group climbed aboard, reluctantly. Finally, Tracer went back down to get Goat, standing quietly ankle-deep in the river by the ramp. They returned together and climbed in the van last. The lonely two-vehicle caravan rattled up the Diamond Creek road towards the rim.

4

Back to the Office

The Japanese samurai text *Go Rin No Sho* states that a warrior should maintain the same calm, unwrinkled forehead, whether he faces battle or breakfast. That is what Harper sought now as he drove back into Santa Cruz to his office. A post-river Zen state, free of expectations and worry. Maybe he would have received a check for that tank closure job, maybe not. As he cruised down the hill towards his office for the first time in a month, he tried to remember his email password. Since he arrived back in town from the Canyon, he had slept, showered off the dust and road grime, and shaved. Then, after he daubed and bandaged a few scrapes that lingered on his knuckles and feet, he put on socks and lace-up shoes. While his first load of wash was in, he rifled through his mail and unloaded his truck. Paddling gear was dumped in a big sandy heap on his back porch.

His shorts were still brick red from Supai Formation river silt. River memories were clinging to all his river gear, waiting for cleaning and storage.

A funk of canyon withdrawal was lurking, a mix of missing his river trip companions, facing his work and personal life demands, readjusting to his shoes and finding his location in time and space. Harper knew from experience that going to his office might not be fun, but it would move this process along. He already had received the bitter disappointment (mixed with concern) of a phone message from Shira, canceling their reunion dinner date, because she was flying to NY to see her grandmother in the hospital. Shira was the foxy Jewish girl he was courting, so far with only delightful encouraging but chaste responses. She sounded rushed and unhappy, but closed with a promise to call him and reschedule their dinner. He played her message over and over, standing in his hallway, listening for nuances in her voice. She didn't mention the Canyon postcard he sent. She would not be back for a long, long, week.

So, to work he went. Saturday morning would be a good time for an exploratory visit. No one else should be in the office. He could check his PO box, erase emails, sit in his work chair and get acclimated.

Driving past the downtown Santa Cruz Post Office, he smiled to see the bearded Tai Chi Guy doing his mystic routine, a series of dreamy morning dance exercises he performed daily in the exact center of the ring of concentric paving stones in the small plaza there. The Barefoot Bluegrass family was on their corner, with smiling Mom, whiskered Dad, and two barefoot boys carrying stringed instruments. They set up a donation basket, and started playing. A wild-haired, white-bearded journalist wearing a rumpled sports coat with patch elbows, black socks and sandals marched past the Tai Chi Guy without a glance. Harper recognized the long-time local newspaper columnist, going down to his morning coffee shop. All players still present and accounted for. Keeping it weird, Harper thought with satisfaction. This town has more mystics, more crystal healers, more herbal veterinarians than a normal town has accountants. In fact, there is probably an herbal, mystic, certified tax planner around here somewhere.

Downtown Santa Cruz was a skein of memories for Harper, connecting his impoverished graduate student years to the present, via his late 1990's run as an affluent Yuppie to reach his precarious status as an independent geologist. Downtown in 1999 was a funky mix of one-of-a-kind shops, good bars, a stellar bookshop, a decent drug store, and reliably excellent roster of music and restaurant places. The bus station provided functional transportation, a place for drifters, and a gritty side. A block or two out, the commercial center gave way to older Victorian homes in various stages of restoration or decay, ranging from student crash pad disasters, to ornate, four-color, painted lady glory. The cast of downtown Santa Cruz characters was legendary. The vibe still hung in there as the year 2000 approached, despite the influx of Silicon Valley computer money, and the arrival of a few chain stores. The 1989 earthquake caused a rough patch, when buildings fell and stores closed, the bookstore and gift shops operated out of a tent, and the homeless outnumbered shoppers. Now the earthquake damage was gone, downtown vitality and tourism were back, the original neon marquee of the Palace movie theatre was repaired, and rents were up. Chain stores were arriving downtown, too, attracted like moths to the ample disposable incomes of a thousand young software engineers and university students walking around.

Harper parked in his regular illegal spot in the Sentinel newspaper office's Employees Only lot, the most reliable free parking downtown, and walked the three blocks towards his office. His office was a room in a converted Victorian across from the bagel shop, with sunflower yellow paint and wooden sunburst fence gate. His upstairs office room shared a receptionist and a copy machine with a downstairs landscape architect, an accountant, and Sleepy Jake, a music promoter. The music promoter was an affable old hippie who favored Hawaiian shirts, country-fried music, and Birkenstocks. He tended to hog the use of the copier and fax machine, but made up for it with occasional unsold tickets to quirky shows no one had ever heard of, like the Prayer Tent Swamp Gospel Boogie Band.

Harper let himself in and ran up the stairs. He tapped his door sign that read **HLP Associates** affectionately, and collecting a concert schedule from the hallway. It advertised upcoming shows by Throat Singers from Kyrgyzstan, Sons of the San Joaquin, and a country group called Hillbilly Haiku. He swung open the door and entered the strangely familiar quiet of his office. His desk chair and lamp sat waiting as he had left them, loyal abandoned relics.

On the river he had imagined his office, mostly to enjoy a sense of distance from it, and the complete contrast with some spectacular canyon or river habitat he was within. But at those times, he always pictured his old cubicle office cell in San Jose, not this office. This office had been his for only six months and was still a hand-to-mouth financial affair, and so was still a place of adventure in his professional life. He had affection and no resentment for this space, and he looked around fondly at the books and desk, trying to remember how he made a living here.

He reached out and touched a series of small hand-written notes on his phone cradle, secret alphabetic reminders to himself. They were his motivational tricks. The top one said **V.P.O.** (Visualize Positive Outcomes, of course, the Grand Canyon boatman's all purpose mantra). The next one read, **A.F.G.O.** (Another Fucking Growth Opportunity). He got that from a therapist buddy on his softball team, and it provided a useful perspective for difficult demands and difficult people.

The oldest and most faded tab was rescued from his college dorm wall. It said **H.L.P.** in big block letters. The conventional meaning for this was his initials, Harper Lewis Purcell, now his business name, HLP Associates. But it also had a secret meaning. It stood for High Level Performer; the secret identity Harper had given himself. Although he would have tried to laugh it off now, this was the root of his choice of his company name. All he needed was a stretch jumpsuit and cloak labeled HLP, and maybe a cool car that turned into a plane. To Harper, HLP Associates was High Level Performers Associates, a superhero collective of one, and this modest office was his lair. Harper tapped the HLP tab on his phone for luck. Keep on marching, buddy he told himself. He turned to examine his piles of work mail.

His mail had been carefully stacked on the table by the lady who answered the phones downstairs. One pile was his latest professional water journals, hours of articles like *Statistical Methods for Model Validations of Anisotropic Leaky Aquifer Pumping Tests*. In grad school, Harper had discovered an aptitude for groundwater models. He had spent entire semesters wrestling with multi-dimensional variations of imaginary aquifers to make them perform accurately, to duplicate actual well pumping records and then predict future pumping impacts. He created unseen numerical worlds of hidden water that only existing in his mainframe model and in his mind. Now, he realized that his computer modeling skills were already out of date, and that he would probably never use most of them again. As grad school receded in the distance, and new, more complicated methods of aquifer analysis appeared constantly, he was dealing with stuff like billable hours, liability insurance and payroll tax withholding, not aquifer recharge rates.

Here was an announcement for the annual California Groundwater Group's conference in Sacramento, *"Addressing Shortages, Creating Solutions".* It would be the usual deal, a glass conference center with a big hall full of wandering white guys and gals in slacks and golf shirts, with friendly vendors, free pens, glossy brochures and expensive water gizmos on display. There would be a series of smaller rooms with slides and technical talks on the perennial greatest hits of the California water industry: seawater intrusion, groundwater overdraft, and leaking underground tank clean-ups. There would be a 'flavor of the month" session on new stuff like prescription drug contamination of aquifers: all of Southern California really was on Prozac, because it was passing through water treatment, and showing up in the aquifer and then in drinking water wells.

Amidst the envelopes of credit card offers, Harper found one he had been looking for. Inside was a check from a small excavation outfit to HLP Associates for $2000, for sampling at the tank removal and soil excavation, and a signed contract for the next phase of work, for $8000, for monitoring wells to determine how far the plume of gasoline from a former bus garage extended. As he held the check up to the light, he felt a rush of professional pride, like a hunter getting a rabbit. He checked the postmark to see how long ago this had arrived. Two weeks ago. He better call this client and get started on scheduling drilling for the next phase.

The next envelope was even better. In discrete formal block letters was the logo **Arena Corporation**, and underneath, **Sand, Gravel, Concrete and Construction, since 1850**. Harper tore it open with excitement. He found a single page on the same letterhead. It was acknowledgment of receipt of his proposal for the Lagunitas Quarry Water Study. The words *"Thank you for your excellent presentation and careful research."* jumped out at him. The next line offered, *" Your firm, HLP Associates, has been selected to attend an informal field meeting and review of the Arena Corporation Lagunitas Quarry setting, and the Quarry Permit Renewal Plans"*. It was this Thursday! There were directions to the quarry gate; as if he didn't know where it was, a gate code and signature of an Arena Vice President of Operations he had ever heard of.

Christ, he was in the door at Arena Corp! His mind raced. That quarry proposal he had written was for 30 grand! And, that could double with drilling costs, if a new well went in. Should he get a retainer? Good thing he came back in time for the meeting. He re-read the letter and stood up. He had work. A surge of ambition and sense of purpose lifted his spirits. He walked around his desk and brought his computer to life. Time for the part of re-entry that he had been dreading. Harper entered his password (IBDHLP) and he settled in to work through his backlog of email.

As the server paused and reflected on his password, Harper looked at his calendar. He imagined spring and summer full with real and potential jobs, proposals to write, drilling projects that might be coming, attendance at the Sacramento groundwater conference in June, maybe a couple of weekend kayak trips up to run the hairy Class IV Tuolumne River, once the snow melt was happening. When was Shira going to be back from New York? Soon. And, of course, he had to get in the ocean and surf. High Level Performer, baby. That $2000 check was nice, but it was already spent on rent and insurance. Better get ready for that quarry meeting Thursday. He could go surfing up north at The Landing tomorrow. He looked back at his screen. The email inbox blinked and said **526 New Messages.** Harper sighed, put his finger on the delete button and started scrolling.

5

The Landlord

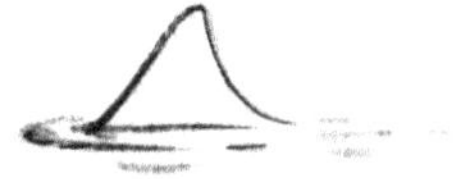

Even in sunshine, the Pacific Ocean feels cold going down the back of your wetsuit. In morning fog, it is a serious icicle. Paddling his longboard out, Harper arched to avoid getting splashed, and crested a feathering wave. It broke into foam behind him as he splashed down outside. He pushed up from paddling, and sat balanced on his board a little uncertainly. He had been back in Santa Cruz from the river for almost a week, and it was his first chance to go surfing. Outside the waves, he was the first man out for dawn patrol, offshore at The Landing. He shivered in his wetsuit as he spun his board towards the shore, gauging where to set up. The board felt awkward after his long spell away. This remote spot, a dozen miles north of town, would allow him to get some wave time without a crowd. The ocean broke on rock-bound cliffs up here, with small sandy pocket beaches sandwiched between point breaks. In the winter, this spot could be trouble in big swells, with close-out waves and no easy way in. For now, it was part of his re-entry plan.

Ocean waves could return him, mind and body, from the Canyon, without loss of spirit. The north coast was rougher, windier, and wilder than the town surf spots, where wave-hogs kids with aerial moves on airbrushed short boards were as thick as kelp. Town surfers joked nervously about the shark attacks that had occurred up north over the years, about the Great White sharks that were known to patrol the elephant seal colony a few miles further. "Watch out for the Landlord; he'll be collecting rent for his ocean one of these days" they said from their parking lot clusters. It kept the crowds down. It was nice to have some room, Harper thought as he looked around the empty sea, but one or two other surfers would not be unwelcome.

Still, he felt good to be wet. The dawn patrol ritual of coffee for the foggy drive north, scouting from the truck in the parking lot, pulling on the wetsuit and booties, walking the sand, hitting the cold water and paddling out was soothing. He was outside. He sized up the wave potential, and looked off towards Japan, considering the infinite ocean.

The Pacific was calm and cold this morning, under low grey overcast. The ocean was the color of a piece of metal. A few baby sets had arrived, promising something workable as the tide dropped. The roof of fog hung low, hiding the sun and there was no wind. A fuzzy glow was starting in a low corner of the fog already, so Harper knew the sun would burn through soon, way before lunch. The headlights of other cars were arriving back on shore, so this spot would not be his alone for long. He had managed to keep his head dry on the paddle out, but his hands were stone cold. His wetsuit hung loose on him in the middle. He must have lost a few pounds during his weeks of canyon paddling. His neoprene-clad body was warming the water it had trapped, but a thin current of cold water ran down his spine inside the suit, chilling his core. He blew into his hands again, reluctant to paddle into one of the small waves and fall into spray just yet. This was his meditation time. He had to admit, it felt good. There is nothing like the privileged vantage of a surfer.

The days since he driven up the Diamond Creek road from the river were a blur. Initially he had taken a perverse pleasure in the cultural shocks of re-entry: buying gas from a computerized pump under the Muzak speakers at futuristic freeway maxi-marts, navigating multi-lane traffic after entering California, and enduring radio commercials. Waiting for a clothes dryer at the laundry mat had made him grit his teeth, close his eyes, and envision the bald eagles trout fishing in Marble Canyon. He was a wolf inside the settlement, a returned Anasazi, a primitive hunter-gatherer river man with the enhanced clarity of the desert clinging to him, suddenly forced to find correct change for the dryer. But, the novelty of annoyance with the modern world was worn off once he washed the reddish grit out of his hair. He resolved again to take the positive feeling and the sense of achievement he brought back from Lava Falls and to apply it here. Every day above ground was a good day, and he was above Lava Falls on another cycle of unknown duration.

The first real disappointment of his re-entry was that phone message from Shira, saying she was making a hasty trip to NY and would be gone for another week. Harper had steeled himself and faced the supermarket after his trip to his office yesterday. The merchandise choices overwhelmed him, but no one else seemed to notice. He moved carefully through the aisles at first, avoiding eye contact. Soon he relaxed and filled his cart with bachelor food staples and treats. He began selecting delicacies and tastes he had missed; peanut butter cookies, cashews, relishes. Unknown intruiging new beer types had appeared on the market. Hunting and gathering was never this easy, he mused, looking at a box of instant Miso soup mix.

He felt energized and hopeful about work. After grinding through a backlog of phone messages, e-mail, and disappointing bank statements, he was back. In a trade journal from his mail pile he noticed that his old firm Envirocon had won a multi-million dollar contract to do groundwater cleanup at several federal ammunition dumps. That would mean big drilling assignments, lots of overtime, and probably some fat budgets (and bonuses) for groundwater modeling of clean-up system design. He felt a pang of professional jealousy, and guilt at having jettisoned his fledgling career at that firm to start his own outfit, surf more, and go paddle 225 miles of gorgeous river canyon. He needed to produce some actual work product on his own. Time to get in on some water wars, meet clients, get signed contracts, bill hours. His office phone had a message from Tony Armstrong, the Environmental Compliance officer for Arena Construction calling about the sand quarry project. Tony was English, dashing, and enthusiastic. His accent made every statement seem like a diplomatic corps press release. No contract yet, but he confirmed the invitation to a scoping meeting at the quarry site with the project team. He rang off the message with a friendly "Carry on till then". Harper knew it was an opening. If this project worked out, maybe he would treat himself to a new surfboard when the winter swells arrived.

The Top of The Food Chain

As he floated there thinking ambitious thoughts, something moved in the still ocean just before him. A boil in the water, then a grey fin emerged from grey water, gliding forward steadily. Harper's brain screeched to a halt and reeled in from his daydream, but balked at what it was seeing. The fin rose soundlessly, inch-by-inch, bigger and more impossible each second, as it moved steadily past, only 30 feet away. No! Hell, yes, it was a fin. Smooth, dark, and thicker at the leading edge which cut the water, thinner, papery, a bit ragged along the pale back edge. He stared, hard. It could not be. Not for real. He looked for a breath hole just before the fin, which would make it a porpoise. He looked around for other fins, for a group of fins. Happy, arching pods of dolphins occasionally appeared and scared the daylights out of surfers. No dolphins. The tip of the fin rose steadily up until it was six inches above the water, no more. It showed no sign of ending, no spine, no back, no indication how much more fin was still submerged. Then it held that level, a steady cutting glide for a few long seconds of travel. And the fin sank smoothly down out of sight and disappeared completely without making a ripple.

As he stared at the spot where it had disappeared, his brain screamed, **SHARK**! But, Harper made no sound except a gacking noise in his throat. Menace swept over him like a set wave. Another part of his mind assessed, wheeled and turned. It was not swimming towards him. It was not swimming away. It was close; it could be on him in an instant. It could be anywhere. Maybe it was gone. He pulled up his feet as he scanned for a reappearance, for the fin, a boil on the surface, for an enormous, gaping, heavily toothed mouth emerging under him to engulf and crush his body with unbelievable force and rip his legs off. Nothing. The calm, undulating, unbroken surface of the ocean was suddenly a horror. He was very alone. He was the exposed mouse in a cornrow, who heard the whisper of wings as an owl descended. He was in the food chain, and he was not at the top.

Trying not to whimper, he quickly lay flat on the board, centering his weight, and withdrawing his legs and hands entirely from the water. Unfortunately, it was not possible to keep every part of his body entirely out of the water without becoming unstable on his board. He started to wobble, overcorrected, made a splash, and cringed. He was forced to move a big toe and a few fingers to edges of the board to steady himself. Thank God, he was on a longboard. He looked in towards the surf line, the first line of breaking waves he was just outside of. The Promised Land. He absolutely needed to get inside that line of breaking waves, now, and get to shore. He tried to paddle without putting his hands too far into the water. This caution conflicted with his objective of getting the hell out of there.

A Discovery channel TV special, *"When Sharks Attack"* flashed in his mind. There had been spectacular shots of huge sharks biting swimming sea lions, and information about sharks sensing wounded fish movement. He tried to keep any irregular rhythm hinting at desperation out of his paddling stroke. His hands dipped in on both sides, dainty and rhythmic, like a dry cat touching water. He brought an errant foot that had wandered off the edge of the board back in. All this occurred in seconds, as he tensed his body to prepare for the explosive shocking impact from below and the bite that would end his thoughts forever. It did not come, so he kept paddling, and kept waiting. Oh, god, why didn't he just surf in town like everyone else?

An eternity and a few quick, strong, non-desperate, non-splashy paddle strokes and he was inside the surf line. A little junior wave jacked up behind him, and he accelerated to catch it, paddling like he was catching an overhead wave at Mavericks. He made no attempt to stand, but lay carefully hugging the board as he dropped onto its face. He trimmed his weight back so as not to bury the nose. There was no way he wanted to pearl and be dumped off the board right now. He belly-rode in with the foam until it became mush, and paddled again to stay with the weak wave. Finally, he jumped off in shallows and ran through the beach break, glancing from side to side, onto the wet sand of the empty beach. The dry sand felt good to stand on. He dropped the board.

He spun and looked back out. There was nothing remarkable: empty calm grey ocean and small innocent waves on rocky headlands. The waves slid ashore rinsing the sand. He looked up and down the beach for witnesses, and found nobody. Some dog walkers were visible far down the tide line, walking away from him. Up by the cars at the overlook, there was a cluster of guys in hooded sweatshirts looking out towards the ocean, but their body language showed no excitement. Harper looked out at the ocean again. His heart was still racing, his mind struggling to remember the exact shape and luster of the wet fin, to replay what he really had seen. He was his own, his only, witness to the drama. In his mind, the fin broke the surface again, raced past, slid down into water and disappeared, leaving the unbroken ocean. He slumped a little looking out, and blew out a deep breath. His favorite break had lost its innocence. Now it felt edgy. Now it would always be there for him. He wondered when he would be able to paddle back out. The Landlord was real. He blew out a breath and shivered. Picking up his board, he began to walk up to the cars.

6

Morning at the Landing

Adrenaline turns to melancholy as it leaves your blood. As Harper trudged back up the beach path to the parking lot, trying to avoid dinging the nose of his longboard on the sea wall, the shock and thrill of the shark sighting oozed out of him, leaving him subdued. He sighed as he saw a bright red bumper sticker on the guardrail, "Stop The Quarry", pasted over faded "Team Donna" and "Last is First" scrawls. Harper had seen a lot of those red quarry stickers around town since he came back. A cluster of local Landing boys was hanging out in their usual spot. They stood around the flames licking out of a fire barrel with their sweats and zipped-up hoodies, with surf and construction company trucker-hats in place, chatting sociably in the fog. They watched him come up from the beach. His ex, an almost famous local named Donna, used to surf here, and had taught him and introduced him to these guys, so he and his truck were accepted visitors. He was not, of course, a full Landing local, but at least his truck stereo was safe (as long as he never showed up here with a kayak on top of his truck).

He wondered if he should stop and talk with them, to warn them about the shark (if you even saw one, a doubting voice in his brain added). He didn't know if he had the energy to deliver the fin story, not like it deserved. None of them looked in danger of pulling on a wetsuit, anyway. These guys could watch waves and drink beer all day.

These were the men of the Landing Alcoholic Surf Team, The LAST. Their social club and local dominance resulted in the *"LAST shall be First"* graffiti on various nearby retaining walls. First at what, it did not say. Cirrhosis, perhaps. They were not first in the waves unless the swell got good enough to provide a challenge. Until then, LAST provided parking lot paisanos, a shaggy group of mostly-friendly petty felons and surf philosophers with no set schedules. They claimed the prime viewing corner of the Landing parking lot as their spot, and used it to genially scare off tourists, University long hairs and Valley surfers. They watched the tides change, and occasionally even went surfing. Their informal leader, Wayne, had inherited a small wood frame house in the old worker housing section of the nearby cement plant. Several of them lived there together on whatever assemblage of day wages, disability checks, and panhandling income which fortune provided. They were an endangered species on the coast in these days of Silicon Beach, but they still ruled this beach niche.

Harper recognized a large guy named Jesus Rocha he knew, wearing an Eastside Homeboys hat, and poking at the driftwood fire. The path back to his truck took him past their corner, so he waved tentatively without intruding. Several of them nodded non-committedly. Jesus grinned a silver–toothed smile and waved back at him for the group, his tattooed knuckles holding the morning's first 40-ounce malt liquor can.

"You sure came out fast today, Huevon. Que pasa? Too cold for you?"

Harper stood hesitating with his long board tucked under one arm. " I thought I saw a fin." He declared it more firmly, testifying, "I did see a fin. I'm sure. Not a dolphin, either."

They eyed him and looked back and forth at each other. This was some news, worthy of further discussion.

"Dude says he saw a fin, brah."

"Yo, how big, man?"

"You sure? How far out was it?"

"A fin at low tide, that's pretty heavy."

"You sure, you sure?" and then, "Hey, where's Donna at these days, brah?" and ribald laughter.

Jesus addressed him again from the fire barrel circle, "Hombre, seriously, you think you saw Whitey?"

Harper nodded yes.

Jesus saluted with his beer. "Nobody seen a shark here since last summer. But, my man Chewy, he saw a 12-foot long shadow swim right under his board. He was riding a set wave, on that good three-day swell the end of last summer. And Chewy, he never been back up here to the Landing since. He surfs Capitola now. But hey, they always here, right? It's their ocean, we just visiting it."

"You look like you saw something, man" contributed another member, not unkindly. "I seen you come in riding that little wave on your belly. Paddling like yo' ass was on fire. Look like you saw a ghost."

"Well, I saw something. A grey fin, that's all. It was real close, then it was gone. So I came in. " spoke Harper, drawing some affirmation and strength from their attention.

The whole group turned and considered the silvery ocean now. They waited a few heartbeats and watched waves quietly. Nothing broke the surface outside of the line of small surf.

They respectfully considering the scene, then opened an earnest discussion of all things sharky: the history and lore of sightings, visual encounters here and nearby, chumming and the effect of blood in the water, number of sightings versus bitings, and of course, the famous shark attack that had occurred right here at the Landing a decade before, when a visiting surfer survived a vicious mauling ("that dude said he was a Montana surfer, man, as if there is such a thing").

Harper listened to one of the crew deliver an eyewitness account of that famous attack ("The dude had a huge chunk of his butt bit off. Only one cheek left, man. He washed up next to his board in a cloud of pink water, crying and rolling around, wetsuit full of blood, just chumming the ocean you know..."). From the corner of his eye, Harper saw a white Econoline van pull into the far end of the parking lot.

Surfers know each other by their vehicles. Everyone at a spot carries a mental inventory of local rigs, so when you scan the parking lot, you know who is surfing. Harper did not recognize this van, but after a quick glance, nobody else commented or looked at it. It was like a standard vanilla work van, but brand-new. Fresh paint, clean tires, and shiny bumpers, just off the lot. It had locking hubs on the front wheels for four-wheel drive, a reinforced safari rack on the roof to hold extra gear, and two military surplus five-gallon gas cans bolted in brackets on the rear bumper. No surf stickers. Except for its showroom condition, it was a stealth vehicle that would not draw much attention, almost interchangeable with a million vans, but clearly set up for driving off-road, and for carrying equipment. And, it was the Goat Boatman, Harper's Grand Canyon river buddy, unmistakable in a grey ponytail, driving it.

Goat drove the van down to the far end of the parking lot,

almost out of sight. He pulled in and killed the motor and lights. A scruffy fellow in tan overcoat peeled off quietly from the fire barrel group, leaving a discussion of whether a shark would rather attack a kayak or a surfer. He walked to a faded yellow Buick Skylark, got in and drove slowly to the far end of the parking lot, to park next to the van. Everyone else in the group studiously ignored the rendezvous, and began to recount interesting things that had been found in the stomachs of dead sharks. Jesus claimed that a shark caught in Florida had a suit of armor and gold pieces from the Spanish Armada in its stomach.

Harper nodded to himself. Goat must be dealing weed again. Maybe more weight than before, judging by his new van. Better give him space. Hope he's being careful, he thought. Harper walked back to his own truck, put his board on the roof rack, and began to peel his wetsuit off.

Soon the yellow Buick cruised back up the parking lot, crunching over the gravel. The car stopped, collected a few worthies from the group at the overlook and departed. The white van remained at the far end of the lot. Harper was out of his wetsuit now and into his sweats, with his board lashed on the top of his truck. As he sat in his cluttered truck cab pulling his sneakers on, he considered the propriety of walking down to talk with Goat, to admire his new van, and check on his re-entry progress. Goat would want to hear about the fin. He decided to let Goat make the first move, as he was unsure what business was underway. Goat knew he surfed here, and would notice his truck.

To his surprise, another familiar vehicle pulled into the parking lot out of the fog. Now it was Dr. Dukie, his raft buddy and retired University of California geology department renegade, in his big red American pick'em up truck, with a

"Cowboy Up" license plate holder and *"If It Wasn't Grown, It Was Mined"* bumper sticker from a Nevada mining group. That was vintage Dr. Dukie style, getting in the New Age face of privileged geology undergrads at the U. Dukie's truck drove down next to the white van. There was someone else in the cab. They rolled down a window to talk into the van. Soon, the van's motor started, headlights came on, and the van rolled out quietly. Instead of driving over to visit at the fire barrel as Harper expected, the van rolled slowly to the exit. Goat looked out to Harper as he drove by, and gave a discreet wave, then placed an index finger against his lips in the international "shhh, don't talk" gesture, as he drove away.

"What the hell? " thought Harper, standing next to his truck and watching him go. Why was he talking to Dukie but not him? Don't talk about what? What did he care if Goat was dealing dope? He wanted to talk about the damn shark fin he just saw, and about their return to society from the river, and check out the new van. Why was his friend avoiding him?

Then Dukie's truck pulled up next to him and stopped with the engine running. The windows were fogged up, and when the driver's side window came down, he saw Duke and recognized his white-haired passenger. It was Ed Larson, the Planning Board commissioner he had last seen at Dukie driveway before leaving on the river trip.

"Yo, Harper, how's the waves?" called Dukie.

"Hey, fellas. " Harper replied cautiously. "A little spooky today. I got cruised by a fin and came in. Hey, what's up with the Goat? And where did he get that new ride? Wasn't that him in the van?"

"Oh, yeah, that was him. He's got no phone at his cabin, so we met him here to talk about a river trip. He said he got the van for contractor jobs. " Dukie answered. His eyes shifted nervously to his passenger and back. "Goat's on edge. He never fits in, you know, especially after a river trip. You know how re-entry is, Harper. It's worse for him, since rivers are pretty much all he has. We were offering him work, but he says he needs to quit guiding and make some real money instead. He says he's leaving town next winter, after he builds up a down payment to buy a property in Baja. "

Dukie killed the engine and gestured towards his passenger. "Harper, this is Ed. We were trying to get Goat to go back to the Canyon to be motor boatman on a research trip next month, but he says he can't make it. Hey, you know the Comish, don't you? " Dukie sat back and gestured to his passenger. "Ed Larson, County Planning Commissioner and Save the Earth do-gooder, meet Harper Purcell, a kayak scum and pretty decent groundwater man. Me and Ed are going back to the Canyon next month, Harper. An old geology student of mine got tenure at UC Davis and got us places on his research trip with USGS motor rigs next month. It's a government boondoggle at its finest, two motor rigs and 8 staff, doing a month-long stream sediment survey at the Little Colorado, and then motoring down to Diamond to take out. We got one boatman place left, but it has to be a licensed Grand Canyon Guide. Any idea what Tracer is doing next month, Harper?"

"Hiya, Ed." Harper waved. "You can try asking Tracer, but he said he was heading to Moab. There's a girl there, named Billie. Wow, Congratulations on your Grand trip coming up, Ed. It's the right thing you're doing. You guys should carry extra cases of beer on the motor rigs and bury them below Lava for our next raft trip. Dr. Dukie, two trips in three months. I'm jealous. I got no guide card, so I can't do it. Besides, I gotta do some groundwater work for a while. Hey, looks like I might get a piece of that quarry job, Dukie. Thanks for the lead."

"Hello, Harper", said the passenger, speaking across Duke. " I heard you guys had a great trip. Dukie told me you are a fine groundwater man and are starting your own firm. What quarry job are you referring to? A good gravel mine can be more profitable than a diamond mine, I'm told. "

" Oh, I'm talking about Arena Construction, their Lagunitas plant expansion. The one everyone hates. " Harper said with a grin. "It's complicated and I know their plant is in a vulnerable coastal setting, but I'm not hired yet."

"Be careful what you wish for' said Dukie obliquely, before Harper could continue. "And we can't talk business with the Comish here, cause he's gotta vote on all our projects."

"Ah, you talk plenty, Dukie. And I can always talk off the record." said Ed, turning back to Harper. "I know you geologists need to make a living, but you both better be careful who you get in bed with around Arena Corp. Dukie thinks he is immune to their charms, but they want your soul, not your technical advice. That reminds me, Harper, what do you know about the water meter controversy down in South County?" asked Ed, leaning forward. "All the growers down there are angry over the District directive to install water meters on every well. They say it is the first step to a water tax and it will drive out family farms".

Harper brightened at the familiar topic. Dr. Dukie slumped at the wheel, plainly disinterested in the latest episode of local water politics plotting. Harper stepped up to the window and addressed the cab eagerly. "Well, Ed, the south county growers pump ten times more water than any domestic users in Watsonville, and nobody measures their use. So, nobody can do an accurate water budget. The coastal wells are going salty and there is an overdraft problem, but how bad is it? You need to get meters on wells, especially on big ag wells, to do a good water balance and to know how bad the annual overdraft is. And, of course, yes, the District will probably put a cost on water pumping once they get meters in, just like the growers fear. But it won't be a tax. The Water District hates the T-word, cause since that Proposition passed, they need a majority public vote to put new taxes in place. It's a user fee, I believe." He paused, and looked into the truck for the effect. The Comish nodded, interested, giving Harper the green light to continue. Dukie sighed and slumped lower in his seat. Harper took the bait. He was riffing on his pet topic, like a housewife describing her favorite soap opera.

"To me, the truth is, that south county water fight is not family farms versus corporate. It's inland versus coastal growers. The farmers inland of Highway 1 irrigate three crops a year with great wells; they get free pumping, and no salt problems. They don't want pumping limits and they don't want to pay for their share of overpumping the groundwater basin. They've been paying nothing but the cost of drilling their well and their electricity. Meanwhile, the coastal guys got the perfect strawberry soils and climate. Only dope growers and maybe lettuce make more profit per acre. They get richer every berry harvest, but the salt is coming in farther each year. So, the coastal guys have to drill new wells farther inland every generation. They watched Granddad's old well, then Dad's well turn salty as the seawater front moved inland. The whole basin just keeps pumping, but only the coastal guys get hurt. The coastal guys, second and third generation farmers, are not dummies. They are ready to limit coastal pumping, even if it takes the government.

They want a supply pipeline to Hollister to connect to the state water project. Which takes water project money. Meanwhile, if their well goes salty and their land goes from berries to growing artichokes, they just lost thousands of dollars per acre each harvest. And their land value tumbles. " He paused for breath.

"OK, so what's the fix? " ask Ed, his white eyebrows lifted.

Harper was rolling now, showing off on his favorite soapbox. He said, "Well, it's all one basin, right? The whole valley aquifer system is interconnected, so the inland farmers and their pumping gotta' be part of any real fix. How to get them to pay, and how to give them some benefit for their increased pumping cost, is the problem, cause the salt is still 40 years away from hitting their inland wells. Logic says: let's make the water cost more, make all folks pay to use water. Then, either the District collects money that it can use for a water project to connect to other basins and buy water, or growers will pump less to save money, or both. And they better do something. The groundwater is salty in a half-mile from the coast in Pajaro, and it is three miles up the Salinas Valley. Three miles inland! Still, nobody's paying any pumping fees and nobody's backing off on the pumping. If I don't pump it, I know my neighbor will. The aquifer still gets hammered. It's the Tragedy of the Commons, a race to the bottom of the well. It's why every groundwater basin in California, or in most of the entire west, is in pumping overdraft."

Harper stopped. He had participated in this kind of off-the-cuff recital of the west's water problems many times. He knew the fix was not simple. But no question, the status quo was a mess. Nobody except water geeks and farmers really cared. Like other slow motion environmental disasters, most folks ignored this one because the dropping water levels and incoming salt front were invisible, hidden underground. There were no visible impacts to shock them, like shoals of dead salmon, or burning oil rigs.

He shot a grin at the Comish and Dukie, "Or you can just subdivide those coastal berry farms into 5-acre residential ranchos, and build cute stucco houses, each with a nice RV and a Quad parked at it, with a trampoline for the kids. Perfect for folks who feel San Jose's gotten too crowded. Take couple thousand farm acres out of irrigation, and add homes and golf courses. That will reduce pumping. You know, farmers use more way more water per acre than residential use."

"Great idea," said the Comish ruefully. "Except for the traffic impact on Highway One. And the visuals, and the loss of open space. If I suggest that at a Planning Commission meeting I'll get strung up by the neck. I already hear proposals for 300 homes and a golf course at every Monterey and San Benito County planning meeting I sit in on. People propose three hundred homes and a golf course like it is an order of burgers and fries. Imagine the morning traffic between Salinas and Monterey if a couple of those projects get built. I think I'll stick with recommending drip irrigation, and water meters and, uh, maybe user fees for pumping."

"Yeah, well, folks keep discovering this place." Harper offered.

"We have met the enemy, and he is us." Dukie chimed in.

"Thanks, Pogo" answered Ed with a smile.

They stopped talking and looked out at the ocean from the parking lot. Maybe they should switch to talking sharks, and let the fire barrel guys solve the water problems for a while, Harper considered. It would all come out about the same.

The sun was burning through the fog now and the tide had dropped further. Blue skies were visible inland as the fog wall was backing offshore. The small waves were working nicely on the reef. Each had a cheerful white foam cap when they rolled into the beach. There was no one out at the break, but several surfers had arrived and were changing into wetsuits. Harper heard one of the crowd by the fire barrel call out "Breakfast time for the Landlord". Jesus made chomping motion with both arms extended as jaws towards some surfers from the University walking past. The crew at the barrel all laughed, and the college guys ignored them. Harper looked out again at the break and tried remember the fin. It was hard to imagine that there was any threat in such a charming ocean scene.

Dukie started his truck engine. "Thanks for the water lecture. I needed a nap."

"See you around Harp," the Comish called and waved as he sat back in the truck seat.

"Go big in the canyon, Comish." Harper said." Play safe down in there. I'll try to contact Tracer for you, Dukie. We're going to meet up to do a high water run on the Tuolumne in a couple weeks, while I'm still fresh from paddling the Canyon. "

Dukie's eyes met Harpers for a moment. "You going to the project scoping meeting at the quarry site on Thursday?" he asked quietly. " Harper nodded. "That's what I heard. Maybe I'll see you there. Good luck with those guys. They're still trying to get out of doing any environmental review at all, you know. Don't forget to double your fee, and tell them to back off if they try to put words in your mouth. " Dukie gave him one of his old smiles, piratical and remorseless, then looked away. "Those bastards don't respect our technical bullshit much, but they do respect a high billing rate and bit of spine." He waved and rolled his window up as his truck rolled off.

7

Meeting at the Quarry

The next Thursday morning, Harper drove north again on Highway One, headed for his big meeting. As his truck passed the turnoff to Dukie's ranch, then passed his favorite surf spots at the Landing and Waterfalls, he couldn't help glancing at the ocean. There were no corduroy lines of ocean energy. There had been no swell for days, but hope springs eternal in the surf scout's breast. He had a quick stop to make on his way to the quarry.

Glancing at the rows of sprinklers chugging away in the artichoke fields, he pondered the shortsightedness that allowed the farmers of the year 1999 to pump valuable groundwater from the coastal aquifer, free but for the electricity, then spray it into the wind and lose half to evaporation before it ever touched soil.

"Slow learners. Everybody's racing to the red light," he muttered to himself, downshifting as the truck hit a grade. A bluff temporarily hid the Pacific Ocean from view. He slowed to turn off the highway, pulling into the driveway of a bungalow on a windy bluff. Artichoke fields stretched away behind an old hedge of Nopal cactus and Aloe plants sheltering the yard. It was the ancestral home of Johnny Twice, his guitar and surfboard repair guy. Johnny came out of the sway-backed shed near the house as Harper pulled up, a barrel–chested man with a snow-white ponytail. Styrofoam dust covered his arms like anthrax powder to both elbows, and a respirator mask was pushed up on his head. He waved majestically as Harper came to a stop. Harper climbed out and shook a powdery hand.

"Hey, Johnny. How you doin'?"

"Yo, Harper! I got that little guitar all ready, bro. But first come check out this sweet ride I'm working on. "

Harper followed him into the Shaping Shack, the inner sanctum, where Johnny shaped custom longboards. White dust coated every surface, including signed posters of famous surfers on the walls. Curved plywood shaping guides with obscure pencil marks hung from low rafters. A mammoth surfboard blank lay on the shaping table, with triple mahogany stringers running nose to tail, and a tail block of fancy wood cut into the foam base. A set of Johnny's trademark curved salmonoid side fins lay on the table, ready to be glassed in place on either side of a massive central fin.

"Yow! It must be 10 feet long!" Harper exclaimed, running a hand along the rail.

"It's a 9-9, bro, but it will carve like a dream. Longer than the one I made for you. Plenty heavy once it's glassed, but I put in extra rocker, so it can still make a steep drop without pearling.

That tail box is old-grain curly Koa wood from the Big Island, from my special guitar wood stash."

Harper touched the custom woodwork jealously. Johnny was one of the last real longboard artisans around. He still finished his boards with hand tools and they moved through the water like steelhead. Johnny picked up the twin side fins with his knurled hands and held them in place on the base of the board.

"Probably the fanciest board I ever did, right here. It's for the CEO of Waveform Software, the computer guy who bought the Locatelli Ranch last year. Nice guy, and he pays cash. He hardly ever surfs, though. I don't know if he ever took off on anything bigger than an ankle biter at Cowell's. But he says he's gonna learn to surf at The Landing this winter."

"Hope your board survives the winter. "

"Yeah, well, I'll be glad to make him another one. Two grand for this baby. My old regulars are pissed, cause I doubled my prices. But, I need it to pay off the hospital bills from my heart thing. You know, I almost had to sell Mom's house last winter."

"Good to see some new folks appreciate your work, Johnny. Speaking of which, what do I owe you for my travel guitar repair?" Harper asked.

"Two thousand dollars" Johnny deadpanned. His friendly face suddenly looked serious. Harper gaped, his mouth hanging open. He recovered as Johnny's lined face broke into his old roguish smile. "Gotcha! You almost choked, dude! Yeah, everything in Santa Cruz is up two thousand percent, right, so why not guitar repairs? No, I just had to adjust the truss rod and put on lighter strings. It was a little warped in the neck. Gimme 50 bucks cash, no tax. And play a song for me." Chuckling to himself, Johnny sauntered toward the house.

Harper followed his friend's broad back across the yard

thoughtfully. Harper almost never went to the doctor, except for stitches when his surfboard nailed him. Johnny was sixty, and a legend among shapers and big wave men, but that didn't provide health care benefits. He knew Johnny had had a series of heart attacks and a bypass operation the winter before, almost taken out by cardiac arrest after decades of surviving big waves and hard partying. It must be hard to cover the cost of heart surgery on the income of an itinerant surfboard and guitar craftsman, he realized.

Counting out the cash in the cluttered kitchen, Harper said, "Johnny, you're a freaking artist. I saw that board you made last year for Miklos, with the airbrush and abalone inlay. You should be doing all high-end stuff. Maybe get a young apprentice to do rough board shaping, so you can focus on the finish work."

Johnny looked at him wryly, "Right, as you get your quickie guitar repair for cash, and are out the door. Shit, Harper, I'm glad to still do dings and guitar repair for easy money. And maybe I won't get an apprentice, but some machine in China. This guy in Pasadena called, wants to pay me to put my logo on shipping container loads of finished boards, to sell on the internet on his " Old School Custom Shaper's Collection". He has four L.A. shapers signed up and wants to add me. I send them one finished board shape, and they scan it into a machine and make a hundred more. I might do it, too. Could make some real coin. He documents your board shape on his software and files it, so no else can claim it."

Harper stood at the door with his guitar case, uncertain what response was expected. "Modern times, amigo" he said, shaking his head.

"Yeah, well, I don't know. No soul in a machine board." Johnny said, stroking the grey cat that leaped up onto on his counter.

Harper looked at him, directly. "Plenty of soul in whatever you do, Johnny. Thanks again for getting my little guitar fixed."

Johnny grinned again and shook hands. "What river were you on where you dunked that guitar? And gone for a freaking month?"

"Colorado River through Grand Canyon, amigo. Greatest journey under sun and stars. You gotta go."

"Maybe I will some day." Johnny nodded. "Until then, you find a nice little overhang somewhere down there and say a prayer to the ancient ones for me."

"Will do, my friend. Me and this guitar. I'll try not to put it on any rafts that are going to flip next time."

Back out on Highway One, Harper continued north to the quarry gate. Trying to look professional, he had unloaded his surfboard, scraped off a peeling Grateful Dead sticker, and removed all food scraps and litter from the cab. Harper had read a stack of sand mining and water reports for his quarry proposal and he nervously reviewed mental notes as he drove. This was no routine gasoline tank pull. This quarry deal was more like an invitation to step into the biggest local shit-storm. Controversy came with all California water projects, but the hot button issues were bigger and closer to home for this one.

The Arena Corporation Lagunitas Sand Plant was 20 miles up the coast, north of the Monterey Bay's calmer waters, but still in Santa Cruz County jurisdiction. The working face of the quarry was hidden from sight behind a locked gate of sturdy tubular steel, inland of Highway One, only a couple miles north of The Landing parking lot. Arena owned the Lagunitas coastal creek watershed from the ocean to almost a mile inland. The automatic steel gate had a keypad system and opened to a paved lane up to the mine. A branch off this access road led to a rusty older gate with a chain and padlocks, on a dirt lane that ran under the highway, along the creek and towards the ocean. This ended next to the coastal marsh by the pocket beach of sand.

That one was the kind of private locked gate that surfers and steelhead fisherman gazed at wistfully while driving to crowded public spots. This tiny Lagunitas Beach, cliffed out north and south, was unvisited except for Snowy Plovers and trespassers seeking the sand bar, where perfect offshore barrels formed from northwest winter swells. The Quarry's security guards trucks were vigilant, and the Plant Manager was a legendary tyrant. Surfers caught crossing the sand were detained, identified, and had their boards confiscated or worse, snapped in half. It was possible to paddle down from beaches up the coast, but too arduous (unless you were in a kayak, Harper mused). As a result, the Lagunitas Quarry break was famous, and was talked about more often than it was ridden. A few clandestine keys to this rusty gate were rumored to exist. Their existence and possession was the topic of late-night keg party ruminations in kitchens at surfer parties up and down the coast. Harper had never met anyone who actually had surfed Lagunitas.

The Lagunitas Creek was tiny, almost dry most of the year, and blocked by a beach sandbar all summer. It flowed into a coastal marsh of rushes and blackbirds, with a postage stamp of a clear lagoon that breached and fed sand out to the ocean after big rains. Behind the new gate, where the paved road ran up onto the terrace above the creek, big yellow machines sat around a rusty tower with a series of conveyer belts, and a string of wash water ponds surrounded by rushes. Bare sandy ground was everywhere.

Arena Corporation mined high-quality, ancient beach sands

from the Santa Margarita Formation, a pure silica deposit of windblown, well-sorted fine sand, with a few Miocene-age sharks' teeth and sand dollars. The Santa Margarita sand quality was famous, a fossil beach, now sprinkled in valleys and pockets of the coastal mountains throughout central California. Twin hunters sought this former beach sand: the sand mining industry and well drillers, for was an excellent aquifer, when it was buried, saturated and thick enough. The sand was under a crossfire of dual development pressure.

The sand hunting had almost done in the nearby basin of Dutch Valley, where a thick aquifer section of Santa Margarita underlay a string of 1980's shopping malls, big box stores, and 1990's housing developments. High-yield wells drilled and screened in the clean sand were pumped harder each year for the water supply, dropping the water table like a falling tide. Sand mines ringing the town scraped away accessible clean sand from above the water table, and asphalt parking acres capped the rest of the sand, cutting off recharge from winter rains. To top it off, rusting underground tanks at local gasoline stations leaked into the sand from above, adding hydrocarbons and organic chemicals with names like BTEX and MTBE to the drinking water. Now, the saturated aquifer section was thinner and smaller, municipal wells on the perimeter of the basin were dry or contaminated, and several mines were closed where the sand had been scraped down to the hard mudstone that lay below.

Dutch Valley's local government was no longer handing out building permits to any developer with a bulldozer and a loan. They had also realized that the mudstone bedrock under their sand aquifer was a lousy water supply. A big municipal wastewater treatment plant was built to treat sewage water for aquifer recharge, and to provide an expensive alternative water supply that nobody seemed eager to use. The same water engineers that had so effectively drained the sand aquifer had drilled a series of expensive, deeper wells around Dutch Valley. Meanwhile, there was a moratorium on new water connections in Dutch Valley, and local government took a sudden interest in water conservation.

Other groundwater geologists shook their heads, wrote papers on the damaged aquifer, and gossiped about the bad professional advice the City had followed for a decade. Aside from a few angry newspaper letters from retirees and the owners of dry wells, most Californians kept driving down the freeway to the beach, fiddling with the radio and getting a tan on their window arm. They took little notice of Dutch Valley's lessons. Water still came out of kitchen faucets, and their sprinklers chugged away on golf courses, artichokes, and lawns. Rallying communities to act about unseen changes in underground water levels was a tough sell, even in communities of folks that recycled bottles every day and paid extra to get a sea otter stamped on their license plate.

Meanwhile, the clean, fine silica of the Santa Margarita sand was in great demand for specialty concrete mixes, and for optical glass production. Because several Dutch Valley mines had closed, the sand became scarce in Central California, and brought a premium. Best of all, it was right at the surface in the Lagunitas drainage, mined by simply scraping it up and running it through a wash system to be graded. Arena had been quietly mining sand here behind their gate for decades. After twenty years, their county mining permit required renewal. With a booming market, Arena wanted to add several new mining areas, access new hillsides and terraces of sand, scrape deeper, increase production, add an upgraded wash system, and get their permit renewed for the next twenty years. They had tried to run the mining permit through the county process as a routine renewal, without environmental review, but the local tree huggers caught wind of it and raised a ruckus. Now, the county planning commission was voting over whether to require a full environmental review. A coalition of strange bedfellows had come out against the quarry mining plans, and battle lines were forming.

Steelhead fisherman had distributed the now-common "Stop The Quarry" stickers far and wide. They were against the increased water pumping, saying the Lagunitas Creek and lagoon steelhead habitat were threatened. Harper knew that several environmental groups Shira belonged to were also involved. North Coast farmers were normally indifferent to the mining and bemused at the ranting of environmental extremists. Instead, they were speaking out against the quarry's new well application, fearing their own existing wells would suffer from increased pumping. A Monterey Bay Surfer's Coalition (which included a surprising number of surfing attorneys) was filing briefs against the continued removal of sand, fearing it would change the sand budget, diminish the offshore sand bar, and alter surfing breaks along the coast, as well as damage wildlife habitat. And of course, the vociferous Citizens to Save Santa Cruz, the usual suspects of all anti-growth battles and planning commission controversies, were strongly against it, because they were against everything.

8

Behind The Gate

Stopping at the quarry gate, Harper felt like a salesman knocking on a rich house as he sized up the ornaments. He punched in the key code he had received, and drove up the quarry road as the automated gate closed behind him. A cluster of green Arena company trucks were waiting above wash ponds at the top of the terrace, like scouts guarding the entrance. He saw Dukie's red pickup truck nearby, but no Dukie. Time to meet the clients. His heart was racing. Taking a calming breath, he recalled floating in his kayak on the long tongue of water leading into Crystal Rapid. This was nothing, compared to running Crystal. He parked a polite distance away, climbed out with his clipboard and strode over towards the trucks.

A group of four men were studying a sheaf of plans laid out on a truck tailgate. They turned as he arrived. A tall,

69

confident, gap-toothed bloke in an Arena Corp windbreaker stepped forward and greeted him with an English accent. Harper recognized Tony Armstrong, the Arena Environmental Coordinator. Harper had met him once at an Earth Day meeting of environmental groups, where Tony had spoken as an industry advocate for recycling or water conservation. The London expatriate had discovered a perfect habitat in California, where a sun-drenched feast of girls and women loved his British charm. In addition, his employer, Arena Corporation, had an endless string of excavation projects that needed all the environmental buzzwords he could utter. After his speaking bit at Earth Day, Harper recalled, Tony played the dashing rogue to the hilt, meeting half the room, handing out and collecting business cards, and then guiding one of the single ladies out to his Triumph Spitfire and blazing off out of the parking lot. Now, he received Harper with a hearty handshake, and said,

"You must be Harper Purcell, our water man! I'm Tony Armstrong, Environmental Compliance officer for Arena. Welcome to the Lagunitas Quarry. Most scenic sand plant in America, what? Dr. Gerhardt has told me much about you, Harper. He's looking for active faults traces just now, wandering about up on the terraces, I believe. I know people at your former firm, Envirocon, and reviewed your proposal myself. "

"Hi, Tony, " Harper replied. "Thanks very much. This is a great view. It's my first time up here, but I've read whatever I can find about your proposed project and permit application. Including the latest bumper stickers in town."

" Ah, yes, we mustn't worry about them. As long as you don't have one on your truck that is, Harper. Some loyal opposition is expected. After all, we work within the system. This quarry is in a special location. Coastal Zone, wetlands, and what not, eh?"

Tony flashed his snaggle tooth smile. " We'll do a top job and no harm will come to the bugs and bunnies. Or frogs and fishes, I suppose I should say, eh, Ralphie?" Tony gestured to a drab, quiet man in a Gore-Tex raincoat and rubber boots standing nearby.

"This is Ralph Longbotham, from Significance Evaluations. Ralph is our consulting biologist. He works on all our quarry permits."

Harper nodded and shook hands with Ralph. He had heard of Significance Evaluations, often jeeringly referred to as Less Than Significant Evaluations. They never met an environmental impact that could not be easily mitigated. Tony paused and spoke with gentle stress on his syllables to Harper.

"Remember, it's a permit renewal, Harper. We're calling it an *existing project renewal*, not a permit *application*. After all, there's been a sand mine operating up here since before America entered the Viet Nam war." Tony smiled significantly, turned and gestured to two company men standing behind him. The older one wore a work jacket and battered steel-toed boots with metal peeking through the toe leather. He was a mean dog, weathered and pugnacious. The younger man held a file and maps. He looked the part of the crew-cut young executive, the kind of guy who has a fantasy baseball team, and a watch that was also a calculator. The bulldog shook hands with Harper first.

"Harper, This is Hitch Owens, the quarry operator. Hitch has been here twenty years. He was here before we started the Specialty Silica department, and he built up this whole sand wash and pond system. Before that, Hitch spent a decade with Arena at the Gonzales gravel plant. And this is Gary Covington, the new project manager. Gary will take over Operations at this plant once Hitch retires next August, hopefully after we renew."

Both men considered Harper. Harper felt them shaping an appraisal. He resisted the urge to look down at his shoes. Instead, he smiled into their eyes, and said "Hi Hitch, Hi Gary. Good to meet. How'd you get that name, Hitch?"

Hitch hiked up his trousers. " Well… I always used to say to my crew, 'Let's hitch up and get started'. I don't like down time. Let's put the Cat in drive and load some sand trucks before lunch, I say." He glared at the biologist and back at Harper. " But now we gotta do a month of biological assessment before we can move a grain. And do a pumping test on the old well, and on every well in the section and who knows what all else before we can get back to work here. Why do we need a new well when the old well does three hundred gallons a minute? But, hell, I'll be retired in ninety days, anyway. And I doubt we'll move any more sand before then. Dealing with trespassers and consultants will be young Gary's headache then, I suppose. "

Gary and Tony smiled at Hitch patiently, like dutiful parents of a dim child. The biologist looked at Tony and said calmly, "There are several special-status species to address on this site, and we are assessing the potential impacts of renewed mining on all of them. There are Snowy Plover nesting grounds on the beach, red-legged frogs in the lagoons, plus possible steelhead habitat in the lagoon and creek. The good news is, that gives Arena grounds to keep everyone out, to prevent disturbance. But the Feds just listed a new lagoon fish, Tidewater Gobies, as Endangered, so we have to check for them too, and for salt marsh plants in the lagoon. As long as the mining plan says no grading or sand removal on the coastal side of Highway One, and the increased water use doesn't change water levels in the creek or lagoon," (Ralph paused and everyone glanced at Harper here) "Well, then there won't be any unmitigatable significant biologic impacts, I expect. Of course, we still have to do an assessment over several weeks for red-legged frogs in the wash ponds and in the creek below the quarry. If we confirm frogs there, you'll have to do pond mitigations and replace habitat elsewhere to avoid a finding of a significant impact. And the County is requiring that their biologist observe our biologic assessment, both daytime and nighttime. We have to arrange their access so Hitch doesn't try to arrest them this time."

Hitch snorted. "Those county fellows were just surfers! Had two boards in the back under a tarp. Parked here to check the waves in a county truck! And endangered frogs? There sure are plenty frogs, for them being listed endangered. Most mornings when we were running trucks there were three or four squashed out on the Highway or on the access road." He lit a cigarette and looked at Tony sideways. " I guess we don't need that part in the damn biologic assessment, huh?"

"I'm sure the biotic assessment will go fine", Tony said airily, " As long as our impact is 'Less Than Significant', what? " He turned back to the maps. "Lets go over the mining plan and water demand with Harper, shall we Gary?"

They clustered around the maps. Gary Covington gave them a detailed briefing of a sequence of Five-Year mining plans, with working quarry face elevations, new sand grading and wash plant water demands, water recycling plans, and plant reclamation guidelines. The existing well was thirty years old, located on the terrace in the remaining sandy ground amidst the quarry operations buildings. Questions flew and they fanned the sheaf of maps back and forth to find various elevations or plans. There was no record of the well screen or well construction available, but Hitch rattled off the well depth, submersible pump depth, well yield and seasonal water levels from memory.

As Harper had suspected, the current well was only a little over a hundred feet deep, and static water level in the well was roughly 50 feet down, about the same as the creek and a little above sea level. Hitch said that during heavy pumping, the water dropped to the top of the pump, fifty feet below sea level, and recovered overnight once pumping stopped. There was no well log with screen locations, but given the depth, the well was likely screened in the saturated sand to the bottom of the Santa Margarita. That meant water came from the same sand that the mine was scraping the top of, and the same aquifer that provided baseflow water to the creek and lagoon in summer months when no rain fell.

The Arena staff listened carefully as Harper discussed the scope of work and the deeper test well he had outlined in his proposal. A new water supply well would have to be drilled deeper, through the sand and through mudstone that underlay the Santa Margarita, and sealing off the surface layer, to prevent connection to the creek or lagoon. That would prevent steelhead impacts, and with no connection to the ocean, prevent seawater intrusion during pumping. After he explained the test well drilling, monitoring well measurements, extended pumping test and stream and lagoon water level monitoring he proposed, the quarry guys looked at each other and at Tony.

"How much will all that work and a new well cost?" Gary asked.

Harper began to talk about how well seals, screened interval, and casing size could affect cost, looking at their expectant faces. At the same time, he was trying to remember what the last big well he had worked had actually cost.

" …But, realistically, a three hundred foot well, five inch

casing, completed and equipped, will be at least fifty grand." he concluded. " Maybe over fifty grand if we don't get good production beneath the mudstone and have to drill deeper. That's just drilling and construction, but the test pumping and permitting work costs are presented in my proposal. And, you will probably need to buy a new pump and maybe get a new electrical drop for permanent use. We can rent a pump and generator for the test phase. Of course, we'll keep the old well open and use it as a monitoring point during test pumping the new well, but it is likely that the existing well is in hydraulic connection with the creek, and therefore with the wetlands…"

He paused, and tried to sound confident as he continued, "Without a deep new well, and without a comprehensive well testing program including stream and shallow aquifer monitoring, and without a convincing and professional report presentation, you will have no answer to the question about water impact, get no mining permit and have no project."

The men were quiet. Tony looked at Gary and said, " He's quite right about the deeper water supply you know. No skimping on this one, fellows. Everyone is watching, I'm afraid. Water supply is the key point, as usual. We only have three friendly votes of seven on the Planning Commission, and we need four to get a permit. We have our work cut out for us. Our capital costs projections for the new twenty year mining plan include a new well, and include our permitting and testing costs amortized over the projected life span, eh? "

Gary nodded, "We can pay for the well, as long as we get the mining permit and can sell the sand. It cuts the profit margin, but the demand for the sand is solid. "

Hitch looked at Tony and said "But I thought you said there was another possible yes vote next month and the alternate fellow on the Commission was our guy."

Tony shot him a harsh look. "Alternate Commissioners only vote when regular commissioners are absent, Hitch. That's why we didn't get our renewal back in January, remember? Now, then,…" Tony switched on his grin and stood up from the maps, as if all was settled. He said, " Right, Gary. Lets give these lads the green light. And don't forget, we're saving a bundle using Harper here to do the testing program instead of his old firm. Ralph, we want a schedule from you to complete the biologic assessment and Harper, get us a workplan for getting new well drilling bids and costs for a complete water supply testing program. Onward and upward, men."

The Arena guys all shook hands with Harper again, this time with more warmth and familiarity. Tony handed Harper a rolled set of the plans, like a lord handing a tenant farmer rights to a plot. Harper acted calm and competent, as he realized excitedly he had passed some kind of test, and was entering in a new stage. As Tony walked him back to this truck, his mind reeled with questions he should ask, including about a signed contract and timing and budget. But Tony was saying something else.

"We'll authorize you for just the first task in your proposal now, Harper, to get you going on the drilling bids and writing a workplan for the rest. Eight thousand dollars, isn't it? Our legal group is still working on an appeal about the requirement for full environmental review, so no actual drilling will occur till that is done. Not much hope there, of course, with the County political situation the way it is, but that's the word from Legal. Meanwhile, I'm to get started on the Environmental Review. We'll use our standard contract, of course. We have Arena company terms and conditions you must sign, a confidentiality statement and so on. And once you sign the Arena Master

Agreement, I can throw you some other assignments as well. We have water issues up and down the coast we could use you on. Say, that reminds me, could you appear in Salinas next week for a Monterey County Planning Board hearing? On an hourly basis, bill us for time and materials? We need to muster our consultants for a different gravel quarry issue there. A great project, really, a 100-year mining plan, nothing out there but cattle and scrub now, the EIR is all done, but there are comments and responses of course. Be at the Monterey County Courthouse, Salinas, next Thursday. We need faces to put in front of the Planning Board. I'll email you the details." Tony smiled winningly.

"Oh, and one more thing, Harper. As our consultant, I can share our beach condo with you now, you know. Arena has a lovely little corporate place at Las Olas Beach. You're a surfer, I believe? The Las Olas condos are right on the sand, you know, built back in the 70's, with the foundations poured just a month before the Coastal Commission Act took effect in California. Our corporate office usually has it booked for retreats or for some highway official before a freeway bid opening, but I'm allowed to use it when available. It's fabulous for the ladies, even has a hot tub on the deck that's guaranteed to get them out of their knickers. I have it for this Saturday, but it turns out I'll be away at a conference in Fresno." He winced. "Fresno, Good Lord, the sacrifices I make. Anyway, why don't you use it for a night? Call it a celebration of us hiring you! And much success to all concerned. You do have a bird you can take there, I hope?" Tony arched his eyebrows delicately, indicating discretely that he could be some help in this department, if needed.

"Uh, wow, that very generous, Tony. I think I might have somebody, yes. A beach house at Las Olas? Saturday night!

Great!" Harper pumped Tony's hand again, eagerly. Cracks were appearing in his professional reserve. "Thanks a million, Tony. Yes, send me the Arena contract forms and the e-mail about the Salinas job. I'll be there! Much success to all concerned." He waved at the others and started for his truck, sensing he was dismissed.

"Onward and upward!" saluted Tony, watching him go. Harper resisted the urge to say Cherrio or something equally ridiculous and he climbed into his truck. As he made his escape down the quarry road back to the highway, he felt as if he had completed a scary whitewater run for the first time, one that had intimidated him while scouting it, but had turned out to be easy. He reviewed his proposal in his mind, already calculating the bills he could pay and weeks of work he could do for his initial eight thousand dollars, and making plans for the drilling and testing stages that would be required once his full workplan was authorized. It could be months of work, a full summer of billable time.

Hey, plus a night at the beach condo! Las Olas was a swank place, a private beach that was supposed to have a fun beach break that caught both summer and winter swells.

Harper thought of Shira, the curvy Jewish woman he had met at a Wetlands Watch press conference. She had dancer's curves, tasteful make-up, intelligence and fun in her eyes. Could he ask Shira to come to the condo? What would she say? He imagined her floating in an embrace of hot tub bubbles, her curves artfully hidden and then revealed by the effervescent water of his imagination.

Shira was not his girlfriend, but he had hopes. She had looked him right in the eyes and lifted her eyebrows slightly as he offered her his business card. She smelled great, like a lemony mango. The power of her gaze was palpable, dark eyes in a classical face from a desert tribe, ringlets of hair spilling down, a generous nose, with silver necklace and earrings. She looked like an Israeli movie star, not a California hippie chick. Santa Cruz girls mostly tended towards jeans and pullovers, but Shira had worn a swishy knit dress, and looked able to stop traffic. And when she gave him her business card, he was surprised to see she was a Registered Nurse and Midwife, not the bugs-and-bunny biology student he took her for.

As he punched the exit code into the quarry gate and pulled out onto Highway One, he glanced once at the lower beach, at the forbidden gate leading to the dirt road under the highway and access to the Lagunitas Tubes beach break. He decided he would need a key to that gate too, to do his fieldwork, and made a mental note to ask Tony about it.

9

The Wandering Poet Pub

Harper opened the door to the Wandering Poet Pub. A blast of talk and Frank Sinatra's voice escaped. Inside was warm and smoky pub air, with a row of intent dart players facing their boards along one wall. There was a good crowd, with a smell of Guinness stout, bodies, and lit cigarettes, which were still enjoyed at the bar here despite the new state law forbidding them indoors. He was looking for Shira's face, but did not find it.

Harper avoided the dart's airspace and made his way to the bar. He could see the bear-like shoulders and balding head of Chris McCann, the owner and life force of the pub, drawing a pint behind the bar. Mac was a former Santa Cruz city councilman, a lover of drink, of spirited women and of spirited discussion, a pontificator and a confessor. He had a short, colorful run as a local politician, but he was born to run an Irish pub. It was said that he knew half the town, and kept about half the secrets he knew. Now in his third decade of service behind the bar, with his own drinking days behind him, he could still cut a wide swath through a crowded room. Harper had seen him toss an argumentative customer out the door, getting the fellow clear over the hood of the first car in the lot. During grad school years, when the earthquake shattered downtown was empty, Harper had been something of a pub regular, nursing a pint and playing darts to avoid working on his thesis. Mac had told him plenty about life and how Santa Cruz worked then, including which loudmouth regular was the no-good son of the family that owned a string of downtown property, which poor divorced bastard alone at the bar was an unsung hero in the early development battle that stopped the Lighthouse Beach from being a hotel, and how to drink an Irish Car Bomb (drop a shot glass of Bailey's and Bushmill's into a pint glass of Guinness, and chug). Lately, Harper had been surprised to see Mac in the room at the City Council meetings, quietly taking notes and nodding to folks up on the council seats, as the upcoming General Plan review was discussed.

Finding a seat at the end of the bar, Harper nestling in beside a large black man in a woven reggae cap with dreadlocks spilling out. The dreadlocked man was saying to a nervous skinny blond guy next to him, " Yeah, mon, I should have bought Microsoft at 35. Jah as my witness, it will never be below 60 again. " His friend replied, " I know! Right? My broker was an idiot on that one! You should check out this new company doing online grocery shopping! It has an amazing business model! It will be huge. The initial stock offering is next week. My broker says he can get me in at the same price as employees." Harper sighed and turned away.

Wild guitar music with gypsy singing came on the jukebox. It seemed to suit the mix of students, bikers, longhairs, and dedicated Guinness drinkers at the bar. Who even had a real job in this town, Harper wondered, as he surveyed the crowd. And why did Shira pick this place to meet him? He waved and caught Mac's eye. The pub owner shambled down to see him, handed him a pint of Guinness and shook his hand.

"Hey there, Harper, long time, no see. Good to still see some familiar faces still in town with all the new money coming in. You've been on the river with Dukie, hey? Have a pint on me, to celebrate your new business. I hear you've hung out a shingle now, and are having a go at private water consulting. Should be enough water fights around here to keep you busy and pay those student loans, hey?"

Harper laughed, "Chris, you are amazing. Nobody even knows I started a consulting business except you. Running my own company is my dream."

"Well, of course it is, bub. This is California. Everyone has a dream. Some are dreaming of the perfect wave, and some are dreaming of buying a multi-unit rental property with good income potential with a no points, low-interest loan. I'm dreaming of a Democratic governor and affordable health care for poets, workers and self-employed Irishmen. I hope your dream works out. Plenty of competition, I reckon. I know there's lots of geologist in this town, cause they all come here for their pints. There's probably a half a dozen geologists playing darts right now. Good customers, you geologists are. And Dr. Dukie in one of the best, of course. Now he's been in meeting his lawyer clients here. He told me some river trip stories last week."

"I've hardly seen him since we got back." said Harper. "Remember, Mac, the best river trips stories never get told. You should come on a trip with us."

"Oh, I could never leave this place for a month. Running a bar is like being a daily miracle worker. The sun would not come up here without me around. Hey, our Dukie is running with some big shots lately. Huddling in the corner with the Arena Quarry boys, he was today. And you've started going to all the water board and council meetings now, I see, Harper. You going to start in with that Arena gang like Dukie? I don't know if they like your kind. I hear they like consultants that write the conclusions first, then do the work later, or not at all. "

"Well, that's not Dukie. And I don't have a contract yet." Harper said. "But I could use some work with folks that pay their bills." He sipped his beer and wiped his lip. "Actually Chris, I am trying to get hired on that Lagunitas quarry job. It's a big scope of work. Using a small local outfit like me could give them credibility. And doing a decent technical analysis on a job like that could put me on the map for water studies around here. And I'll do a good job."

Chris looked at him. "Credibility, is it? Well, you got to find work, I know. Tough enough to survive in this town without a trust fund, or commuting to a job over the hill. But watch out for Arena. Their lad Tony Armstrong, that English wanker, he comes in here acting like he's half Irish, and talking like he's John Muir's brother to boot. But I know those quarry folks he's with, from way back. They got their boot on their non-union worker's necks, and the rich SOBs that own it are just out to grab more dollars. Devil take the environment, and the hindmost. You keep your nose clean with that lot." With that, the barman nodded and walked back down the bar.

Harper drank his beer and shook his head. He was barely even hired, for the best job he had a shot at, and the grief was piling up over working for Arena Construction. He realized he was not looking forward to telling Shira about it.

Then he saw her come in the door. The music did not stop, but it seemed to walk beside her. She strolled through the crowd like she was in her own living room, straight to the bar, and leaned over to kiss Chris McCann on the cheek. Harper was taken aback. He had not thought the Poet was her kind of place, but clearly he was wrong. She talked to Mac like an old friend, and it gave Harper a chance to watch her. He drank in the curve of her neck and shoulders as she leaned forward, watched the way she laughed at something Mac said. Mac gave her his big smile, leaning across to hear her question, then turned and pointed down the bar towards Harper. When they both turned to look, Mac made a comic face behind her, pointing at Shira with huge raised eyebrows, saying, Well, good on you, lad.

Harper gave a shy wave and stood up as she moved down the bar to him. She hugged him, kissed his cheek, graciously took his seat as he stood next her. She was wearing a simple dress with a scoop neck and the same silver necklace he remembered. He smiled at her and tried to keep his eyes from following the clean line of her collarbone to the peek of perfect hollow between her breasts. Mac came down the bar, bringing her a glass of red wine and a pack of Spanish cigarettes.

"Better enjoy these now, Shira." He said laying the pack and some matches on the bar. "I got a court hearing next month with the State Liquor Board, and if I don't get a smoking waiver, they say I have to stop the indoor smoking or lose my license. My attorney says it's all hopeless, but he's still working to pay off his bar tab, so I keep him on the case."

"Mac, you are still the Patron Saint of lost causes, aren't you?" Shira said fondly, tearing open the pack, tapping out a cigarette and holding it to her lips. Mac lit the cigarette elegantly for her, and smiled wistfully. " Oh, I've won a few along the way, darling". He looked at Harper and said seriously " You be nice to this lady, Harper. She's one of the good ones. And she helped my daughter at the birth of my first Grandson, Eamon, so she's family." And he smiled at Shira again and left them.

Harper looked at Shira holding her cigarette and coolly blowing smoke and was at a loss for words. He could not have been much more surprised if she had taken out a sparrow and bit off its head.

"You smoke? " he managed. "I thought you're a vegetarian. You know Mac? He has a grandson? You were his midwife?". He realized he was sounding foolish.

"You drink beer?" she said in mock horror, looking at his pint. " We better get you another one." She poked him in the ribs and grinned. "Sorry for not telling you about the cigarettes, but it's a nasty habit from when I lived in Spain. I know you're only supposed to smoke weed in this town, but that just makes me sleepy. The Poet is the only place I can get these horrible Spanish truck driver cigarettes that I used to smoke. I get such a nicotine rush from them." She took another long drag and then stubbed out the remaining half a cigarette. "Oh, it's so bad. They make me want to speak Spanish and drink wine, and dance like crazy" she said with a spark of mischief in her eyes.

"Here, let me light you another one then. " Harper said, reaching for her matches. "Take two. Teach me how to smoke them, why don't you".

"Stop it " she smiled, swatting his hand away. "I like being myself with you. I don't have to drink for that. Beside, I can't drink too much, I'm working tomorrow. "

She sipped her wine and considered him with gorgeous brown eyes. "Harper, you look great! You've been gone forever. How was your river trip! I got your postcard and it was lovely. You sounded so…. reflective. And very sweet. What is the big news? You said in your phone message you wanted to tell me something?"

"Well, first I want to hear about your trip back east. Everything all right? I mean, is your Grandma OK?"

"Yes, she's OK, thank you. She was in the hospital for a week, but just as a precaution. Bubbe is 90, so when she gets sick, you don't wait around. She had a bad cough and fluid in her lungs, but she is fine again. My Mom sees her every day. They both want me to move back to New York. " Shira paused " And, I told her about you" she added with a smile.

"What? Me? What did you tell her ? What did she say?"

"I told her I met a nice man, a geologist. I told her she could meet you when you came back from the Grand Canyon and came to New York with me. What did she say? She said, What, you work in a hospital, you couldn't meet a nice Jewish doctor?"

They laughed, and they sat and talked for a while, becoming comfortable around each other again. Mac visited their corner regularly and kept an eye on them from wherever he was at the bar. Harper felt good to be near her. He got the sense that they were safe together, that there was no rush, that neither would do the other harm. They looked at each other faces often while they talked and they listened to each other. Harper told her some of his river stories from the trip, about hiding the Groover and getting run over by an empty raft at Lava Falls. Shira told Harper about a difficult birth for a first-time mother that had been scary and then turned out well. After they had talked for over an hour, Shira finished her second drink, looked at him kindly and said she had to go home early, and asked again about his news. Harper coughed into his hand and looked up.

"Oh actually, I got a couple new jobs, and one of them gave me an offer of a place to stay, as a bonus. A free overnight at the company beach condo at Las Olas, down near Moss Beach. I'm, um, I'm working for a big developer on a new water well installation. My first big local project. Their Environmental Rep gave me the key code to their place. And it's mine for Saturday, tomorrow night." He watched her for a reaction. " It has a hot tub. And a balcony. There's a very nice beach break there, good waves with a south swell. I thought I might take my board down, stay over tomorrow night and surf it at dawn." He paused, out of steam. He took a breath and looked at her carefully. Her brown eyes were enormous, gazing at him, honest and clear. He met them, fell into them. "Shira, would you, please, Shira, like to come with me tomorrow night to stay at a beach condo at Las Olas?"

She gazed back at him for a long moment, still looking serious. "Well, that's great that you have some new projects. " Then her face broke into a merry smile. She said, " An overnight date? With a hot tub? Why Harper Lewis Purcell, are you propositioning me?"

"Yes!" he gasped, nodding vigorously. "Oh, yes! But, you know, with dinner first." he stopped, not happy with that, and tried again. " I mean, Shira, I wanted to see you more, do more first dates first, but then I was gone, then you were gone, and now this beach place is only for tomorrow…" he stumbled to a halt. She was actually smiling at his distress.

"Dinner, too! Lucky me!" she said charmingly. She stood up and collected her things. She looked at him mercifully. "Thank you Harper, that is sweet. I am considering your offer. And, congratulations again about your new job. I want to hear all about it. But right now, I have to go. I have to work tomorrow early, and I am going home now." She paused. "About tomorrow …well, I have office visits all day tomorrow, and I'm on call tomorrow night, too. I have two women who are about to go into labor any moment, so I can't promise you anything about tomorrow night. I may be at the hospital all night. But that sounds very nice. I would like to meet you. "

Harper nodded, hopeful, trying not to look desperate, not saying anything. Shira continued,

"So, if you call me tomorrow and you give me the address and the key code, I will come to the beach condo with you, if I can, when I am done work tomorrow night. OK?" She looked at him very directly and simply, with kindness and warmth and no artifice, and she kissed him. He was relieved, melting with happiness and kissed her back and smiled. He was thinking that Shira could say lots, or she could say lots without hardly even talking. He liked both. She waved down the crowded bar to Mac and smiled again at Harper and then she was gone.

Harper watched her go, yelled a late goodbye, and then plopped down in her still warm seat in a daze. He reached for his beer. The suddenness of asking her, and then of her departure left him weak. He reviewed the situation. She said yes, didn't she? She had received his postcard from Phantom, she liked it, she told her grandma about him, she had looked in his eyes and smiled like that when he said please come to the condo. That was all good. She looked so terrific. Such a kiss! He felt bad about asking her to stay overnight so fast, about not telling her about working for Arena. Now she was gone, but she had said yes, about tomorrow. Probably, anyway. She said to call her, to tell her the address and key code. She would come after work. He should call now to give her the key code. He reached for his coat and found his cell phone buried in a pocket. The battery was dead, again. He sighed; he would call her tomorrow. She said yes. He grinned like a fool, and finished his beer.

10

Las Olas

Harper had never used such a perfectly clean enormous steel refrigerator before. He ran a finger along the flawless brushed metal surface. There was not a single cute magnet on the fridge. The place looked like a movie set. He was exploring his overnight Las Olas beach condo; the spoils of his new consulting assignment, feeling more like an intruder than a guest. He prowled the place slowly, peering into cabinets and opening doors. The Arena Corporation's beach pad was decorated in California Elegant. Cool pastels and modern art on the walls, nice wine glasses above the sink, stainless steel appliances in the kitchen, a shiny barbeque grill on the deck, and jazz on the kitchen CD player. There were ocean views on three sides, on each of the top two floors. Nothing but chilled air and fancy mustard, a jar of pearl onions and three kinds of barbeque sauce were in the shiny refrigerator. Unfortunately, Harper was also alone. Shira was with a laboring mom at the hospital, and had not arrived yet by sunset.

He dined alone glumly on take-out Thai food, and then sat in the hot tub until he was prunish and shrunken. He climbed out of the tub, opened, sipped and then gradually finished the bottle of Spanish sparkling wine he brought to share with Shira. Leaning on the balcony railing and staring at the dark ocean, he followed the half-circle of the Monterey Bay past brighter clusters of towns at the top and bottom of the bay. Along the shore in both directions, the string of beach lights suggested similar elegant hide-aways. In each one, he imagined shining conversations, where confident men stood laughing as glamorous women shook their sparkling earrings over tanned bare shoulders, sipping wine and witnessing the great offshore darkness. Shira had called him before dinner and said that her patient's water had broken and labor was starting. She was dilated to 6, (whatever that meant), and so Shira would come to the condo if she could, maybe late. Maybe even tomorrow. She was apologetic, rushed, with hospital loudspeakers echoing in the background. Harper had made understanding noises into the phone, swirling his finger in his wine and looking at the layer of fine water beads that formed on the bottle in the silver ice bucket.

After she called, Harper had worked his way through the bottle of wine, crystal flute by flute. At first, he had been philosophical, contemplating the mystery of the ocean, allowing the phosphorescent purr of arriving waves in the growing dark to accent the clean, metallic taste of the wine. Then, he estimated the cost, the down payment, and monthly mortgage of a place like this, plus condo fees. He though about what he would have to earn in a year to buy one. He concluded he could never afford it.

Then again, he considered, wrinkling his forehead. What if he scored a bundle of cash and could double his down payment. Maybe, then? Hey, what if he married money? He imagined what powerful institutions or wealthy families owned adjacent beach houses, and all of the lovely and inviting beach places he could see from the balcony. With a pair of binoculars he found in the kitchen, he scanned other houses, then the floating pelicans in the purple offshore. His eyes followed a single woman and her Dalmatian across the sand, among the last wanderers on the darkling beach. Did she live here at Las Olas, or were she and the dog guests like him? Was she a wealthy heiress from a dynasty, a carefree gypsy girl, or a foreign tourist just enjoying the sand between her toes? Did she care about the outcome of land use planning, water battles, and traffic problems? Putting down the binoculars, he considered calling up a couple of his surfer friends to share his condo bounty, to bring some beers, turn up the tunes, and taste the fruits of his first consulting efforts. He could give them the gate key code to party in the borrowed palace, and then all go for a dawn surf session. But it was already late. He missed his guitar, and cursed himself for leaving it behind.

A glass of wine later, he realized he still had his ex-girlfriend Donna's number on his cell phone. He also remembered her athletic body, slipping out of her wetsuit after surfing. He thought about her quick breath and warm pulse against his skin, and how she always loved getting comped with a pro deal. They had never actually broken up, just faded out. He considered the old Donna speed dial button, as he filled his flute glass again. But he sighed and dropped the phone on the table. He didn't want to see Donna.

He imagined Shira working now with the laboring Mom, focused, competent, a sheen of sweat on her brow, the nervous husband hovering, the mother panting, and Shira in the center, at home with the Doula's ancient feminine role amidst life and death, more desirable than ever in the power of the birth scene. Truly, he was in awe of her. He thrilled to imagine that her hands, hands that could sew sutures and could bring a baby safely into the world, could unbutton his shirt and run across his chest. Maybe she would come over later.

The moon was rising, leaving a track across the waves. It was too late to call anyone. Perhaps he should just go surfing. He had his surfboard out in the truck, and could paddle out for a moonlight session. Floating in the ocean at night was scary but fantastic. He could work off this buzz in the surf, get a good sleep and be ready for Shira in the morning. He topped off his glass with the last of the wine, and placed the empty bottle upside down in the ice bucket. He carried the glass inside and made an unsuccessful search of the cabinets for more booze. Gradually, an amorphous melancholy took him, a distance from the unknowable people on the beach and from the glamorous windows he could see from the balcony. He felt distant from his family back in Pennsylvania, from his married sisters working conventional jobs and raising children back East, from the stars that twinkled and were reflected in the ocean, then blurred by the line of surf. He padded barefoot to the sofa, set down his glass and reached for a folded down duvet cover. He lay down and sleep took him.

Much later, he heard Shira's voice. It was in his dream. The soft pillows, cover and velvet fabric of the sofa cocooned him, and the wine hung in mists. In the dream, he was alone in an old rowboat, perched just above a rapid. He could see rocks and foam below him, exploding water and noise, but his boat was frozen in place and would not move into them. He scanned the water, alert, worried about the low freeboard and awkward hull of his craft, searching for a clean line, or a killer hole to avoid. He pulled again on the oars and wondered why he was not moving. He heard Shira's voice, and searched the boat and the river for her, but he was alone. Then the sofa shifted and he felt her warmth as she crawled under the cover next to him. He surfaced from his dream to find her cuddling against him. "Is that my delightful Shira darling?" he murmured sleepily. He felt the confusion and hesitancy of awakening in a strange place. He needed to finish rowing the rapid. He became more fully awake when she softly whispered "Hello, handsome" into his ear and spooned against him. His mouth was dry. She was soft and warm and incredible. The last mists of his dream curled away.

He turned to make room for her hips on the sofa, and put an arm around her. She curled against him in green scrubs, still wearing her sneakers. Her face was tired in the moonlight, and she smelled faintly of sweat, blood, hospital hallways and the mysterious and powerful forces of birth. "Sorry I missed dinner," she said, "I know that was supposed to be part of the seduction."

"Hmmm, I think you have seduced me anyway" Harper said. He smelled and then kissed her neck in an exploratory way, and they both shifted to bring their bodies and faces closer together.

"You surfer boys are so easy. " She nuzzled him back. "You smell like champagne. I really did miss the party. But, Sheila gave birth to a lovely daughter. How about if I take a hot shower and meet you in the bedroom?"

" Oh yes, oh yes, oh yes, that would be wonderful" he said as encouragingly and manfully as possible. He was feeling dizzy, his blood pressure rising. She untwined from him, slid off the sofa. He sat up, his tongue sticking to the roof of his mouth. "I feel like I rowed twenty miles in my sleep. I had the strangest dream."

He drank water and moved to the bedroom, then waited forever while she showered. He heard the shower turn off. Sitting on top of the covers in the dark, he took his shoes off, but remained dressed. It was not clear to him how she would return and how dressed he should receive her. Then, she came from the shower and glided to the enormous master bed, dropping her towel in the moonlight. She was nude as a pearl from an oyster. Her bare feet were silent in the deep carpet and she glowed majestically, with dark shining hair. She looked like a granted wish, and his eyebrows popped up. He tried not to lunge at her, a starving man, but he could not contain a delighted series of Oh, Shira, yes, oh yes escaping him as she approached. She smiled at this litany, accepted it as her due without any embarrassment, and sat the bed next to him, relaxed, pulling covers over her. She was comfortable in her skin. Two strands of thick dark hair fell across her shoulder. He reached tentatively for them, brushed them off, touched her arm, and kissed her shoulder. Touching her skin lit up his brain like Times Square.

She said, "Let get you out of all those clothes" and began pulling his shirt over his head. Harper lifted his arms to help her, and as her hands slid over his chest for the first time, he commanded his brain to remember every nuance of this.

Later, after she had calmed him down and he swept her up, after he joined her under the covers and they found each other, and after her curves, her kind and eager hunger, and her generous little love cries were forever in his memory, Harper lay next to her with his sweat cooling. Their bodies were loosely wrapped together in luxurious sheets. He floated on a cushion of wonder and relaxed lust. "We are a love burrito," he said, pulling the sheet around them.

"This place is too fancy for a burrito, we are a love crepe," she corrected. He kissed her neck.

"My little strawberry. But, you taste too salty to be a strawberry. You must be a pickle". She smiled and stretched, elegantly, a tigress within his arms.

" Who are you calling a pickle, Mister Pickle?".

Harper gazed at her in honest delight. He felt a sense of awe that cast halos around her. "Shira darling, four thousand years of Jewish history and culture have reached their pinnacle in your perfect breasts".

"Why, thank you, kind goyim" she said demurely, "Thank you for appreciating them." She lay on one elbow, posing for him, the gilded nude painting above the saloon bar of his dreams. She smiled playfully, "You do mean the twin pinnacles, don't you?" He grinned and leaned forward against her, appreciating them with kisses. His nose pressed against her sternum, breathing in her scent and making nuzzling noises against her breasts as she giggled and squirmed and then hugged his neck, trapping him there. He did not resist, and she rolled on top of him and pressed him into the pillows. He was content to stay buried in her cleavage and to feel her weight settle onto him. She hummed softly, leaning forward, her rich hair cascading down around his face. Her hips were atop him, and she traced her nipples across his face. They went down his jaw, across his lips, back to his nose. He chased them with his mouth making little kissing noises. She let him catch one, and he closed his eyes in bliss for a moment, enjoying the firm flesh between his lips, then opened them as she rocked back and sat atop him. Their eyes met as she bit her lip and began to breathe faster, shifting her position atop him subtly and then settling her hips back down atop him. Their mouths found each other. Harper was amazed and breathless again, drunk on her skin, letting her set their pace, as his hands explored and memorized her. He guiding her onto him and was guided into her. Her curves were velvet softness on the surface, with a web of muscles just beneath. Her movements began building smoothly, then urgent, increasingly fierce, and then just perfect. Later they dozed, and the early sunlight found them together fast asleep.

11

Dawn Session

———

Deep, soft pillows, and the smell of clean cotton sheets. Harper awoke to Shira gazing at him. He was at the condo. She was there. It was early morning outside, blue-grey light in the sky and purple tones rolling on the quiet ocean surface. She looked composed, rested, fantastic. She considered him as if she was waiting for something. He realized it was for him to awake. He opened his eyes, and kissed her good morning, happy but trying to find a handle on his situation. She said, "Good morning, handsome. You know, you really have to come to New York now to meet my Grandmother. "

"OK, um, yes, great" Harper ran a hand through his hair and cupped her buns with his other hand. "When do we leave?"

"Well, maybe this summer. If you want keep company with me, that is. I have about 200 relatives back in NY, but you have to meet my Bubbe for starters. ”

"I would be honored," said Harper, realizing he meant it and looking straight back at her. He let the glow of being next to her wash over him. Gradually, he realized he could hear the crisp unmistakable sound of breaking waves from outside. The swell must have come up overnight. He sat up casually in bed and peaked out the window at the ocean, spilling the covers off them. Yup, nice clean lines on the water, with no wind, and a lovely beach break, peeling left and right. Two guys out already.

He looked back at Shira on the pillow next to him, more glorious than ever in the soft morning light, and then back out at the swell. He had not surfed in over a week. Truly, an embarrassment of riches this morning. He felt her watching him, and he dove back under the covers with her and scooped her up in his arms.

"Smart choice, mister " she said wryly, " I thought I lost you to the waves for a moment there. But, I'm sorry to say I have to leave you in about five minutes. I have a checkup appointment with Sheila at the hospital that I can't miss."

"Five minutes? Leave?" Harper protested, nestling against her and tickling her ribs, trying not to whine. "No! Are you sure it can't be fifteen minutes? Fifteen minutes is good. I am quick like a bunny in the mornings. Twenty minutes, perhaps?"

Shira laughed and squirmed away from him, but not far. "Harper, you are a horndog in the mornings, you mean. And at night too, I noticed. And I like that. But no, I'm already late. And, we don't keep first-time nursing mothers with a newborn baby waiting." She settled down on her pillow and looked at him. "Don't worry, you can see me again soon. And besides, now you can go surfing like you really wanted to. But seriously, I have been waiting for you to wake up. I promised myself I would not rush into things with guys anymore until I knew more about them. But, now here I am again in some cute guy's bed, wondering all about him. Can I ask you something?"

He nodded yes, and lay looking at her face, wary.

"Well, for starters, what do you want out of life? To make you happy, I mean?" she asked simply.

He exhaled slowly and considered.   Talk about your lightweight pillow talk. This woman was really something. Don't rush this, he thought. Breathing in, he began tentatively,

"Well, this is good. This moment is a very good one. I would like a lot more of you in my happy life." He paused, glanced at her. She looked back, eyebrows up, expectant, waiting for more. "From life? " he asked. She nodded, waiting. " I guess, " he continued, "I am pretty greedy. I want a lot. There's a toast that I like. I heard it in Mexico. It goes, *"Love, health, friends, money and time to enjoy them"*, he said hoisting an imaginary glass. " I want that, I guess. I want it all."

"Amor, salud, amigos, pesetas, y tiempo para gustarlos." she said with a smile. "That's Spanish, actually. So Spanish. And it does seem to cover it pretty well. They know something about life." She looked back at him "As long as you include family in the love part. Plenty of family."

"I'm fine with family. Definitely, family. " Harper thought about it for a moment and looked right back at her. "But, really, I think the challenge is balancing it. How does a man work and make time to play, and to enjoy his family, when the American career system wants you to work 55 hours a week? Or, if you skip the career, how do you afford good river gear, boats, surfing trips, and decent beer, and a warm palace for your lover and family, too? Balance is the challenge, I say. And you? What do you want out of life, Shira?"

Her brown eyes were enormous, her face composed, serious, heart-breakingly wise. "I just want to find a man who is strong enough to be kind," she said finally.

"I, will be that man," said Harper firmly, emphasizing it with a tender one-handed squeeze on her buns. She looked back him at silently, and he felt their hearts beating together, hers saying, well, maybe you could be. Then she broke the gaze and slipped away.

"Oh, no, you can't leave now!" he moaned as she moved out of bed, dragging all the covers off and away with her. He was left bare on the bed, curled up alone as she grinned wickedly and flounced away. "Come back! That was my best romantic declaration ever!"

"It was very nice. You are so romantic. Maybe I will give you a chance to prove it." she said merrily over her shoulder as she disappeared into the bathroom. She seemed to swirl her skirts as she crossed the room, dragging the covers but not wearing anything. "Keep it up, handsome." Her head popped back out from behind the bathroom door for a moment, an impish grin in place. "No pun intended" she said, and she disappeared again as he howled in protest.

After she showered, and dressed faster than any woman he had ever known, she kissed him and ran down the condo steps, back in her scrubs. She stopped at the bottom and turned back.

"Hey, Harper, I almost forgot. Wetlands Watch needs someone to do a water evaluation of that horrible quarry expansion north of The Landing. We need to show that their water pumping is already killing steelhead and red-legged frogs. It's part of our strategy to stop them from mining the coastal bluffs. I think it would wreck a good surf spot, too. Anyway, I told the board that I know a groundwater geologist, and they want you to do a proposal. They don't have much money, but they are trying to get a grant to pay for it. Tell me what you think, OK?"

Harper felt sick. He opened his mouth weakly, but before he could answer, Shira waved again, blew him a kiss, and ran out the door with her keys in hand.

After she left, Harper pulled on his wetsuit, and headed for the ocean, his pleasant morning daze now confused and unsettled. What did he want out of life? How about a quickie? He knew he should have told Shira he was working for Arena. But, it's not like he even had a chance, he told himself. He was asleep when she got here last night. Too late now for excuses, though. He sighed. Everything was going so good with her. It was a new experience not to be looking forward to the next time he saw Shira, and he did not like it. Hmmm.. Time to paddle out.

Walking directly out to the sand from his house was another new experience for him. Beach property prices in California currently started at above a million bucks, and were climbing faster than Yahoo stock prices. His feet squeaked pleasantly on the clean sand. Out in the line of surf, a teenaged kid on a short board took off on a wave, made a casual late drop, snapped a perfect turn and sped down the line past floating pelicans in a comfortable crouch. Born to shred.

The ocean was sunny, glassy, with no clouds, no fog and no wind. There were a couple of surfers out directly in front of the condos, but lots of space up and down the beach. He spotted a rip tide flowing out between two cells and he trotted up the beach to it, and paddled out. He was swept out past the breakers without getting his hair wet, and he sat up on his board outside. A mixed flock of pelicans, gulls and terns were diving close to him where the riptide churned food out from the shoreline. He looked farther offshore for the enormous clouds of Sooty

Shearwaters that should be arriving soon, tiny seabirds that made a ridiculously long voyage from New Zealand to summer on the Monterey Bay each year. Sometimes in summer, the shearwaters would fly past at water level in dense whirling clouds that went on for minutes, surrounding surfers but never striking them. He liked thinking of the birds moving back and forth around the globe, crossing the Pacific to find the Monterey Bay each summer without a GPS.

Then he remembered the fin up at the Landing, and the ominous feeling of the blank ocean after the fin had sunk. Well, this is the ocean. Sharks live in it, and there is nothing anyone can do about that, he thought matter-of-factly. He looked around at the birds, the distant surfers down the beach. His feet tingled, down in the water, but he resisted the urge to bring them up onto his board. Relax; you're just a link in the food chain, like everything else in the ocean.

Harper felt too large on his short board, instead of the comfy longboard he normally rode. But, longboards were for old men, or for making it into big point breaks. Fast steep beach breaks were more fun on a short board, and he was not that old yet. He had a 7'0" pintail, a fun shape with forgiving rails, plenty of rocker, and a loud Tequila Sunrise airbrush job. He realized he had gotten a little lazy, paddling into set waves up at the Landing on the big modern longboard Johnny had shaped for him. The beach break was quicker, steeper, jacking up on a hidden sandbar, then peeling quickly left and right in clean sections.

When a wave came up under him, he started late, then was too far forward, was pitched out and he went over the falls. The wave and the board came down on top of him, as he curled up instinctively underwater to avoid impact. He got a little

Maytag, a good morning hold-down, with complimentary cold water brain freeze. When he surfaced, he was already washed 30 feet inside. He checked automatically if anyone had seen the wipeout, and then collected his board at the end of the ankle leash. If you made a kook fall like that on an easy wave at a crowded break like The Lane, nobody would let you get another wave for the next hour. Luckily, there was no crowd to judge you here. Private beach access was a nice part of the deal at Las Olas.

Harper grinned at himself, and pointed out into the oncoming waves. He ducked the next one smoothly, pushing his board down as the wave covered him, plunging the nose under, so the wave passed over his back. He surfaced, paddled hard and made it out over the next two waves before they broke. Back outside now, he was awake, mind clear, breathing hard, and in the game.

He broke into an involuntary grin at the memory of Shira, as she came across the room to him nude last night. He felt like yodeling. He thought again about her question. What did anyone want? There was a bumper sticker on Shira's little car which said, "For Happiness, Cherish Those You Love". He decided that was a good start. She was a keeper, no doubt about it. Balancing on his board and filling his lungs, he blew it back out slowly, feeling gratitude. Gratitude for Shira, for this morning, for the pelicans diving, for the quarry job, for everything.

It was the clearest and happiest he had felt since returning from the canyon. He thought about what Tracer said at the take-out, about carrying the spirit of the river trip into your life. Always Above Lava. Greeting the day, rigging your boat properly in the morning and then rowing twenty miles, whether that day was in an office writing proposals, standing at a drill rig, or sitting in a public hearing listening to attorneys.

"It's the right thing you're doing" Harper said to himself. Looking ashore at the condo bedroom window, he thought about what Arena wanted, wondered if he could use the condo again. He winced as he realized he had still not told Shira that he was working for Arena, that his work would be used to help permit the quarry expansion. Then, he started thinking about Shira's legs in the moonlight again, when he suddenly noticed a set was coming.

The waves were getting taller. He spun the board. The first wave of the set rose under him as he began digging. The green swell became a steeper wall, with sun shining through and making it glow from within. Excited about the wave, he paddled harder and committed to the drop, his weight forward on the board. A final hard stroke sent him gliding down the face. Up off his belly and onto his feet with a push-up, he stuck the landing, and shifted weight to his back foot to avoid burying the nose. As he hit the compression at the bottom, he cranked his shoulders left to turn down the line. Good morning, wave!

The board threw an arc of spray, buried a rail, moved through a bottom turn and locked into line, down the wave. He grinned at the perfect drop, then looked ahead, seeking focus as the wave tried to catapult him. He let his body react to the unfolding balance changes, no thinking. The lip was overhead now, slowly falling in front of him as he raced by it, a sparkling liquid wall stretched out catching the sun. For a moment, it was falling over him, landing behind and exploding below his rear foot as he sat in the pocket.

A liquid section of lip well ahead started to drop in slow motion. He braced, hunched, and aimed for the falling water with the top of his head. Bursting through it and back onto the green wall, he emerged into speed, balance, light and magic. Moving down the wall on his board, facing overhead power ahead and sensing exploding foam behind, he entered a trance state with breathless heartbeat. Then, the hanging green lip dropped on his head and swept him off the board.

After the hold down, he surfaced to capture his board, and let the rest of the powerful set break over him and wash him towards shore. He was almost back at the sand. Briefly, he considered paddling back out, but his desire faded. Time for breakfast. He had a little bit of a hangover, a little bit of a love Jones, and had a lot to think about. As he floated in, a glimmer of a familiar deep calm reached him. It was his old buddy, The Peace That Passes All Understanding. He breathed a prayer of thanks to the ocean, for all of it, as his feet touched sand. Walking back to the condo to clear out, his booties left a line of three-toed ninja footprints in the sand.

12

Ghost of Steinbeck

The twin poles of power in Monterey County represent the local balance between yin and yang, ocean and the land. The salt spray mansions, Republican golf money, and oceanside military camps of Monterey (and Carmel) balance the Long Valley; the hundred-mile, wealth-giving, deep soil of the Salinas Valley. The courthouse and government center are both up-valley in Salinas, giving a sense of which one truly holds sway, even if the mansions are along the ocean.

Harper had driven fast to Salinas, and worked the knot of his tie against his neck as he circled the Monterey County Courthouse block a second time, looking for parking. He was late, and unfamiliar with downtown Salinas. Finally, he left his truck at a donut shop and hurried on foot to the Courthouse building and into the courtyard. The severe architecture of the government center was gloomy, with bas-relief Greek figures looking down from the Depression-era Moderne facade, blocky and incongruous amid the dusty office buildings and small clapboard houses of workaday Salinas. A covey of hired experts and company flacks were gathered in the courtyard, standing like a flock of suited birds with briefcases. He saw Pete Rastovich, a soils engineer he knew from surfing Moss Landing, talking with a traffic engineering guy he recognized, and then the well-known white hair, shiny suit and weasel face of Jerry Duckam, Salinas Valley land use attorney. Duckam was favored by developers for his track record of getting dubious development projects approved.

He was standing with a cluster of other suits Harper did not recognize. They were probably 415-area code gang that did the Environmental Impact Report, down from their San Francisco Bay office for a Salinas payday. The burly men next to them with corporate rigor and serious faces must be Arena Construction mucky-mucks. Tony Armstrong was at the center of the Arena squad. As Harper arrived, Tony gave him a broad smile of crooked teeth and a cheery "Ah, Good Show, Harper. Here's our new water resource man, then." Harper shook hands with Tony and the Arena VPs, and was handed off to the attorney.

The attorney was staring at a file, planning his script for the hearing. He greeted Harper curtly, sized up his tie, jacket and shoes as acceptable, and accepted his card. He told Harper that today's hearing was mainly for public testimony, and not to present any answers. "Remember, the Environmental Impact Report is done. Today, you're hired just to appear, show your face, hear questions on the draft EIR, and let the commissioners see you. We're doing a show of force to demonstrate the Arena Corp resources behind this project. The hearing is not for expert testimony; it's for a parade of community folks. You know, the union guys saying how good the Quarry will be, then some whiners from Landwatch Monterey, then more of our guys. We'll record any technical questions, ID who will respond, and get out of there. It's all Show, no Tell. Got it?" Harper nodded. Sounded like easy money.

He took his place over with the other experts, standing with their battered briefcases, polished shoes and client- meeting faces on. He nodded to the others. Rastovich had removed his habitual golden earring for todays' gig. Pete smiled and said, "Hail, hail, the gang's all here, hey Harper? You got your board in your truck?"

Harper grinned and nodded. Among local consultants who surfed, pick-up trucks were the preferred vehicles, so one could keep their surfboards and wetsuits present but concealed during work hours. Rastovich was famous for surfing both before and after client meetings, for taking mornings off when a good swell was due, and for scheduling meetings around low tides, as well as for good coastal and soil engineering. Armstrong checked his watch, and signaled the attorney. The attorney gave a wave and the group formed a skirmish line, then trouped behind him into the building and up the steps.

The upstairs courtroom where Monterey County Planning Commission meetings were held was right out of the 1950's, with rows of carved wood seats and benches, dark paneling, threadbare carpet, and gold government seals on the walls. The benches were unusually full today. Normally, planning meetings droned along to an almost empty room, with a few earnest applicants, perhaps some hostile neighbors or lawyers waiting their turns in the worn seats, while a bored-looking stenographer typed away at the foot of the raised dais. A semicircle of Commissioners would lean forward sporadically to speak, while a County staff person at the lecturn would show charts and refer to a stack of reports as he or she walked the room to the preordained outcome.

Thus the planning business of Monterey County was generally conducted, without fanfare or public attention. Today was different. There was a feeling of excitement, a buzz from multiples nodes of conversation, and a diverse range of local people in attendance. Harper saw cops, Chamber of Commerce types, blue blazers, and retirees, mixed with men who belonged on backhoes, in their checked shirts, construction boots and Union Local windbreakers. In the back stood a row of farmhands in faded overalls, with rotund Mexican grandmas in shawls, and ranchers with cowboy boots, clean work shirts, jeans and tooled leather belts, holding Stetsons in their gnarled hands. It was a mosaic of the Salinas Valley, with representatives from each demographic, except maybe the Latino youth gangs. Those hombres only came to the courthouse in custody for trials and sentencing. It was as if the characters out of some modern East of Eden theatrical production had wandered into the Planning Board meeting to read their lines. The Planning Commissioners on the dais in their comfy chairs looked like a bunch of retired folks here to watch dinner theatre, who had somehow ended up on the stage.

The line of hired experts filed into the courtroom together, and took their place in the conspicuously empty front row. They filled the first bench entirely. All the Arena consultants were from the same gene pool: middle-aged, nerdy white guys with fraternity haircuts, a variety of hairlines, ties and suit jackets, each clearly carrying business cards in their pocket and an hourly billing rate clicking away in their heads. A discerning eye going down the line could detect a variety of levels of comfort. The silver-haired attorney at the head of the line was at home, preening in his suit, and making a mental roll call of the Commissioners on the dais with their microphones and nameplates. Down the row, the consultants had their game face on, but Harper looked mildly choked by his tie. The Archeologist kept running a hand through unruly hair and rubbing his glasses furiously with a handkerchief, while next to him, Rastovich drummed his fingers and looked nervously around the crowded room as if he might bolt for the exit.

The Chairman tapped his microphone and called the meeting to order. A few items of old Board business were called and quickly disposed of, while the crowd ignored the dais, filed in from outside, and settled. Harper saw Tony Armstrong working the room with a clipboard, going among the seats and handing out papers and checking a list. He was speaking to the rancher types and then to a Mexican grandmother in a black shawl, black dress and an ancient woven straw hat with ceramic fruit. The *Abuela* nodded to Tony with dignity and accepted his proffered document gravely, as if she handled these matters of great import regularly. Harper wondered briefly what her role in environmental compliance for Arena Construction might be. Finally, the Quarry item was called. The attorney for Arena rose, smiled warmly and addressed the Commissioners like old friends. He introduced the EIR consultants, referred to the completed Quarry EIR in glowing terms, introduced the long row of paid experts one by one, then turned back to the commissioners. These folks were just here to listen, he stressed, but would be the talented team prepared to respond to comments. The Commissioners listened to the attorney dryly, and considered the experts without visible enthusiasm. Harper smiled back at them cheerfully. He had just been introduced to government officials for the first time in a professional setting, working under his new company name. He liked that feeling, and settled in to watch the show.

A young male Monterey County staff planner with a bad haircut and a tall stack of document file boxes was standing at the lectern. He punched a remote control, and the first slide projected. It showed the proposed 100-year mining plan for the Gabilan Gravel Quarry, on the former Hamilton Ranch property. He clicked up a history of the site's review, then a short list of potential biological, traffic and water impacts identified in the environmental review, and proposed mitigations that reduced impacts to less-than-significant for each.

Harper noted that the quarry access road location went directly to an on-ramp for the 101 Freeway that ran down the Salinas Valley, but was off a small side canyon that hid the quarry face from public views. Nice touch by the traffic engineer. Planned traffic upgrades to the access road and freeway on-ramp were included in the project mitigations to accommodate a steady stream of trucks. Preparatory design work on the quarry had been going on for several years now, and detailed traffic estimates included in the completed EIR showed these mitigations would make any traffic impact Less Than Significant. The slides included topographic models of the quarry's working face after 10, 25, 50 and 95 years of mining. The existing granite hilltop within the quarry boundaries was eaten into and shrank in each projection, until finally a modest pond existed in the location of the former peak. The property shape was a large irregular box centered on unnamed Gabilan Range peaks that formed the eastern edge of the Valley, almost reaching to the San Benito County line. One long thin finger of land ran from the heart of the ranch property out into the Salinas Valley proper, connecting the hills to the valley floor. This strip of property was the ranch driveway and access easement. At the end of the driveway, where it curved out of the granite-floored canyon and reached the county road out on the alluvial valley floor, lay the ranch well. A dot on the map here labeled the proposed water supply for the quarry.

Smiling to himself, Harper shot a glance at the row of three older men with weathered faces at the back, the only gringos in the room with cowboy hats, as they watched the presentation carefully. The soils engineer had pointed them out to him. They were the Hamilton brothers, the ranch owners. These old boys were no dummies. They had inherited a rocky hillside ranch from their Oakie dad, with nothing but salt soils and cheat grass, and spent decades raising skinny cattle that barely paid the property taxes. Local valley farmers always said their soil was too poor to raise hell with a fifth of whiskey, but they knew that was a granite mountain under them. Now, they finally found a buyer for their granite mountain, one who needed a freeway on ramp, with a good well site and water rights out in the valley. If they lived to see this quarry deal go through, they could retire to a proper ranch down by King City, one with sweet grass up on a river terrace, abundant irrigation water rights, and a corral full of palominos and quarter horses for their daughters. Their faces were strained with a mix of tension and fatalism, as if they realized the show they were watching controlled their destiny, but was beyond their command.

The commissioners acknowledged receipt of the staff Draft Environmental Impact review, and of staff comments. The gavel banged. Now the Public Hearing parade of comment proceeded as inevitably as the hot summer wind up the valley.

The crowd stirred. Individuals trouped forward to line up at the standing microphones stationed between the rows of chairs. The preparation by the quarry's operatives bore their fruit.

First, the equipment operators union officials spoke of the need for the good wages and jobs the quarry would provide. Next, construction industry business owners and local contractors spoke of the need for a new gravel quarry to supply aggregate at every project they did, and of the current costs in traffic and pollution of hauling gravel in from other existing quarries located out of county. It made sense. Local politicians spoke of the need for gravel for road projects, and the tax benefits of the quarry for decades to come. A teacher's group spoke of the generous elementary school donations they received from Arena, so vital now since state school budgets had collapsed. The ranchers in the back row nodded their heads vigorously in agreement for each speaker. By the time the ancient *Abuela* walked, her twin canes in shaking hands, to the microphone to state, in Spanish, that her husband, *Que en Paz Descanse*, had worked 30 years for Arena, a good company, and that the quarry's jobs would keep local youth employed and away from drugs and crime, the event had acquired the flavor of an Arena Corporation infomercial.

The experts in the front row watched, slightly uncomfortable with their role as silent figureheads, presumably brimming with unspoken technical knowledge. They fidgeted and looked at the row of people still waiting to speak. Some opposition surfaced at last, when an angry man who lived in a new house in the same canyon spoke about the endless truck traffic, the blasting noise and increased water use. A nearby vineyard owner made the same comments. A young man in tweed jacket and a pony tail from a non-profit land preservation group presented an objection to both the quarry itself, and to the systematic loss of prime Monterey County farmland and open space due to both the quarry, and to the future development that the gravel from this project would support. He gave a list of potential grave impacts to fauna (the ranchers guffawed when he said that mountain lion breeding could be disrupted by blasting), and to traffic, air, and water. The Hamilton brothers in the back looked at him sadly and shook their heads no, no, no. Clearly, they felt these concerns were less-than-significant. Finally, the line of speakers was exhausted and the hearing was suspended for the day. Staff was directed to summarize county and public comment for the applicant to respond to. The meeting was adjourned and the gavel banged.

The crowd filled down the stairs, spilling into the late afternoon wind that blew newspaper sheets past and lifted dust to the endless valley sky. A tall, gaunt local man in a checked shirt was seen reading his notes on a pad and talking to himself, black eyebrows arched over sad wise eyes, as he scanned the characters, then faded away into the crowd. Working men held onto their hats, lowered their heads, and turned to walk into the wind. The expert group dissolved, after a quick debriefing in which the distribution of the comments requiring a technical response was outlined. The quarry reps and their attorney left together for the law office, pleased and proud of the hearing, as if they had seen their kids in a school play. The consultants engaged in a little industry gab as they parted, and then drifted off to their vehicles. There might be time to get in a surf check, or get back to knock out a letter report or something that felt a little more substantial before the day was over.

Harper walked back to the donut shop and sat in his truck. He looked at his project file with **Arena Construction, Gabilan**

Quarry written in bold letters across it, and considered making some notes. His big new client. He had said nothing, and done nothing at the hearing, and would bill 4 hours. Despite a hurried review of the Draft EIR before today, he had never been out to the proposed quarry site, and he knew almost nothing about it. Welcome to the Show.

The quarry's total water demand was modest, really. But still, there were always some water issues to be considered. Future pumping for water supply and possible impacts from blasting and taking down a mountainside over 100 years of mining occurred to him. These had been addressed in the EIR already, but there would be further work to address questions, perhaps to agree on a monitoring schedule for future water level changes, and to further define potential quarry pumping impacts on existing wells. Today had been The Show, for the Commissioner's benefit. Later, he and the others might write detailed technical responses to specific comments that no one but the County staff would ever read, to address questions and issues raised by staff and public comments. He could take his professional pride in that part. He understood he was part of the process, but he could not help feeling that today he was just a prop.

Turning his truck down the Salinas Valley and back towards the Pacific to return home, Harper followed the old farmer's turnpike route from the valley to the coast. He drove through orderly rows of lettuce, broccoli and cauliflower crops, with drainage ditches snaking between them and dirt farm yards full of stacked irrigation pipes and parked tractors. He imagined the aquifer beneath him, the thick sequence of sand, gravels, clays and silts over a thousand feet thick, with multiple sandy zones that generations of well drillers had tapped with confidence.

This incredibly productive aquifer perfectly complemented the mild climate and rich soils to make an unbeatable agricultural combination. The Salinas Valley was so fruitful, so wealthy, so unsurpassed as a salad bowl for the nation, but it had a hidden flaw.

Decades of pumping had dropped the water table over a hundred feet throughout the valley, so that the normal groundwater flow out to the sea had reversed. For decades now, the ocean saltwater had crept in under the valley, soaking in where the sand aquifers outcropped offshore in the Pacific. As he drove to the coast, Harper was passing over the invisible underground front, where fresh, then brackish, then saline water mingled beneath him in the 180- and 400-foot aquifers, with the sea creeping through the aquifer pores and slowly migrating up the valley, relentless and irreversible. He was miles from the ocean here, far from the first sight of the coastal dunes, imagining the salty water and ruined aquifer beneath him. Around him in the fields, lettuce and broccoli changed to artichokes, a sure sign of salty wells, then changed to scrub and weeds of fallow fields long before he reached the coast.

At Moss Landing, back at the ocean, he pulled into the State Park amid a row of vacationers in RVs. He parked, and removed his tie. He rubbed his temples. The farms all looked so pretty and orderly, like a vision of plenty at the end of a desperate voyage for a Dust Bowl refugee. It didn't look like they were slowly killing their water supply. He wondered how much longer it could last, how long before the salty wells and rusty irrigation lines and abandoned farm lands reached from the coast clear to the city of Salinas, and the empty fields were taken over by weeds, and bobcats and cautious deer. It seemed hard to believe driving through the thriving valley now, but of course it would happen.

And once the cities shrank and the fields went feral, pumping would be stopped for a hundred years. The rains continued, the aquifers would fill back up. The earth would survive whatever Man might do. The walls of Grand Canyon had taught him perspective, deep time; a sense of how temporary was all human folly. We are dust specks, full of our own importance.

"But I want to be a better dust speck!" Harper said to himself with a smile. He restarted his car. There was too much onshore wind to surf. The waves were blown out and choppy. He had to get back to his office and finish some work. He was going to the mountains to kayak with Tracer this weekend, anyway.

Tracer had called him last night, from a noisy phone at the Iron Door Saloon in Groveland, outside Yosemite Park in the High Sierra. It was like a blast from another dimension to talk to Tracer, with a bar band playing in the background and the dirt road down to the Tuolumne, sweetest Class IV river in America, outside. Tracer had demanded that Harper drop whatever he was doing, stop work, drive up and go boating. It was the early Spring snowmelt runoff. There was deep snowpack all over the West this year, which meant a good whitewater season, but it would not last forever. Harper smiled to himself, remembering Tracer's grin coming over the phone. It had been a demanding week for Harper. He even had to wear his tie today. It was time to go big in some whitewater. Of course, Bay Area traffic would be nasty Friday if he left too late, and there was a flock of well permits to type up before he could leave. He put the truck in gear and left the lot.

13

Creekers

Every good whitewater river needs a decent whitewater parking lot. Not one big and smooth enough to invite RVs, or God forbid, raft company headquarters, but a nice dirt space. Lots are the homely but functional counterpoint to the beautiful river they pair with, and often the only gaps in the private land ownership monopoly for miles. There is a network of good lots at the high gradient rivers of all the western states. These tiny free spaces serve as a combination of car shuttle spots, hangouts, free sleeping spots, and impromptu social scenes. The Tuolumne River is one of the finest whitewater rivers in California, and the unofficial Tuolumne paddler's lot is in the granite dust and pine trees off Highway 120, behind the log cabin that holds the Casa Loma coffee shop.

Harper was just a half-hour short of the gates of Yosemite

National Park when he pulled into the Casa Loma parking lot. Tracer's pale yellow van was parked under a big Ponderosa Pine out back. No sign of the actual Tracer. He rubbed his eyes, turned off the car stereo, and slowly motored across the pine needle and dirt. He had been driving hard for 5 hours, escaping the Bay Area with Friday traffic, and he was wiped. The sinking sun was hitting the pine trees, and less than an hour of light remained.

A fleet of old school buses was based in the back lot, a flock of shuttle vehicles for weekend commercial rafting. With giant steel racks welded on top and bright purple paint on their rounded profiles instead of the institutional urine yellow they were born with, these river buses had gone native. Next to them, a group of relaxing paddlers formed a folding chair circle around a spanking new SUV. A fleet of colorful, blunt kayaks and scarecrows of drying paddle jackets lay around them. Reggae music blasted on the car stereo. Two lean guys and a girl looked up from their chairs as Harper rolled in, all in custom sunglasses, paddling shorts, tight shirts, and Class V attitude.

Creekers, no doubt. Resting after a day of heroics on the Cherry Creek run. The Casa Loma lot and the shuttle road down to the river shared two populations. "Normal" kayakers heading for the standard Tuolumne whitewater route all started here and went downstream. Creekers, the elite who ran the dangerous Class V series of waterfalls, holes, ledges, and rock flakes that formed the Cherry Creek run, all started higher upstream, ended here and usually did not bother to go farther downstream. The Cherry Creek run was a Class V test piece for ambitious paddlers eager to improve their river resume. It was a potential man (or woman)-killer. Many a kayak disaster tale started out, "So, last summer on Cherry Creek, …".

The Cherry Creek run started high in Sierra headwaters, where water was released from an ancient stone dam and hydropower gate. The creek ran 8.5 miles of steep gradient whitewater, in a remote wooded canyon, with multiple individual rapids graded Class V, the knarliest level (the next highest level, Class VI is defined simply as "unrunnable"). Creekers then took out at Meral's Pool, a calm spot where the access road hit the river, where the main Tuolumne run began, and where most boaters started down their adventures in the "still pretty damn hard" Class IV main Tuolumne section.

Harper gave the Creekers a friendly wave. They eyed his rig, with his sun-faded, three-years-ago whitewater kayak on top, his Santa Cruz plate-holder, Grand Canyon River Guides sticker, and cluttered truck contents. They nodded non-commitally and returned to their conversation. The tall, skinny guy with shoulders like a linebacker was using both hands to describe a waterfall-leaping boof move he made into a do-or-die eddy below. They had profiled Harper with a glance: older, coastal not mountain, a weekend kayaker, maybe an old guide, trying to get down the standard Tuolumne run on his day off. In other words, not one of them. No offense, but no love from the Creekers circle. Harper grinned faintly and drove on. Let's see those fancy day-trippers run a 225-mile river and come out with their expensive sunglasses on straight, he thought to himself.

There was a note on the windshield of Tracer's van, with his trademark Anasazi logo and the words:

"Your Corporate Masters cannot control you now.
  Leave your kayak and paddling gear here,
  Drive down to meet me at Moral's Pool.
  Bring more Beer, your Bike

And your Good Vibe, Happy Face.

Harper peeked inside the van. There was a short, blunt kayak inside, with several paddles, and bags of padding and camping gear. Why were the kayak and van here, not down at the put-in? Why leave his kayak here and bring the bike? What chaos factor was Tracer generating now? There was a plan, no doubt. Since it was a Tracer Plan, the possibilities were endless.

Harper was tired, road-weary, and ready to drink one of the tallboy beers calling to him from the ice chest. He wanted a campfire, a beer buzz, a seat under the Sierra stars, and then to fall asleep amid the building excitement that only sleeping at the put-in of a whitewater run could give. Maybe Tracer wanted to do the Rainbow Falls waterfall drop tomorrow, a popular play spot near the road with a 15-foot "easy" waterfall. He untied his boat and threw it up on the van, then found Tracer's hide-a-key under the van bumper. He stuffed his bag of paddling gear and his paddle into the van.

But if we are paddling Rainbow Falls tomorrow, why sleep down there? Harper sighed, got back in his rig, pulled an icy 16-ounce aluminum can of Dutch beer out of his cooler and popped the tab as he pointed his truck down the steep Forest Service road to the Tuolumne River. Let's go find out, he told himself.

One and three-quarters beers later, at the bottom of the truck-bouncing downhill trail ride, he found Tracer sitting at a campsite table, with candle lantern and book, by the calm put-in pool of the main Tuolumne. Harper climbed out of the truck, and stood quietly for a moment, relieved as always to have arrived at the banks of the river. The indigo sky showed the first stars. A cool rushing sound came from the rock garden waiting below Meral's Pool. Cricket song and the fresh night smell of river came to him. The noise and dust from the truck arrival faded. Harper blew out a breath. Tracer stood up and stretched also, and they clasped hands. Harper produced two fresh beers and handed one over.

"Greetings, Brother Harper. Way to escape your Monterey Bay eddy. Ah, Oranguboom lager, my old friend. You got my note, I see."

"Tracer, my friend. Cheers. Damn, I almost forgot how good this river sounds. So, tell me why are the boats at the top and we are at the bottom?'

"Because, we are at our take-out, my friend. Tomorrow we will leave your truck here for take out, bike or hitch up to my van, drive up stream and paddle back down. Hard to hitch a ride with two boats"

"Paddle back? From Rainbow Falls? Is there enough water below that drop?"

"Not Rainbow Falls, man. I thought we should step it up and try the Cherry Creek run. Cherry Creek to Meral's Pool, brother. I did it today, solo, kinda, paddling along with some visiting young guns from Sacramento. Folks are pouring in from the Bay Area this weekend to get their Class V ticket punched." Tracer paused and took a long pull on his beer. "You told me after we ran Crystal, you were ready for to lose your Cherry this season. "

Tracer looked over in the near dark and continued,

"Uhh, I mean if that's what you want, Harp. You're in peak paddling form after 18 days in canyon, right? That's 225 miles on the Colorado, no swims. You were solid in everything we ran down there. I wouldn't suggest it if I doubted you. " Harper gazed into the dark and listened to the river sounds. He said,

"Everybody wants to be Hank Williams, but nobody wants to die."

"Meaning?"

"Everybody wants to have paddled Cherry Creek, Trace, but not everybody wants to paddle it."

"Hmm. Wise words, amigo. " Tracer sipped his beer in the dark. ""Well, it's your call. If you go big, you gotta be clear on why. It has to be for yourself, nobody else. We can always put in right here, do the regular Tuolumne run tomorrow, have a blast. Surf every damn wave from here down to Don Pedro Reservoir. Might catch some wild trout down there."

Harper hesitated. He felt a need, for something. Assignments, proposals, phone messages, billing timecards were waiting back at his office. The quarry job, county meetings, and what to do about Shira spun before his eyes. Meral's Pool and the standard Tuolumne run seemed suddenly… mundane. His skills were not in Tracer's league, but still. He had run the Grand Canyon three times, and had never paddled better than on this last trip.

"Cherry Creek, huh? I saw Creekers lounging up at Casa Loma. It might be the medicine I need. How was the run today? "

Tracer paused and considered, and then gave his evaluation. " Weell, it is a powerful stretch of water, I kid you not. You better bring your A game. Good news is, it's optimum water level right now: medium low, but not bony. It is easier than at flood water or at low water. Still, it is nowhere near easy. Technical and steep. Very cold water, so swims are dangerous. Continuous whitewater after the second mile, with narrow lines to hit to for your entries. This is not like Grand Canyon, with 30-foot wide slots through rapids. Some true no-go routes down there, that you cannot enter unless you want to be sieved through boulders. Follow my line, brother. Probably 20 individual drops of 5 feet or more in the nine miles. For all the true Class V drops, you gotta nail the line, and also be ready to hit your roll, cause swimming is just not an option. If you swim there, you are fighting for your life. Then, there a bunch of easier Class IV to V-minus sections, fun, heads-up boating, where you can still catch an eddy and rest. Boat control and mind control are required. We should probably carry around Mushroom at mile 5; it has a big waterfall, a terrible hole at the bottom at this level and a deadly swim below. And, we will definitely carry around Lumsden Falls, running that's for psychos only." He paused and looked over at Harper with wicked grin. " Oh, you're gonna love it."

Harper tasted his beer again doubtfully. "Christ, that sounds encouraging. Can't we just drive to Rainbow Falls, smoke a fatty, paddle off the waterfall a dozen times and take hero photos of each other?'

"Another time, my friend. Cherry Creek is doable, with focus. We can scout the big drops, take our time, hit the lines. You can always bail and walk out the old logging road. Or if you don't feel up to it, we can skip it and have a surf party down to the Res on the standard stretch. "

The quiet river noise hung in the air as Harper drained his beer and looked out at the dark pool. From out of the tiredness of his drive and the tangled skein of his goals, he felt a rising sense of … hunger. Wildness, powerful longing, a fuck-it-all desire to take the leap. He had behaved, he had followed the prudent course, he had colored inside the lines, been tamed too often. He was more than that. He did not need anyone's permission to risk his own life.

" I want to paddle Cherry Creek," he said. " Yup, I want it, Trace".

Tracer nodded calmly, as if hearing what he already knew. "There it is. Well, then, I'm gonna' get some rest. We can leave your truck here and catch a ride up top in the morning. Then we'll take my van up the Cherry Creek Road to the put-in. Sweet dreams, brother. "

14

Rough Swim

No Breath
And no roll up into sunlight
My mind races and turns, lungs surge
till I pop the sprayskirt and swim.
Leave my little boat.

So strong, so cold, the water.
Now I must swim.

Fighting the icy water for a breath, Harper thought, so, this is what drowning feels like. Horrible, not at all peaceful. Without air in your lungs, everything stops being fun. It was before lunch and he was swimming, stuck in a Cherry Creek hole, out of his kayak. He was shocked by the stunningly cold water, and already nearly exhausted. Despite his big red life jacket, his head barely surfaced in the violent aerated water. It was so cold that he could not feel where his bleeding knees had struck rocks, and so powerful that he could not avoid the crashing hold-down. He had to get out to survive. If only he could.

He had fucked up, bad. He knew Tracer could not help him now. Focused on catching a little eddy, he bumped a hidden rock, and flipped his kayak in the chute to Corkscrew Rapid. So, he entered the first Class V drop on Cherry Creek upside down and then gone over the Bad Side drop backwards. It was a terrible place for error, before he even got in the really hard part. He and Tracer had scouted it carefully on shore with adrenaline building. They planned out a ferry move hard right across current into a sweet little eddy at the top of the drop, to miss a 5-foot waterfall into a nasty keeper hole. He had been boating awkwardly all morning, but nothing as stupid as this; tipped downstream in a careless instant by an underwater rock, a nothing sleeper, as he focused on following Tracer. He never made it across the tongue to the micro-eddy.

After he flipped, he had rushed his set-up, as horror at his exposed position ricocheted in his brain. Haste blew his first and best chance for a roll. Seconds later, he went over the waterfall, backward, upside down, with his paddle still sweeping for some purchase. It was a sick feeling, falling blind into the reversal at the base of the waterfall. Their whole scout plan was about missing this.

His secret brain voice was saying, bad, bad, bad, but in a still hopeful tone as he went over the falls, half waiting for a crushing blow to his head and neck. That did not occur. He landed in the plunge pool tucked, head down. Hydraulics got rough in a hurry. He rolled up at once, but was stuck in the crashing reversal under the falls. He managed to get a look and one solid breath, before his boat was windowshaded over, flipped violently, trapped in the perfect hydraulic curl at the base of the waterfall. In the glance before he went over, he saw with horror that he was in a keeper bowl below the waterfall. It was a narrow deep plunge pool of falling water with side walls of Sierra granite. The heavy curtain of water, tight space, and high walls made a trap. Drowning pools, they were called. The waterfall created a uniform reversal, churning back on itself within the walls. No outlet flow started until at least 10 feet downstream from the falls, and he could not reach it. Bad, bad, bad, his inner voice said again, as he set up for another roll. His paddle failed to find any purchase in the churning. Harper felt a first blast of naked fear push through his thoughts. Upside down in his boat on the edge of the pocket, still in the plunging hydraulic, the waterfall was booming down onto the exposed underside of his boat like a jungle drum. His helmeted head struck the rock wall, but he found no bottom with his paddle. His lungs contracted inside his chest. A first involuntary surge in his lungs sought a breath he knew he could not take. Panic fought to squirm loose in his brain.

Enough of this upside-down shit, he thought. Let's go back up where the air is. Feeling angry and mean, but trying for poise, he bent forward and set his body up for a roll. He knew he could still hold his breath; you could always hold it longer than you thought. One good roll! Now! He initiated, swept confidently into his roll stroke. Wham! His paddle was blocked almost immediately, striking underwater against the wall at the edge of the deep plunge pool pocket. Too tight to sweep. His head also struck the wall as he flailed, struggling to complete the stroke. No roll, no breath. Bad, bad, bad. He really needed that one. Time to come out. He had to swim for it. Abandoning poise, he tore at his spray skirt, pulled the seal, and wriggled hips and legs out of the tight cockpit. At the same time, he was fighting not to breath too early and get water into his lungs.

Popping out of his kayak, still underwater, his lungs screamed for air. He kicked up and broke the surface, waterfall crashing on his head. Gasping like a manic, eyes bulging, he tore in a breath that was half water. The shock of the cold water on his body and legs, filling under his paddle jacket, was paralyzing. Immediately, he was smashed by the force of falling water and sucked under by the reversal. It was shaking him like a rag doll at the same time. It was much more violent out of his boat than he expected. He felt his shoes get torn off. Surfacing along the wall for a moment, clutching his paddle, he clawed the smooth wall with his free hand for a grip, but found nothing. The reversal quickly took him under again. His life jacket seemed to have utterly no effect. Now, he was getting scared.

Harper had been pummeled in big water lots of times, in ocean swells and in river whitewater. It made him proud of his ability to take a water smackdown, but this kind of overwhelming impact that he could not outlast or escape was new. Ocean waves stuffed you deep, and then passed by. Most river holes did the same. Beginning kayak play in Grand Canyon was called recreational drowning, due to the rough swims in big rapids that beginners had to learn survive. But, those big river holes washed you out. You held your breath, stayed relaxed but in warrior-mind, then fought to the surface and swam hard when you felt it let you go. Here, there was no letting go. He was trapped in a tight, ugly place, pushed down by a powerful relentless force created by the broad sheet of falling water. He was disoriented, exhausted, freezing, held under, and tumbled like a shoe in the dryer. It could not last much longer.

Underwater, he blew out some air to orient himself and fought to follow the bubbles back up. His head bumped his boat. Grabbing at his kayak in the tight space for a purchase, he got hold of the cockpit edge and tilted it. He surfaced under the cockpit for a quick breath, then another, his head shielded from the falling water. Then the boat shifted and danced away, with him clutching at it. The water beat on him like a fire hose, he was sucked under, his wetsuit socks were torn off his feet. He could not hold the smooth boat. He had gotten a breath, but the cold and the power were winning. There was no air pocket behind this waterfall, no cozy secret room to surface in, and no way to survive in this pool. He knew he had to go down, to get out.

He tucked his legs and dove deep to the bottom of the reversal, head splitting in the cold water. He was grateful for the lungful of air he had captured, and used it to swim hard, first straight down, then over. Down there in the dark, water was moving to the exit point of the pool. He surfaced with a huge breath ten yards downstream, but out of the constricted plunge pool. Already, he felt himself accelerating into a fast broken whitewater channel.

Out from under the waterfall, things did not look much better. His kayak was still trapped in the reversal. He scanned the river skyline for help as he swept out of the drowning pool. Tracer would be trying to reach him, but it was almost impossible to get to a swimmer in water like this. He had to rescue himself. He kicked for a passing eddy, but was swept past in the current.

He had another glimpse downstream. No joy. The next stretch was violent crashing water as far as he could see. He went into it as unprotected flotsam, holding the paddle as a staff, without his boat. He was a scared animal now, battling from one breath to the next, crashing off underwater rocks, bracing for impacts as he protected his face and head, gasping before being swept under, amazed at the speed and violence he was moving with. The strength ran out of him like wine spilled from a dropped flask. He grabbed at midstream rocks, but they were scrubbed flawless by the water. He washed past them like a leaf in a storm. Coming around a bend, he struck a midstream rock hard, and was wedged under it by the current for a bad moment, thrashing free in desperate anger and washing on. He began to focus on just getting breaths, and on protecting his face. He withdrew his feet from traps whenever he felt contact. His bare feet were smashed, then quickly numb and useless. His legs were bleeding from rock strikes. Pinballing this way, he covered fifty yards from the first waterfall in two or three breaths. He was drowning, he was alone, the river was merciless, it was killing him, and there were no eddies in sight. He felt a final flare of anger, shading into despair.

A horizon line was coming, and then he was flung over it, another small waterfall. It was a clean drop as tall as himself. This time, the landing was not a plunge pool, but a heap of broken rocks, with two distinct outwash channels. He went over the drop feet first. In his brief instant of airtime between the lip and landing, he saw two things. He saw that he would land on rocks, hard, but would not stay there. And he saw that if he bounced left, he would die. On the left, the water shot into an enormous jumble of big and small boulders and dropped into a mix of twisted trees and rocks, then reappeared ten feet below. He would be driven into the big holes at the top, but not come out the bottom. The left side was a death strainer.

On the right channel below the falls was a flume, a smooth fast plunge of white water that dropped the same 10 feet in a curving granite chute carved in the rock. He still clutched his paddle in one hand, from habit learning to kayak in Grand Canyon (never let go of your paddle). As he fell and landed barefoot on the rock jumble, he stabbed the paddle into the rocks below, and braced the other blade of the paddle against his chest life jacket. He fell onto it like a spear, stabbed but cushioned by his life jacket padding. The paddle blade cracked, and broke the force of his fall. It tumbled him right, away from the strainer, towards life. Into the outwash chute he went, landing a clattering fall out of control in a jet of water. He lost the paddle, and was swept down the chute feet first.

Made it, he thought, barely. His next thought was that he might not survive much longer. He could barely move now. He was no longer swimming, just passively floating and grabbing air. Breathing was all quick gasps and gacks, and another horizon line was coming. This river was pure Sierra snowmelt, and the cold was sucking the life force out of him. He was hitting rocks without protecting himself now. The next drop was close.

A bump appeared in the water just before him, above the horizon line of the next falls. It was a smooth, humped rock protruding barely above the surface, domed like the back of a sea turtle. As he washed over it, he realized it was his chance. Squirming to drag his chest atop it, he slowed down and clawed as it went by. Both hands searched the rock face, but found no purchase. His hands swept across the top, the sides, the edges. In horror, he felt himself being drawn past the rock, slipping gradually over it, leaving it behind. His eyes and hands desperately prowled the rock edges. Years later, he would recall in dreams every facet and crystal of that wet, smooth rock and that searching moment when he needed something to hold onto. He found a crack. An open, straight crack, almost hidden under water, split the lower half of the rock.

His hand found the crack in the turtle shell, stabbed into it and made a hand jam, just as his body washed off the end of the rock. His hand stayed jammed, his wrist, then his arm took the load, and suddenly he stopped flowing. He hung, rather comfortably, paused in the current just above the next waterfall. His body swayed with his outstretched arm connected to his anchor, like a student laying in the river and waiting for teacher to call on him. His body was undulating in the slightly protected space just behind his savior rock. His legs were fully extended, toes almost at the very lip of the downstream waterfall drop, but his face was out of the water and he could breathe. He breathed, gasped, spit, and he breathed again, one arm out, still swaying in the current. A candle of hope lit in his brain. A sly, purposeful gleaming look came into his eyes. He caught the rock. He could get out of this. Nothing else had ever mattered like this next part mattered.

Carefully, so carefully, he rotated his body around his shoulder joint, thankfully still undamaged. With his arm still extended and his hand in the jam crack, face down in the water now, he pulled steadily on the hand and brought his head back upstream onto the rock. He surfaced, spit out a breath, and looked intently into the crack and at his jammed hand from inches away. It was beautiful. His entire future hung on that hand. He reached in, and matched his second hand in a jam just above the first. Also solid. He drew himself upstream until his chest and hips were the smooth turtle back rock. Then, delicate and focused as a diamond cutter, humping and balancing weight and keeping both hands in the crack, he got his knees on the rock, then one foot. One numbed, bloodless, ice-cube almost useless foot stood on the rock, and then the other foot, and he removed his hands and stood up in the center of the current, balancing like a man on a wire. He stood on top of the deadly smooth and slick savior rock and looked at the shore, just a dozen feet away. It was maybe his greatest achievement ever.

He trembled and waved his arms for balance as his knees straightened. Christ, don't fall now, he thought. The next waterfall and the maelstrom below, the next quarter-mile of whitewater, were clearly visible once he was standing. He didn't think he could survive that swim if he fell. He looked back down at the crack at his toes. This was the knife's edge. Nostrils flaring, almost weeping, he embraced the intensity of focus it took to just stand there. Not yet. A quick glance upstream, and he did not see Tracer. This could not wait. Just twelve feet away, across a thin channel of ripping current, lay a small, everyday eddy and the shoreline of Cherry Creek. He wanted that eddy with a fierce and ruthless wanting. Gauged the leap, he swayed and waved one arm wildly. Inadvertently, he had leaned too far towards the shore. He was falling. His toe was on the lip of his savior crack, and as he fell, he converted the lean into a mad dive. Flying off the rock like a drunken Tarzan, he made it almost across the current to the edge of the eddy in his first splash.

In four quick strokes, kicking hard, he crossed the eddy, felt gravel under his knees, swam farther up, touched dry leaves and dirt and then continued to swim a few feet more, using a crawl stroke across the ground, until he was tangled in the holly bushes. He was out. Choking and coughed racked him now, his whole body shuddering, his back heaving. A surge in his belly interrupted, and he vomited a small amount carefully beside him into the leaves and gravel, spit, breathed, and shuddered more gently. Collapsing onto his side, he let his ragged breathing become less desperate, coming under control and slowing. Lying in the dirt, he looked back out at the river and felt a feeling of happiness wash over him. He breathed experimentally once, then deeper. He felt a painful presence high up inside his chest on one side, which discouraged deep breaths. Probably some water aspirated into his lung. No problem. Water in your lungs could cause infection or pneumonia, but it would pass. His arms and legs worked. His knees were a bloody mess, but intact. He rubbed one of his feet and felt the sting of blood moving into them.

Already his breathing was calming, approaching normal, with an occasional sob breaking the rhythm. It was very nice here in the dirt, lying in the shade. Birdcalls mixed with the sounds of the rapids. He was done with Cherry Creek, forever. He would not get back in his boat today. There was a timber road uphill somewhere, and he could walk down the canyon to his truck. He would drive home, in the mundane world of radio ads and traffic. He felt very, very happy about that. As feeling started to come back into his feet, they hurt and he was glad about that, too.

That is how Tracer found him, just a bit later, laying on his side next to the eddy and grinning. Tracer looked shocked and scared, like a guy who has seen a dog hit by a car and rushed over through traffic. He crashed in from the current, spun a tight eddy turn and stopped in the pocket of still water. He looked at Harper with concern and understanding.

"So, how do you like Cherry Creek so far?" Tracer asked from his boat. His voice was too high and cracked a little. Unbelievably, he had found and retrieved Harper's paddle, broken blade and all, and he tossed it over onto the gravel next to him.

Harper smiled and cried a little then, the tears coming easily and running down his face. He sat up and looked at Tracer. Leaves clung to his jacket and arms. He laughed and coughed, wiped his face. He felt so happy. "It was all my fault, Trace." He started to say more, stopped, then said simply, "I'll think I'll hike out from here."

Tracer looked at him, drinking in the sight of him with relief.

"Fucking Harper. You gave me a heart attack. Well, you won't be the first to hike out of here. Lets get your boat first. It washed out of that trap and is upstream on a log. You can drag it uphill and use it to hitchhike with." He looked at Harper's bloody knees and shoeless feet. "You lost your shoes, man? <u>Rough</u> swim."

Harper nodded dreamily, tears flowing freely. He said smiling. "It was really, really bad, Trace. I almost stayed in that first pool. What about you? How was your run?"

"I saw you flip. My heart stopped when I saw you go over that drop upside down. Then your boat never came out. Christ, Harper, I thought it was gonna be a body extraction. I was thinking about having to call your Mom and all that shit. It took me a while to get out of my boat and get to the top of that rock with a throw bag. Then, you weren't there, and I saw you way downstream, shooting down a flume like a greased donut. I jumped back into my boat, paddled over the right side, and powered down after you."

"Sorry to put you through that. Tracer, I blew that eddy move up top. That was a really bad place I fell into. I…. I'm not Class V. I'm done. What are you gonna do?"

Tracer looked a little surprised at the question. He looked around, like there was someone else Harper might be asking. It was obvious. "Finish the run, I guess. I paddled this run solo yesterday, so I'll run it again today. Don't worry, I'll be careful and carry around Mushroom. Definitely gonna carry Lumsden Falls. You just did a demo on the severe consequences of swimming in Cherry Creek. You going to be able to hike? You're in shock, you know."

Harper used his paddle as a staff and stood up, wobbly, checking his knees and his feet. He nodded. "Sure, I feel great. If this is shock, chain me to the wall. I love breathing. Just help me get my boat."

Later, after Harper had walked and crawled barefoot several hundred feet up the steep hillside, dragging his kayak and paddle through thick brush to the sunlight and the heat, he stood sweating at the dirt road. It was a lovely spring day in the Sierra. Looking back down into the Cherry Creek drainage, he could see the route of his swim. Tracer was gone from sight. It was a postcard view, with snowy peaks in the distance, steep timbered canyon hillsides running away both directions, and below him, the green pools, tiny waterfalls and white threads of Cherry Creek, looking like whitewater heaven. The happiness to be alive had not gone away, but had settled down. He was no longer on the verge of happy sobbing. A steady buoyant feeling stayed, a sweeping goodwill, which kept him cheerfully humming while he was crawling upslope through prickers. "Maybe I should consider golf," he thought, looking down at the creek run that almost killed him. He picked out the waterfall hole at Corkscrew and his swim route down to the eddy. Standing up here in the heat, it seemed like something that happened a long time ago. Part of him considered that the remote glow and the distance from the event he was feeling were due to shock.

"But not bad shock" he thought to himself. "This is the good shock. The happy-go-lucky shock." He looked hard at Corkscrew Rapid again, and found the line that he had blown so badly. He put himself back there and he ran it in his mind again. The fear rose in him as he did, but that was OK, it had been there before, too. This time he crossed the tongue aggressively, and caught the tiny eddy at the top. With powerful smooth strokes, he peeled out in a tight turn, and ran right down through the broken, steep section, bracing left and right in his mind. "Visualize Positive Outcomes" he muttered fiercely to himself, shifting his hips and boating it. Fast and flawlessly, he followed the correct line past his savior rock, and continued down to where the river turned out of sight.

Maybe, just maybe, he thought, it was time to seek some new challenges that did not depend on expert kayaking. He could cultivate skills that required a different blend of abilities, but were just as demanding. Flying a plane. Raising a family. Building his business. Playing fucking golf, even. Why not, if he approached it as an interesting challenge, with sincere effort and an open mind? He could be a soul golfer, seeking a perfect drive.

Just then, a pickup truck of teenagers came around the bend of the timber road in a cloud of dust, with Van Halen music blasting. God bless the US Forest Service roads, Land of Many Abuses, Harper thought. They stopped their truck at his energetic wave, stuck their heads out and gaped at him, and his bare feet, cracked paddle and funny little boat. Harper smiled hugely, shook hands through the window, made friends, tossed his kayak in the back and climbed in. He knew he would paddle other rivers, but not this one. Probably not this one, he thought. As the truck rattled down the dirt road, the teenagers handed him a cold beer, turned the music down and asked him how he had cut his legs. He pointed down at the tiny thread of whitewater at the bottom of the canyon. "Cherry Creek kicked my ass!" he shouted and they all laughed and pounded his back.

15

Parting with Tracer

The truckload of metal heads dropped Harper and his kayak off after 6 miles. His new friends gave him a high five as he pulled his boat off the back of the truck, and they tossed him another Coors Silver Bullet for the road. Then, they tore off up the road towards Highway 120, to go smash mailboxes or scare pedestrians in Groveland.

Tracer was already there at the takeout, sitting like a Buddha atop his kayak, in shade beside the green water. Harper dragged his boat over and joined him in the shade. Looking upstream of the calm pool towards the bad whitewater Tracer had paddled alone, Harper realized, finally, the gulf of paddling ability between them. All it took was near-drowning to make him see. There didn't seem to be much to say, so they shared the Coors, then loaded the boats into Harper's truck, and drove up the dirt shuttle road.

On the drive, Tracer apologized at once for suggesting the Cherry Creek run. Harper accepted his apology, then said no, it was good. He had needed to learn his limits.

And it was true. He was glad that he had tried it, but he realized now that it was not good for him to paddle Class V. Tracer nodded back like he understood. He was kind but not intrusive on the drive with Harper, an old friend riding with a convalescent. A comfortable silence settled between them, and they listened to Emmy Lou Harris sing stories of loss and heartbreak. The dirt road climbed out of the river canyon into hot sunshine.

In an hour and a half, they were back at Tracer's van at the top of Cherry Creek. They had launched their kayaks there just that morning. It seemed like ages ago. The other vehicles ranged from expensive foreign SUV's to battered mini-trucks, and they all had empty kayak racks on top, and paddling stickers on the windows or bumpers.

They stood by their vehicles, keys in hand. Harper had changed into dry clothes, put on sneakers, and was moving like an old man. As his adrenaline faded, he became aware of a wealth of body pain. He found little cuts on his knuckles from his hand jam into the crack, which made him smile fondly at as he considered them. The beer had made him light-headed, and his belly was empty. He still had to drive back across the state to sleep at home tonight. He stretched and breathed deep.

"Where to now, Tracer?"

"Moab for me, brother. There is a river gal there named Billie that likes me. She's tough as nails, daughter of a Mormon rancher, a guide on Cataract Canyon. She has a sunny smile and a wild streak a mile wide. I had a card from her at Phantom

Ranch last month. She said I could stay with her this summer. How 'bout you?"

"West into the sunset. Back to town, to my office and my corporate masters. And Shira, I hope. Sleep in my own bed and heal my spirit. Maybe go paddle in the ocean to get strong again. Hey, you got time for a burrito before we part ways?"

"Casa Loma is closed. But, there's good burritos and coffee in Groveland".

"I need food. Coffee would be good before I drive home, too."

"I know just the place. Follow me".

"Follow my line?" Harper echoed with a rueful smile. "I'll probably miss the turn and drive off a cliff."

"Aw, keep your chin up, brother. Anything that doesn't kill us…"

"I know, I know. Only postpones the inevitable. Now, lead me to lunch before I keel over."

They drove back into town, to an A-frame restaurant that combined the coffee, pizza and burrito food groups, with a wooden deck out back. Harper was soon beaming at an enormous carnitas burrito, and a large frothy mug of coffee and steamed milk.

"I always suspected you were a latte-sipping Yuppie dog." said Tracer as he sat down next to him.

"Hmmm." Harper took a big sip. "Was it my Prada paddle jacket that tipped you off? This is already healing me, by the way."

Tracer tore a triangle out of the plastic lid of his coffee, blew on it, and sipped as he looked at Harper. "You know, after a swim like that, you might have bad dreams for a while. I did."

"When did you last have a bad swim?"

"Two years ago, I almost died in a drowning pool like that one you were in. Doing the steep creek run on the Clavey at high water, with Rok Sribar and some crazy men in from Slovenia. That was the last time I swam."

Harper swallowed a bite of carnitas and picked up his mug. "You never mentioned it".

"It was rough. But I kept my shoes." Tracer sipped his coffee and shivered. "Early spring, high water, snowmelt runoff like today, freezing water. I missed the line above a drop, went into a keeper hole, and swam out of my boat. You never swim in flood stage Clavey. It is deadly. I did some rock bashing and washed into a deadly little soup pot with a fatal boulder sieve outlet. I caught the wall, and stopped, where I could just hold on and get my head out of the water for a breath. My legs were getting sucked into the sieve. I hung there until I was so tired, Harper, I swear I almost just let go. The dark force was sucking me down. "

"Christ, Tracer. Clayey Creek is all waterfalls and smooth granite walls. How did you get out?"

"I got a toe in a foothold, and I climbed out of the pot to the lip. Just pulled it, with my last strength. It was like a 5.7 climbing move, balanced on one toe. The guys couldn't see me from shore, but they got a rope across the current to me once I was out. They pulled me across. We never even found my boat. It just disappeared under the boulders. After, on the ride home, I got hives all over my body from stress, then I had dreams about that pit for a year. So, you might have the dreams."

Harper shook his head slowly, setting down his mug.

"Is it worth it, Trace? What we do for fun, I mean. Like, last week out in the ocean at the Landing, I saw a shark swim so close, I could almost touch it. It could have bit me in a second. Just chance that it didn't. Today, I swim in Cherry Creek. Things come in threes sometimes, so I'm officially due for a third death threat. I don't know, maybe I should switch to golf."

"And get struck by lightning?"

"Or get run over by a drunken accountant in a cart, probably.
"

"I know what you mean. Nothing lasts forever, including a Class V career. I though about quitting rivers, after that Clavey swim. I had to really ask myself what I wanted. Have you been back out in the ocean since you saw the shark? "

"Yes. I stayed overnight at Las Olas down near Moss, and had a great dawn session last weekend. But inside the Bay is different. I still gotta' go back out at the Landing. You say you thought about quitting paddling, huh? But you didn't. Instead, you paddled Cherry Creek solo today, Tracer, after it almost drowned me. Which is a bit psycho in degree of exposure, my friend."

"For me, Cherry Creek is still in my range. It is easier than high water Clavey. I didn't quit paddling, but not because I want to take big risks or die. That's stupid. On hard rivers, when my judgment and my ability are all that keeps me from drowning, I am most alive. Like anybody, I enjoy what I am good at. Rivers is what I am good at. And you are the same way, my friend. You just have a world of other things to be good at, like running your damn aquifer models that I can't even understand. But you need to use your abilities, and to do hard things. That is why you wanted Cherry Creek."

Harper looked back at him glumly. "Well, I am over Cherry Creek, now. Maybe I will learn some new aquifer algorithms for a while. Damn, that is good coffee."

"How's your consulting gig doing?" Tracer asked. It was rare of him to acknowledge Harper's career, except as a barrier to paddling.

Harper shook his head. "Good. Be careful what you wish for, eh? It's been slow, but all of a sudden it's like, too much funky business. I'm getting better jobs, moving away from just doing samples from tank yanks, and get this big quarry study. And then I met a great girl, Shira, and she likes me. She is this cool hybrid, glamour girl and tree hugger. Lipstick, heels, dress with matching belt, and everything. Only, it turns out, she is working to stop the quarry that I just got hired to do a water study for. And I didn't tell her about the job before she went to bed with me, which I know I should have.

"Oh, you gonna pay for that."

"Yeah, well, meanwhile, everyone, including Dukie, is telling me that this quarry client is going to twist my work and make me sell my soul. All I want, is to do some good work and maybe get a little rich, so I can afford to live in Santa Cruz, surf, paddle, ride a mountain bike and have a love shack with Shira. "

Tracer looked like he wanted to spit. "You're working on that quarry now, too? Dukie cracks me up. He should know what he's warning you about, because he already sold his soul to those Arena guys."

Harper was surprised by the anger in Tracer's voice. He set his burrito fragment down. "How did you know about it? And what are you talking about? Dukie is the one that warned me about them first."

Tracer considered Harper over his coffee and said scornfully. "Since every one of my consultant friends now is working on that same stinking quarry, I guess I know plenty. And you, Harper, you're kind of innocent, with your 'I just want to do good work and get paid'. Dukie is working both side of the fence on that gig, taking money from the quarry to get them a permit, and taking money from other folks to stop it. And he's got Goat in on it now on one side, and you on the other, and you're both getting hooked on the money."

"What? Goat? I thought he was dealing green bud to surfers. I saw him up the coast at The Landing, doing a deal with some of the LAST crew, with a brand new van. Dukie was there too, in fact. Did you hear Dukie is headed back down in the Grand on a research trip? He was trying to get Goat to drive a motor rig. And Goat said no, which makes no sense. I told Dukie to call you to drive the motor rig. What the hell is going on, Trace?"

"Well, let's just say what Goat is dealing, is not for smoking. But it's just as valuable. And dangerous. I tried to get him to stop, but I can't even talk to him anymore. He cut himself off up in his cabin in the hills. He's like everyone else in Santa Cruz now, trying get rich before the dot.com bubble bursts. He wants a big score, so he can leave the country and build a house down in Baja.

Tracer looked sick and angry, talking to his plate and twisting napkins into knots. "And yes, Dukie did call me about that driving a boat on that motor trip. That trip is not what he says it is. He is playing games with high rollers, and I'm staying out of it. I can't say more. Ask him about it if you want to. He says he needs the money to pay off his divorce attorney, and retire, but that doesn't make it right. "

Tracer finished his coffee and stared off uneasily into the middle distance. His face was gaunt, unshaven, and uncomfortable. Harper realized again, Tracer was a different guy away from the river. In his kayak, he was relaxed, masterful, and self-assured, though scruffy. Now, Tracer looked like a freeway on-ramp panhandler, stopping in for a cup of coffee and muttering angrily.

Tracer was talking mostly to himself now, and Harper listened in, "I was born in California, but I'm sick of it. All the greed, subdivisions and quick scores. Everybody is doing a deal, working crazy hours for stock options before the public offering, or selling Mom's old house in the Westside circle streets to clear fifty grand. I can't even afford to insure my truck. Everybody else is trying to grab their personal gold nugget out of a stream and cash it in, easy as pie. I just want time in the canyons and on the river waves. That's what life means to me. So, fuck it, I'm going to Moab to live in a trailer with my Mormon sweetie. Maybe find work and try to get back down in the canyon this summer".

Harper listened to his friend run out of steam. He tried nodding with understanding, but he was not sure what had set him off. Still, it was clearly his turn to be the reassuring one.

"OK, Trace, I hear you. I hope Moab works out for you, buddy. I am dug in back in Santa Cruz, and I am going back there to try to make something work. Just make sure I hear from you. You are my Grand Canyon brother. We gotta keep our connection. "

Tracer came back from his sour reverie and looked up.

"Keep the faith Harper. You are a good man. I guess it's different for you, with a career and all. You still are a pretty good kayaker."

Harper shook his head, not sure whether that was a compliment or not. He knew it was hard for Tracer to get why Harper cared about work. For Tracer, nothing mattered more than not having anything that would control your decisions. Even if independence cost you everything else. The meal was finished and they stood to leave. The two men embraced awkwardly over the table and clasped arms. Tracer looked Harper in the eyes.

"Listen, since you didn't drown in Cherry Creek, and if you don't decide to quit kayaking now, I have a plan. I've been thinking about a special river operation this spring. It might require your support. It is still undercover, but it could be epic. Maybe a perfect mission for you, me and Goat. Can I call you if it develops?"

Harper held his arm and his eye. "You got a plan, Tracer? Is it legal? Why am I am not surprised? Will there be snacks? Is there health insurance? Of course I am interested! Tell me!"

"Well, you know Lake Powell is near full this year. Almost too full, and there is record snow pack in the Rockies, right? Tons of water, all in storage upstream of Grand Canyon. The fucking BuRec engineers have been holding back flows all winter, but they finally authorized increases in daily dam releases from Lake Powell, up to 18,000 cfs. That is enough to pick everything up a notch down in Grand Canyon. But that is nothing. They are going to have to spill serious water soon. Lots and lots of water. Dukie's motor trip is launching in two weeks and they might get some of it. Depending on storms, record releases from Lake Powell and Glen Canyon Dam into Grand Canyon could happen in May and June. If the melt and runoff hit early, it could be the highest releases and biggest flows in Grand Canyon since 1983. It might, could be, ideal conditions for a Speed Run. And Goat has a river dory stashed. For our Speed Run! One boat, three-four guys, a dory for speed, non-stop Speed Run from Lees Ferry to Diamond! I'll be looking for some crew."

Harper stared at him for a moment, stunned by the idea. "That would be wild, Tracer! You are a scary genius. I'd love to go. If we get a permit."

"Well. Sure, if we get a permit. And if the snow melt happens and the river comes up, and the dam holds, if you are not killed by a golf cart. Then, the heavens may favor our plan. So, be ready. I'll let you know. And, hey, way to battle and not die in Cherry Creek today, amigo."

"Thanks, brother. Thanks for being there for me at the end. Safe trip to Moab, and good luck with that Mormon gal."

They hugged again, left the restaurant deck and walked to their separate vehicles in the lot, each one marked from the common herd by a small kayak strapped on top.

16

Home from the Hills

What are the legal standards for driving while partially drowned, Harper wondered, as he pulled out of Groveland in his truck? All the traffic seemed too urgent. He was wary of other moving vehicles, and sought the slow lane. A cautious, stunned feeling persisted, overlain with a greyness clouding his perception. Some part of his brain was still scared and wary, groping for an explanation of what had happened to him in the violent water. He knew from experience that this would fade gradually, maybe after a good night's sleep. Meanwhile, be careful driving. This Sierra-to-the-Sea route back from paddling was usually one of his favorite drives. He could leave the mountains, pass through the valley's summer heat, and arrive home by sundown, to sleep again in coastal cool at his condo on a wave cut platform. A long jam from Allman Brothers *Live at Filmore West* began to play as he tilted down his sun visor, and drove into the sun.

There are few day trips equal to a California transit by auto. A half-day of driving took in a swath of changes in elevations, culture, landforms, and geologic terranes. Leaving wood-burning hillbillies and ski towns behind atop the Sierra Microplate, dropping out of the mountain pines, you first rolled through miles of foothills, framed by volcanic ash flows, tall pastures, and shade oaks. Then, leaving the Sierra batholith completely, you took an arterial onramp onto deep sediments, freeways and Central Valley heat. The next hour was freeway miles, moving at a safe and sane 70 mph, past Basque restaurants, Republican election posters, and rows of irrigated crops, atop bottomless layers of Great Valley Sediments. The crops covered shallow bones of Tule Elk and Grizzly, who patrolled wetlands and swamps just a short time ago. Then, at the San Luis Reservoir, full of trapped water from northern California waiting to move south, drive west again, crossing the San Andreas Fault onto the Pacific Plate. The exotic, fault-tortured rocks of the Franciscan accretion complex stand up as the Diablo Range Mountains. Those mountains hold back the coastal fog, and link to Harper's familiar stack of Cenozoic sedimentary rocks, the salt-threatened Pajaro Valley and Salinas aquifers, and the groovy vibe of the Monterey Bay. A journey across such a mosaic of geologic depositional environments and voter demographic groups could only be made on the Left Coast.

As he drove, Harper wondered about the behavior of Goat and Dukie. He could not sort it out right now, but something was all wrong. They had been together at Lava Falls, celebrating at Tequila Beach, just a month ago. How did it all get so heavy, so fast? He wondered again about the mental aftermath from his swim today. How damaged was he? What would happen the next time he had to roll up in a bad place in his kayak? A good whitewater roll was all about confidence. He thought about what Tracer had said about bad dreams and quitting rivers.

Then Harper recalled the fear, the stark feeling during his Cherry Creek beatdown that he might not survive, the awful sadness at realizing he could cease to be. He tried to clear his mind, to ask honestly and let an answer surface: did he want to stop kayaking?

Hell, no, he quickly thought defiantly, I am not stopping. But, there was a follow up thought. He had seen what drowning is. He didn't want to drown. Well, that was no big surprise. He definitely did not want to be in another drowning pool, he thought with a shudder. So, where did that leave his boating? Only "safe" whitewater? Easy rivers, Class III, with their crowded kayak play spots on "trade" routes, with an eddy full of strangers waiting their turns on the wave. Well. Maybe.

He had to observe limits to his paddling behavior, because his Cherry Creek Paddling Test had come back with an F stamped on it. Safe and warm in his truck with a good lunch in him and Duane Allman's guitar sliding down to the tonic, he knew what he wanted was not thrills. It was completion. Moving in the veins of a great river, riding his boat in powerful forces that he could understand and navigate, but not control, was an earned skill. It brought powerful rewards. It had to be hard, to be good.

The trick was seeking paddling water that challenged you and completed you, but did not kill you, he thought, steering automatically down through switchbacks towards the Central Valley. He was onto something. That balance, that challenge, that was a worthy quest. Challenge and completion. If it was easy, anyone could do it. He was a Grand Canyon boater and a high level performer, damn it. There was no shame in hiking out of Cherry Creek, but it did not have to not crush his spirit.

He turned the music up a little and smiled to himself. A speed run down the canyon with Tracer? In a dory, no less. That could be a mighty fine time-o. But, he remembered the feeling of being trapped under the waterfall. When he had been unable to roll his kayak, then swimming, then fighting for a breath, needing it bad, and being held under. What about the next time? He tried a deep breath again, then coughed painfully, and shuddered a little. Step by step, he told himself. And don't forget to breath.

The neat houses and rectilinear streets of the Central Valley town of Escalon came into view, and he slowed for local traffic. He reached into the glove box for his cell phone, turned it on, and checked it for calls as he drove. There were four missed calls: one from Shira and three from Tony Armstrong. He looked at Shira's number and felt the weight of not telling her about the quarry project. He wanted to see her, to hold her, to tell her everything; about the quarry, his bad swim, about his new perspective and metaphor for life. But not on a phone call. Phones were for work. Instead, he highlighted Tony's number and pushed the dial button.

"Ah, Harper, old boy" Tony's chipper voice came on the line.

"Hello, Tony" Harper shouted at the phone. He didn't trust cell phones and treated them as if his voice had to carry under it's own power. "What's up? I saw you called."

"Ah, well, I need to see you. To talk about your timing and scope of work. We should meet this weekend in fact, if possible."

"Is everything OK?" Harper yelled, steering around a tomato truck.

"Great! Not a moment to lose, the fate of the nation at stake, the planet hangs in the balance and all that." Tony sounded cheerful and rested, not urgent.

"Everything OK with the quarry project? " Harper asked.

"Well, no, nothing is OK there, actually." Tony replied. "Corporate office is quite nervous about it. The lawyers are intent on screwing everything up, as usual. Standard Arena Corporation Operating Procedure. Once the attorneys have pissed off and inflamed everybody, then the problem will be dumped on me to solve. And to you, hopefully. Anyway, corporate office has some questions about your scope of work. About the new well. Could be a problem getting a new well permit. Might need to use the existing well.'

"The existing well." Harper realized he had lost some of his hunger and optimism about this job. "Listen, Tony, I'm driving back from Yosemite right now and won't be home till late. How about tomorrow morning? At the quarry?"

"Very good. But not the quarry. It's closed on Sunday. Let's meet near there, just down the coast road. Do you know the little beachside parking lot one mile south of the quarry road?"

"The Landing? Sure, I surf there all the time"

"Ah, do you? Very good. See you there at 8 AM? I'll be in a green company truck, can't miss me."

"OK, Tony. See you there. And, ah, don't leave your truck unlocked there. The radio might be gone when you come back. "

Harper closed his phone and threw it onto the seat. Work headaches. There goes his hoped-for Sunday morning sleep-in with Shira. And what did Tony mean, problems with a well permit? He sighed and put his turn signal on for Manteca. I guess I'll find out tomorrow, he thought.

17

Dirty Offer

$

By the next morning at 8 am, Harper was alone in his truck at The Landing waiting for Tony. His breath was clouding the windshield. The mist on the glass did little to change the view, which was a uniform cold grey. The fog was in thick this morning, and there was no swell bringing energy ashore. Except for a decrepit RV with exfoliating fiberglass, the Landing parking lot was empty. A few truckloads of surfers on dawn patrol missions had cruised through earlier, paused to peer at the ocean hopefully, and departed.

After his drive back from Cherry Creek, Harper had collapsed into bed, slept like a dead man, then risen early and driven here without shaving. Now he felt rumpled, discontented, and suspicious. The boundless happiness in being alive that had suffused him after Cherry Creek was not in evidence. Harper noted his change in attitude with detached irony. Less than 24 hours in a state of grace after a second chance at living, then back to the same grouch. His surfboard was in the back, but the cold grey ocean was flat. Every time he glanced to sea, his eyes automatically scanned the water outside for dark shapes. Tony pulled up next to him suddenly, halting in a bright green truck with the Arena Corp logo on the door. Harper jumped, then sighed and got out.

Tony rolled down his window quickly, shook hands and said "Jump in, I've got doughnuts". Then he pushed the door button to roll the window back up, so as not to let any more heat escape. Harper climbed in on the passenger side and closed the door.

Inside, the truck was spotless, like a display model at a dealership. Harper looked at the mud on his boots, and wondered how Tony kept his vehicle like this. Once more, he felt out of his element, playing a role for a movie that he did not have the script for.

Tony held out a rolled-up wax paper bag. "American dough-nuts are the best. Just sugar, flour, grease and water. Much more straightforward than French pastries. I got you a coffee, too. I hope you like it black and sweet".

"Just like my women." Harper grunted, taking the cup. He selected a doughnut from the bag, his spirits rising at the smell of coffee.

"Very good." Tony saluted with his paper cup. "Empty here this morning isn't it? Where are the gang of louts usually found over by that barrel? Last time I was here, one gave me the finger as I was leaving. Must be my company truck, hmm? Did you enjoy the Las Olas condo then? A bit of slap and tickle with your girl, I hope? I must say, I had a splendid time there last month, with a lady from the state Air Quality Control Board.

She fairly woke the neighbors with her cries."

"Yes, very good." Harper said, declining to discuss Shira. "Thank you. Las Olas really was wonderful. I appreciated it very much. "

"Glad you enjoyed it." Tony said after waiting for more, sensing the evasion. He changed his tone from jocular to academic. "Listen, Harper, I called you because there is significant public opposition arising to our quarry expansion"

"No shit? Don't you mean permit renewal, Tony?" Harper ate a third of his doughnut in one bite.

"Um, yes, quite." Tony was dismayed by his tone, but continued. "Simply put, we need to know that you are on the Arena team before signing you to our contract.

"Meaning what, Tony?" Harper asked levelly, chewing. He was tired, unsure what was going on, but finally free from anxiety. He let resentment go. He had nothing to prove this morning; in his mind's eye he saw the crack in the rock in Cherry Creek, and his hand slipping into it perfectly, effortlessly.

Tony, paused, looked across the truck, tried again to deliver his best pitch. "Arena wants to be sure you support our goals. That you will contribute towards achieving them." He was doing his best, but it sounded canned.

"Of course, I will." Harper said. "That's what my job is, actually. I just won't lie for you. Or any client."

"Well, of course not, nobody is asking you to do that. " Tony agreed, quickly jocular, backpedaling. He braced, and resumed forward progress. "But, there are always uncertainties regarding subsurface conditions, notwithstanding the technical data. There may be multiple working hypotheses, for aquifer interconnection with the stream, for example. We want to be assured that you will be comfortable expressing alternative explanations, or including those which may tend to support our position, or to reduce the level of our potential impacts. How would you feel about a lesser scope of pumping investigation, to reduce the cost, and to lessen the potential negative outcome for Arena? Say, remove the water level monitoring in the stream, and in additional wells during pumping for instance? "

There was a moment of silence in the truck. Harper nodded kindly, empathetically. He liked Tony, really. The way he treated every opportunity for a fat greasy slice of American pie, for some profit or some pussy, all to be captured and enjoyed was quite. …Californian of him, actually. Perhaps more throwback red meat Gold Rush style, rather than the vegetarian, vitamins and cocaine style now in vogue, but still, he had stylish greed.

Harper realized he had been waiting for this moment. Everyone had warned him about working for Arena. He considered a self-righteous protest, since gutting the pumping monitoring proposal was outrageous. If Tony had given him this pitch a week earlier, he would have been a prick about it. But, now, he understood. What he felt was comprehension, not indignation. He saw the whole of the moon, and the turbulent carryover from his Cherry Creek beatdown was good, because it made him so much calmer about this.

He looked at Tony and said quietly, "Tony, you are good at your job. So, you already know this, but listen. I share your goal of a successful outcome. Your case, Arena's case, to evaluate water impacts from expanding the quarry will be strongest if you conduct a full scope of work, not a weak one. Instead of going in reluctant, kicking and shirking, you must cooperate and engage the county staff fully. Do what they ask and a little more. Complete a great pumping test, with pages of stream and groundwater monitoring. If you complete an honest evaluation of the water issues, and then negotiate over how to fix any problems you identify, you can win. If you try to minimize, to lie, to deny, or fight claims of water impact without even doing a decent test, they can stall you for years. And every damn hippie in the county already knows the problem: your old well is shallow, and connected to the stream and wetland. Duh! More pumping will cause problems for endangered species, for the steelhead and the red-legged frogs. "

"Potentially connected," Tony stressed.

Harper nodded and continued calmly, "Yes, like your hipbone is potentially connected to your leg bone. Further study is needed to clarify the extent. Do you really want to sound like the tobacco companies talking about lung cancer, or the Republican Senators talking about global warming? Clearly bullshit, in other words?"

Tony seemed to deflate a little now that his spiel was delivered. He sat glumly holding his coffee on his lap, steam rising to form a cloud circle of fog on the windshield. He spoke to himself, looking out at the sea. "You know, at University I majored in Agriculture. I studied organic cropping methods. Dad was a farmer in Kent. He wanted me to work for the Soil and Crop Service. But I haven't even had a tomato garden in years." He looked over at Harper and smiled wanly. "I'll tell you something, Harper. If you work in industry, and you are the environmental guy, and you are always telling the corporate office that we have a problem with water, we have a problem with traffic, we have a problem with endangered species, well, they start to look at you as if maybe, the problem is you."

Harper nodded. "I hear you. But Tony, you know the expression, don't piss in your own well? If you lie to the regulatory agency guys, and they know it, you poison the well with them. You bullshit them once and you can never scrape it off your shoe. They will doubt you and fight you on every Arena project for the next 10 years. Tell that to the Corporate office. Those county staff guys never forget and they never leave their jobs. They have a great health benefits package."

Tony sat up, rallying, "Quite. Understood. Dr. Gerhart said something very much like that, actually. Do a complete scope, then negotiate and so on. I agree with you. However, there are situations in which, well, some discernment may be used, and your professional ethics can still be preserved. Dr. Gerhart, for example, refused to budge on his geologic scope or presentation of any geology information, but he has been very effective in other ways. He has been willing to be very creative in the political arena and able in, ah, using his personal connections. "

Harper nodded wearily. "Yeah, Dukie knows everybody. He told you to get me hired, and then he told me to watch out for you. What else is he doing for you?"

Tony smiled " Nothing I can discuss. We would like to both have our cake and resell it for profit later, eh? Why is Professor Gerhart called Dukie, anyway? Some kind of American royalty?"

Harper shrugged and grinned, thinking about the infamous Dukie tapes that were played on river trips. "He is just Dukie".

"Well." Tony considered. "About the pumping test. Harper, I will take your position regarding keeping the evaluation scope intact to our corporate office, and will seek approval for your contract, as it stands. They will make the hiring decision, not me. If you are hired, and work shows that there are water problems that cannot be mitigated, and the quarry application is unsuccessful, Arena will have to proceed in other directions. In return, you must agree that there may be confidential information related to the project, especially regarding future plans by Arena, that cannot be divulged, regardless of your personal sympathies."

"You mean like, Arena's plans to turn the quarry into fancy homes and a golf course when you're done mining? Or, if you can't get a mining permit?"

Tony gaped at him. "Why do you say that?" he asked indignantly. "Where did you hear it? From Gerhart, er, Dukie, I mean?"

Harper snorted. "It's just a guess. Every local realtor could guess the same thing. This is California, Tony. Fancy homes and a golf course grow from old ranches and quarries, like a new Burger King grows from an abandoned gas station on a good commercial corner. There is a natural order of succession of trees in the forest. Or something like that."

"Well, it is strictly confidential, but that is one possible development scenario, yes. Work you are doing now could prepare the ground, so to speak, for the next phase. Dr. Gerhart's work on potential fault activity at the quarry could be crucial to plans for future residential development. And, there could even be some long term financial advantages for you both." Tony looked across at Harper significantly. Harper half expected him to arch his eyebrows, and twirl his mustache like Snidely Whiplash, but he did not, so Harper asked.

"What advantages?"

Tony returned to an academic, diffident tone. It went so well with his British accent. "Future discussions of residential development will center on the capacity of the local aquifer. Number of houses, water demand, and so forth. Work done prior to the residential application, by a credible professional, may have more validity, more perceived validity, than subsequent work done in the heat of battle, shall we say. "

"People would buy aquifer test work done now for the quarry better than later tests done to support houses. Especially if done by a local guy that seemed legit."

"Just so. There is a reluctance to accept water reports that are produced once a development battle is underway. Especially since some of the larger consultant firms we have used have lost credibility by being so willing to be optimistic in their findings about water yield. Hydrostitutes, I believe the term is."

Seeing Harper wince, Tony rushed on. "But to the extent your work, your technical work, conducted as you see fit and without bias, supported our goals, we might arrange some ownership portion of the future development for you. Once the parcel was subdivided, that is. As part of your fee. "

"You mean, I would get a fucking building lot!" Now it was Harper's turn to sit up.

"Well, not one of the view lots. And not for free. But a significant discount is possible. Certainly nothing illegal, no explicit *quid pro quo*. The opportunity for you to participate in an equity position could be quite a valuable benefit. Preliminary designs range from one hundred to over two hundred fifty building sites on the property. That is confidential, too. Depending on water, of course, and on the golf course design. We are exploring a similar arrangement with Dr. Gerhart, and he suggested you might be interested. "

"Fucking Dukie! I would never have believed it." Harper said to himself. But, even as he said it, he realized that he believed it completely. It fit perfectly. And now he believed what Tracer had told him, that Dukie was working for Arena on the quarry, and trying to wreck the quarry application at the same time. Because if the quarry permit failed, and it kicked over to a residential development, Dukie could still win. With an inside deal on a cheap coastal lot, the crack cocaine of California real estate.

Tony's cell phone went off, breaking the tension. He flipped it open, and lifted it to his ear. "Oh, bloody hell! Not again. That same van that's been lurking about? I thought you were hiring men to wait for them. Did you get the plate number? I'm just down the road, I'll be there in a jif."

He closed the phone and reached for his keys. "Trespassers at the quarry. Some funny business. They weren't surfers; they were messing about the stream and ponds. Probably Earth First types from the University, trying to monkey wrench the bulldozers. Hitch is beside himself; he hates people on his quarry. I've got to go."

Harper blinked, sat up, reached for the door. He turned back and shook hands with Tony. Their eyes met and held for a moment. Tony flashed his gapped-toothed grin. The phone call had broken the awkward moment between them. Now in his rush, Tony dropped the legal doublespeak and his essential spirit of shameless fun returned.

"You're a good man, Harper. I'll get you hired for your pumping test if I can. Just help me with the county approval, and we'll let the chips fall where they may. Maybe you can be a hero for the tree huggers, and we can still get our houses. Everybody wins. Onward and upward. And remember, mum's the word."

Harper nodded. His mind was spinning. "Mum's the word," he repeated numbly, and then he was standing in the grey fog of the parking lot as Tony's truck drew away. He looked out at the sea. The ocean and sky horizon was a single shimmer of pale grey, with no clear line between them. He searched the ocean for the Landlord, but did not see a ripple.

18

Big Weather Coming

It was another Friday afternoon at the office, a good time for Harper to finish his to-do lists. At the end of the workweek, six days after leaving Tony's truck, Harper sat in his office chair, going over a list of clients. He had heard nothing from Arena since that intense conference at the Landing. The quarry project was out of his mind for the moment. He had finally talked to Shira about it, and told her, in barest outline only, that he was trying to get hired to do the water evaluation for the quarry. It had put a chill, not quite a frost, on their communication. He felt better for having broached it with her and she sensed he was not happy about the assignment. They were warily moving forward with each other. She had not asked him about working for the Wetland Watch group again, but at least she laughed when he asked if he could still meet her Grandma. Tracer was holed up in Moab, Dukie had left town for his Grand Canyon motor trip, and the month of May was on him. Summer was coming into sight, his liability insurance premium was due in 30 days, and he felt the need for income.

Harper was trying to round up consulting work. Since hanging out his shingle, his bread-and butter clients had been local guys removing underground fuel tanks. Most service station cleanup work was the territory of big firms with national contracts, but rusty old tanks were also present in dozens of small gas stations and truck stop properties. The cleanup of any leaking fuel tanks became a prerequisite for a commercial property transfer in the 90's, and in the overheated California real estate market, the damn things turned up everywhere: truck stops, ambulance companies, shipping centers, old hardware stores, even ranch houses had old tanks buried nearby. Harper collected the mandatory soil and groundwater samples during tank removal, and provided regulatory guidance, additional sampling, and sometimes sympathy and emotional counseling, when the tanks had leaked.

As a small operator, he drew a quirky mix of clients who could not afford, or were suspicious of, bigger firms. Currently, he was working for a grouchy Asian lady who worked nonstop to operate three convenience stores and treated him like he was stealing every dime he charged her, a group of asthma doctors who had a very successful investment sideline of buying old gas stations and opening Burger King franchises (the Burger Kings, he labeled the file, and he always imagined waiting rooms full of wheezing patients when the Doctors called to quiz him about their latest property), and a pair of elderly brothers trying to sell their gas station and retire. All these clients had problem sites, leakers with gasoline down in the groundwater, and no easy fix.

At his former employer, Envirocon, Harper rarely talked to clients and almost never met them face-to-face. But Envirocon was a 200-plus person billing machine that did everything from building landfills, collecting samples, gas chromatography analysis, designing, building and operation of a cleanup system, to expert witness testimony to blame the gas station across the intersection and collect their insurance funds. Harper was a one-man shop, focused on clean water aquifer testing, and tank leak discovery, water monitoring if required, and fast cleanups to achieve that Holy Grail, the regulatory closure letter.

Sometimes he felt like a cross between a dentist and therapist, alternating expensive painful of drilling in the early stages, and the ecstasy and relief of closure at the end. He scanned his list of tank projects and realized he had to call the brothers, Jim and George.

As he dialed, he pictured the last black rotary telephone in Sunnyvale ringing on the counter at Jim and George's Garage. Their place was a survivor, a relic of that former staple of every town in America: the competent mechanic and busy gas station on a downtown corner. No mini-mart, no beer, no propane fills, no lottery tickets. Outside, an air pump and a couple of soda machines. Inside, a dusty office with Girlie calendars and a cash register, with a candy bar dispenser and a pull-lever cigarette machine, for Christ's sakes. Piles of oil and air filters boxes sat with magazines of buxom girls in hot pants leaning on motorcycles and polished cars. Every auto parts catalog for a Mopar, Ford or Chevy car was stacked nearby, with a smattering of foreign ones. Strung around the ceiling and on top of display cases were scale plastic models of U.S. military planes and tanks, in tribute to Jim and George's World War II army service. They bought the place after they got out in 1949, and had worked there side by side for 50 years. They were in their 70's, finally ready to retire, and their Sunnyvale corner was worth a couple of million, if they could just satisfy the County that they had dug up all the gasoline that had leaked over the years. They still fixed cars, but didn't even sell gas anymore, having pulled the tanks a year ago. Now, Harper was their point man, to get the tank closure letter and sell the joint. The Chili's and TGIF restaurant chain was interested in the corner for a franchise.

Harper call went through and made an antique jingle of a real bell being struck inside the phone at the far end. Jim answered quickly with a brisk, "Jim-an-George-Garage". Jim was the older brother, 73, a terrier, wiry, red-eyed, volatile and talkative. He suspected all government of sloth and all businessmen of greed. He worked the desk, ordered parts and supplies, approved bills, and dealt with Harper and the gasoline cleanup. George was the horse, massive, shy, still powerful at 70. He worked out in the bays, fixed the cars, glowered silently in the background, said little, missed nothing.

"Hello, Jim, this is Harper Purcell, your groundwater cleanup guy at HLP Associates. Listen, we got a letter from the County, with their response to our report. Did you get your copy?"

"Well, young Harper, how are you? Find any more oil wells lately? " Harper heard him cover the phone with a callused palm, rear back and shout, "Hey, George, it's Harper, our Gee-ol-o-gist!" Harper heard an air wrench pause in the background, then return to making a racket. Jim came back to the phone.

"Yeah, yeah, Harper, we read it. It says we gotta keep them little wells you drilled in for another year at least. Send in water samples and reports and maybe, pretty please, in a year we can be done and sell this place. If we live that long."

"That's pretty much it, Jim. One full year of quarterly monitoring, in three perimeter wells. If no further hydrocarbons are detected above regulatory action levels, we seal those wells, get closure, and you're done."

"Action Levels, huh? A coupla parts per million of gas never hurt me. We rinsed our parts in gasoline for years. What happens if the gas or the, uh, the benzene concentrations, say, comes back into them little wells?"

"Well, Jim, we excavated all the contaminated soil, got clean samples, and there are no tanks left anymore, so that is unlikely, But if it does happen, the monitoring period will be extended. Maybe for another year."

"Uh huh. You know, for guys our age, Harper, a year is a pretty long time to wait around. Did I tell you I rode across North Africa on the same tank as General Patton when we took Tunisia? I was younger than you are now. We're living history, kid." Jim paused and broke into shouting unexpectedly, making Harper flinch and jerk the phone away from his ear. "Hey George! The kid geologist says another year of sampling before we can get our closure and sell. You didn't want to retire yet anyway, did you? "

In the background, the air gun hammered away wickedly. Jim came back on the line. "OK, kid. Send us the contract for the sampling work, like you did before. My son Harry, he's our C.P.A.; he'll check it out and file it for us. We'll sign it and get started on another year of fixing brakes and changing oil. You're still looking out for us, right, Harper?"

Harper took a breath. "Jim, this final year of monitoring is mandatory, to prove our clean-up worked. It should come out fine. You can use the time to market the site, get a good buyer, and set up a good sale contact for the property. Maybe you can have it set to close as soon as we're done. I talked to your son about it about the letter, and this actually is a good thing, because it means an end is in sight. A buyer can get a loan for the property. And I can provide copies of everything for the bank to get the deal going. "

"Thanks, kid. You're doin' a good job for us. My son says this corner lot is worth 2 million, once we get it all clean. Maybe in a year it'll be worth 2 and a half, way land prices are going lately. You know we gave the bank 15 grand for it back in '49? Had a monthly payment that almost crushed us the first couple years. Now we raised six kids between us, and got eleven grandkids, and we don't pay a dime but the taxes on it. So, we'll be fine. It's you kids that got to afford new places I worry about. You take care." He hung up.

Harper replaced the phone and sat looking at it. Approval for more work, and he knew he was helping those guys. So, Jim rode on a tank with General Patton. Probably never stopped talking all the way across North Africa, too. The tank cleanup stuff was not too complicated on the scientific side, but there were endless complications in every other aspect. He was surprised to find he was enjoying those parts: the real and perceived risks, the contracts, the insurance, the client expectations and the regulatory requirements. Lawyers lurked on the fringes (or dead center) of most jobs, prepared to exploit the massive liability of dealing with contaminated properties.

For a typical monitoring well job, he would do weeks of work; buying well casing, hiring drillers, ordering cement delivery, lab work, and courier services, as well as the tasks of design, permitting, construction and sampling of a series of wells. He would prepare a report with maps, graphs, text and lab results that determined the fate and value of an entire property. All for maybe 15 thousand bucks, total, with a thousand bucks profit.

If he screwed up anything, and a lawyer pounced, he could have a million dollar liability claim. Meanwhile, if everything went right, in a year, Jim and George would have a property worth 2.5 million, and Harper would gain a thousand bucks, after expenses and subcontractors. The routine risks he took consulting were way worse than he took whitewater kayaking. At least his shoes didn't get torn off consulting.

His eyes drifted to his calendar of surf porn, with glossy photos of empty waves at remote surf spots. Maybe he should just move to Puerto Rico, get a little fishing boat. He could find a surf shack and a Latina cutie with cinnamon skin. Drink dark rum with her till the winter swells arrived. His phone desk rang and the beach receded back onto the wall calendar.

As he reached for the phone, he glanced over at his computer screen. There was a flashing notice of an update from SurfCast, the ocean swell forecasting service he subscribed to. He clicked on the blinking icon to open the notice as he picked up the phone. Shira's voice came into his ear, as his screen resolved into a satellite picture and text.

"Hello, Harper. It's me, Shira. Can we do something together this weekend? I wanted to see you." She sounded tentative and far away.

"Wow!" Harper said involuntarily into the phone as he read the surf alert screen. A huge Pacific storm, or rather a sequence of imbricated storms stretching to Japan, was filling the Gulf of Alaska. The swell could be huge, or maybe a windy mess. Very strange for May. It was due to arrive tomorrow, then increase a day or two later. Looked like a whopper.

"Oh, Hi, Shira! Yes, uh, yes I want to see you. I mean, I really, really want to see you. How about dinner at the Asian Star tonight? This weekend? Well.." Harper glanced longingly at the surf alert on his computer and calculated when it might peak.

" What about a morning beach picnic? Well, you wanted me to take you to Ali Baba's Cave, right? It's that secret beach up north you can only get to at low tide. Let's see, when is low tide tomorrow? 6:45 AM, right? Want to get up early and go explore? A big swell is coming, but we could get ahead of it, maybe. Yes, bring the pooch. And maybe a picnic. Hey, if we stay too long, we can't leave the beach till the next low tide. So, bring plenty of snacks. Well, you can always swim out if you get bored. Um, I might bring a surfboard with us, but I can go out later at sunset. OK, great! I'll pick you up tonight for dinner."

Harper hung up and touched the faded note taped to his phone base. H.L.P., High Level Performer. Time to get that written contract in the mail to Jim and George for their year of monitoring work, and then get home for the weekend. He had a date, and a big swell was on the way.

19

Murder and Discovery

Never judge a day by the weather, say the river guides. Saturday morning threatened rain and gloom, but the cozy truck cab was full of warmth. Driving north on Highway One with Shira and the Homer dog, Harper turned up the heater and the music. The Beatles, Harper and Shira all joined voices for a soulful finish on Let It Be, crooning "Whisper Words of Wisdom, Let it Be, Let it Beeeee.." as the piano chords crashed to a close. Homer the dog essayed a yelp from the back. Shira snuggled against Harper on the bench seat, as they sipped mugs of coffee and sped past the landfill road. They were north of town, almost to The Landing, halfway to the secret beach turnoff that was their destination. They had overslept and lingered under the covers together, and missed the minus tide at dawn. It was too cold anyway, more like winter than spring. The sky was bruised purple and dark grey, signs of a coming storm. Powerful swells were arriving and crashing on offshore rocks, and the north coast surf spot parking lots they passed were filling up. Harper looked longingly at the waves. He was doubtful about the hike along the ocean cliffs to reach the beach hideout. And, it panged him to be missing a prime swell. But sleeping in had been worth it. He and Shira had the joy of discovery that only new lovers know. Waking up with her there felt like Christmas morning every time.

Harper was telling about his secret beach. He had found it on a solo kayak outing along the north coast. Until now, he never brought anyone there. He named it Ali Baba's, because the only access was a spooky swim through a rock tunnel. The tunnel started as an open crack, an expanded bedrock fault. A dark cleft in the cliff at the surf line, it did not seem inviting. Ten yards into the tunnel, the starfish and anemone-encrusted walls turned abruptly back toward the sea, expanded, and opened into a stand-up arch looking out at a pocket beach, cliffed on all sides and hidden from every vantage point but the sea. It was a secret pocket beach, known only to sea lions and a couple of surfers.

The Beatles launched the raucous rave-up of "I've Got a Feeling", and Shira was singing along, twisting in her seat and hoisting her coffee cup. She belted out, "If ya leave me, I won't be late again" as Harper and Homer Dog gave her back " Oh, Yeah" voices. Glancing in his rearview mirror, Harper spotted a flashing light, which quickly grew into a police car, moving up fast behind him. He lifted his foot off the gas, checked his speed, slowed, signaled, and moved crisply into the right hand lane. The police car was followed closely by an ambulance, and they both rocketed past in the fast lane, their sirens breaking in through the music. Shira turned down the song and they looked at each other in silent alarm and watched the sirens speed north. Harper sped up again to keep them in view.

They passed the familiar turn out off for The Landing, and Harper automatically glanced over to check the swell. The lot was full and a crowd was standing at the scouting point. It looked too big, with closeout sets breaking clear across the small bay and way offshore. Good day to get a wave spanking. And, it looked like there was no way they were doing the Ali Baba cave hike. Maybe the ambulance was for a surfer rescue? Or a fisherman washed off the rocks? The two emergency vehicles were still visible ahead of him on the long straightaway of the highway, and then he saw their brake lights come on. The police car and ambulance pulled together into the entrance of the Arena Lagunitas Quarry road.

"It's at the Quarry!" Shira gasped "My God, maybe a bulldozer accident? Harper, why are you stopping?"

"I know people in there. Let's see what it is."

Harper slowed and pulled into the quarry road, drawn by curiosity and something more. It was as if he had a sense of ownership of events here, due to the worry and tension this quarry was causing him. The gate was open, and several trucks with Arena logos were parked there. The emergency vehicles had pulled ahead and around the first bend. They were stopped by the sand wash ponds, doors flung open and lights still revolving.

In the bushes back under the freeway, parked against the inner locked gate where it could not be seen from the road, Harper saw the rear of a white Econoline Van, with twin exterior gas cans mounted on the bumper and a steel expedition rack on top. It was Goat's rig!

He was sure of it. The last time he saw Goat he was driving it, weeks before, dealing at The Landing. Goat's cabin was somewhere on the ridge above here, in fact, not more than five miles away. What was Goat up to now? Harper though of the worries Tracer had voiced, and felt a sense of dread.

Asking Shira to wait, he cut the engine, jumped out, and ran along the dirt road to where the vehicles were. A circle of men in uniforms were gathered down at the edge of the wash pond. Harper appeared at the top of the hill and looked down at their tableau.

There was Goat. His body lay facedown, sprawled at the edge of the water, in the center of a circle of kneeling men. His body had the carelessness of death, his face underwater and partly buried in the sand. One leg was stuck up on shore, one lay in the water. There was no movement. He was wearing his river headlamp, and the same tattered old blue fleece pullover and sandals he had worn at Lava Falls. The back of his head was bloody, horribly crushed, misshapen. A dark red stain around the base of his ponytail spread into the sand and the water. It had turned black in places on the dry sand, and a faint pink cloud hung around his head in the water. There was a stout piece of irrigation pipe with a water meter on the end on the sand near him, and a lumpy burlap sack in the water next to him. As in a dream, Harper realized that the burlap sack was moving and making burping noises, while everything else was silent.

The circle of men crouched around the body were a mix of ambulance crew, Quarry security guys, and a cop. They were looking down, focused on Goat's body. All seemed to be held in a spell. Harper realized they were waiting while the ambulance guy held a gloved hand to Goat's neck and checked for a pulse. The paramedic shook his head, a definite clear no, and he removed his hand. They all sagged a little.

Harper saw the no, and the look that passed between the cop and the medic. He took it in, all in a painful eternal instant. He let out a defeated "Oh, no, Goat!" and they all turned together and looked up at him, surprised. The cop came out of the reverie first. He barked to Harper "Hey, you stay up there. I don't want you down here! OK, everyone except the medical team, back up to the road. I want statements from all of you. This is a crime scene. We got too many damn footprints already." Everyone started to stand and draw away from the body.

A little ways down the pond, an old man in an Arena Quarry jacket was dragging a second burlap sack and incongruously hopping and splashing in the shallows along the shoreline. He was hunched over, cursing with intensity, ignoring the dead body and the crowd. Harper's mind was reeling, and it took him a moment to realize that it was Hitch, the quarry manager. He appeared to be trying to catch frogs. They were abundant. Half a dozen frogs were visible nearby, some hopping intermittently. Several more dark heads emerged from the water edge, just beyond Hitch. As Harper watched, Hitch lunged with surprising speed and grabbed one with a bony hand. Angrily, he stuffed it into the sack and turned back towards the pond for another.

The cop spoke into a radio microphone attached to his shoulder. "Yeah, send the Coroner, the Sheriff's Crime Scene crew, and you better page the Detective on weekend duty. And, I got a vehicle I want to run plates on." He stopped talking to the mike and looked up at Harper suspiciously. "Who are you? What are you doing here? You know the victim? Got some ID?"

Harper was shocked, still staring at Goat's body. As he watched, two large green frogs emerged from the throat of the burlap sack next to Goat. They slipped into the water and swam away. Slashes of bright scarlet were visible along the inner surfaces of their sturdy legs. The quarry guard next to the body noticed, hurriedly collected the sack, gathered the neck and twirled it tight, carried it up the roadbed, and set it in the sand, where it lay twitching with life. He glanced at Harper, then at the cop. "They musta been releasing frogs. We seen the van around here a couple of times before, but he always took off. This time we seen the van parked when we pulled in to open up, and we found him lying here".

Harper looked up and met the cop's cynical face. The policeman growled at him.

"Who are you, I asked. I want an ID."

"Oh, sure." Harper fumbled for his wallet. " Of course, Officer. I work for the quarry. For Arena Corporation that is. I'm…I'm Harper Purcell, I'm a geologist, doing a study for the quarry water use. I was just driving by and stopped to see what happened. What happened to that man?"

The cop glanced at his license, his face, then ignored him again and looked down the bank at Hitch, who was standing ankle deep in the pond, still cursing to himself, stuffing another frog back into his sack. Suddenly, Hitch swung the whole sack wildly over his head, and brought it smashing down onto the shore. It made a slapping, wet, meaty sound. Hitch staggered for footing, and advanced a step out of the water, and swung it overhead again. He was crying now, spit flinging from his mouth as he flogged the sack again on the ground with a thwack.

"Sons-a-bitches! Sons-a-bitches! Trying to close my quarry! "

"Hey now, quit that!" The cop shouted and moved down the bank, stopping him and reaching for the sack as he wound up for another swing. Water and blood dripped out of the burlap mesh. Hitch mutely surrendered the bag and looked around blankly. Flecks of spittle were on his lips, and his eyes were fixed and glazed. He did not seem to recognize Harper, the cop or anything.

"Sons-a-bitches tryin' to close my quarry. Just like when they poisoned Granddaddy's well to get us off the farm. This ain't Oklahoma. Nobody got a right to come in here and try to close my quarry down. Twenty years I been here, a- runnin' this here quarry. Sons-a-…sons-a…sons-a-bitches. " He ran out of breath.

The policeman set the bloody bag down, holding it away from his uniform, and looked at Hitch severely. Then he staggering back up the loose bank to the road, loose sand filling into his black uniform shoes. The cop looked disgusted. He had had enough. He pointed at Harper and the security guards.

"All you people except the medical crew, get your asses back over to that gate, and wait for me to take your statement. Medical team, please wait in your vehicle. We're not moving the body yet." He turned back to Hitch, glowered, and placed his palm on top of his gun butt. "You stay here. I want your statement now."

Harper was already walking fast back to his truck, tears welling in his eyes. He got in fast, started the engine and pulled away before the security guards had arrived at their truck. He entered Highway One in a cloud of spitting gravel, ignoring Shira's alarmed questions. The truck climbed a slight rise and dropped, and the quarry disappeared behind them. A half mile further, Harper turned right at the first blacktop road into the mountains and drove uphill, swerving around corners, climbing almost blind, until he finally pulled over into a roadside turnout in a cloud of dust. He shut the truck down. Crying openly, beating on the steering wheel with his fist, then resting his forehead against the wheel, he remembered Goat's body floating at the edge of the pond.

Shira was scared, and stopped asking anything, waiting for him to speak. She rubbed his back with concern and the dog jumped forward into the front seat, nuzzling in between them with a worried nose.

"It was Goat. I saw him dead. They killed him. He's dead. And just so he could make money and go to Baja."

"What? Goat? The man from your river trip? How? Oh, Harper, I'm so sorry. Can I help? Can we call his family?"

" I don't even know if he has any family. I don't even know his damn real name. He was just Goat. He was always alone, except on river trips."

"What happened? Why did we leave so fast? Are you OK?"

"I don't know what happened. I need to call Tracer. Maybe I should go back and identify him. His cabin is around here somewhere, I think. I just left without saying anything. But I did give them my name. Oh, that mean old fucker. I don't know what's going on, except he's dead. C'mon, I got to go home and call Tracer in Moab. "

20

Goat's Cabin

It was a pale and tired Harper that drove back up Highway One later that afternoon, headed for Goat's cabin hideout. He switched on his wipers as a steady rain began. The shock of Goat's death was a dull ache, but he had spoken to Tracer, and now he had a mission.

The parade of events at that damn quarry cycled through his mind. Everybody saw their own gold nugget laying there. For him, it was his shot at a decent groundwater job for HLP Associates. For Arena, it was another twenty years of sand mining, plus 200 homes and a golf course. For Goat, it was a chance to score cash towards his desert hideout. Surfers wanted in on the uncrowded barrels breaking on the sand bar offshore. For many others, it was precious water and rare open space for wild critters. Unfortunately, with real estate prices going up 20% a year, the critters were outbid. Now, Goat was dead, apparently caught and punished for upgrading the biotic species count. A week ago, Tony Armstrong had offered Harper… what exactly? A job? A bribe? A nice deal on a coastal building lot? He was not sure, but it was in exchange for doing groundwater work that supported future residential development. Grab the gold ring and let the Devil take the wetlands. And he was ready to do it. No wonder Tracer had left the state for Moab.

He had spoken with Tracer, reaching him at Billie's trailer in Moab. Tracer had been silent a long time when he told him about Goat, and the sacks of frogs. Harper thought he had lost him. After a pause, he heard Tracer come back on the line, his voice thick.

"Who clubbed him?"

"Maybe Arena Quarry security. Probably. The manager is a tyrant and I think he snapped. It doesn't matter."

"Harper, you have to go to his cabin. Goat was running a scam, planting endangered species for money. He tried to bring me in. Said it was easy money. Last year, he raised steelhead in an aquarium, and released fry in a tributary to the Carmel River. His pay off was five grand, cash, no taxes, from some rich, pissed-off neighbors. The steelhead changed the biologic assessment outcome, the project stalled, then got dropped. Goat got paid, and it was game on. He was hooked. I guess he figured out how to breed Red –Legged Frogs, too, the fat ones from coastal streams, listed as endangered. He said he had over a hundred adults, from about a thousand tadpoles. Anyway, you gotta go to his cabin and destroy the evidence, or the shit will hit the fan for all those sites he worked on. All those folks that hired him will be screwed."

"Why should I care?" Harper asked.

"Well, one of them is Dukie. And all the protests against projects that he worked against will be screwed, too. Anyway, we need his boat."

"Dukie? Dr. Dukie hired him? What boat?"

"Yeah. Our own Dr. Dukie. I'll deal with him later. I should kick his ass. Lucky he's down in Grand Canyon on that research trip. Aw, Harper! I can't believe Goat is dead! I was just going to call you and him, both. To tell you to come out here, like, tonight. We're going!"

"What? Come there? Moab?"

"No, not Moab. Flagstaff. Lee's Ferry. The canyon! The Speed Run is on, Harper! Billie just left for the Park Service office to get a cancellation permit for Monday. Our launch is the day after tomorrow! In, like 48 hours! You and Goat and me and Billie. It was all going to be perfect. Aw, man."

"Goat is dead, Tracer." Harper was still stunned by all this.

Tracer was insistent, his voice breaking and edging into crazy.

"We have to do it without him, then. You have to get Goat's dory and bring it here. Now! Or, OK, tomorrow then! Listen, Harper, it's a great plan. Epic. Lifetime. Glen Canyon is spilling 40,000 cfs. And it is going up to 60,000. Or 70! Fucking huge water! The Little Colorado is coming in downstream at almost 10,000 cfs. Lake Foul is nearly full, the Rockies snowmelt is on and a five-day storm is still coming in off the Pacific. Should be the highest water since 1983. We'll go nonstop in a dory. Maybe one or two quick sleeps. You, me, and Billie. Just like The Factor, Petschek and Wren did in '83. We could set the speed record! We need the dory. You have to bring his boat out. Shit, I wish we could bring his ashes down. "

Harper stared at the phone. The confusion and anger came spilling out. "Tracer, I don't believe you. Goat is dead, murdered, and all you can say is, let's do a river trip?"

There was a pause. Then Tracer replied, quiet and intense. "It hurts, I know, Harper. Goat was like my brother. And I knew this would end bad. Now, a river trip is the only answer we got. It's all I know how to do, and in this case, it is actually, truly, the right thing to do. And you know it, Harper. I don't have to explain. Not to you. Record high water, this window won't last, and we got a permit. The Speed Run is on. Do it for Goat and for me. And do it for you, too. Cut the bullshit, and go up to his cabin and get the dory. This is what matters. Me and Billie are leaving for Flag tonight."

Harper wiped his face and tapped the receiver against his forehead. Christ, 70,000 cfs? Who could even imagine what that meant? A speed run? He almost drowned in Cherry Creek last week. But, what did it matter? Maybe Tracer he was right. Everything was getting away from him. "Be in Flagstaff by tomorrow night, huh? I'm in Santa Cruz, man. I don't have wings. The police probably want to talk to me. Christ, Tracer. I don't know. I just got hired for like, three more tank jobs. I gave the cops my name, then I took off. I didn't even help identify his body. And my lung is still funny from Cherry Creek. Remember, that was your last plan? I never even rowed a dory."

"Me and Billie are rowing, not you! Billie is the trip leader now, and she might not even let me row! You don't know her. She is at the South Rim office getting the permit. You are our high-sider and bailer, man! We need three, and we need the dory.'

"Fine." Harper breathed into the phone. "I'll go get the boat. I can drive there tomorrow and be there by dark. Just don't say any more."

"You'll be back in under a week. This is for Goat. We're gonna do it for him, and for us. But get up to his cabin before the cops do. I can tell you how to get there. It will take them a little while to find where he lived, cause the cabin is his Mom's name. Goat was pretty suspicious of government, you know. He still has family out in Colorado, I think. Hey, Harper, do you know, what was Goat's real name anyway?"

After the call, as he was throwing all his river stuff into his truck, Harper tried to make sense of the whirl of thoughts. Shira would want to come with him to the cabin, but he was afraid of arrest. He felt a duty to make the speed run, but he was not ready to leave so soon. He was excited and scared about the high water, but felt bad about going big for fun when Goat had just been killed. Confused and upset, he headed back up the coast to find Goat's cabin. On Highway One, he went whizzing past the cluster of official vehicles now swarming at the Arena Quarry road, then he turned up into the mountain redwoods on two-lane blacktop.

He had directions from Tracer to find the cabin, but he was not seeing the landmarks. Thick green moss coated the fallen logs along the road. Filtered rainfall from the treetop canopy reached the carpet of needles and brush. Rain was falling hard now, and making a stream on the blacktop road surface. The forest was vibrant green, with a creek lost in a tangle below. Several unnumbered dirt driveways went by, no mailboxes, just chains strung between posts as a crude gate. As he drove past a hillside cabin slouching into moss, ferns and ruin, he couldn't help thinking of a bumper sticker he had seen at a whitewater festival; *"Paddle Faster, I hear Banjo Music"*. The redwood trees kept getting bigger and the blacktop road seemed to get smaller. These mountain gulches were sensimillia farming territory, where growers raised powerful marijuana with names like Skunk Breath, Diesel Fuel, and Lost My Car Keys. Folks up here fired guns at passing helicopters. He had better not pull up the wrong driveway.

In a rare clearing, he passed a trophy house, with an ornate frosted glass door, a wrap-around porch, trampoline for the kids, and several dirt bikes and quads parked around a tarped RV. The level patch the house stood on seemed unusual in the surrounding topography. Harper searched briefly for the outline of an old landslide downslope of the house as he drove past. Dozens of deep-seated, ancient landslides were mapped on these hills, and they formed appealing level spots at their head. Many were so large that there were visible only on stereo air-photos. Local engineering geologists thought they were thousands of years old, perhaps from a wetter climactic period. Lots of people built atop these old landslides, but not many geologists bought those houses.

A cynical staff person at the Santa Cruz County grading office had once told Harper the stages of development for big parcels up in the redwoods: first, an initial Timber Harvest, taking only the most valuable trees (which raised funds to pay off the loan for the land). This was followed by a period of quiescence, until the owner got a backhoe onto the site. Then began a period of backhoe practice, recreational grading, new dirt roads, small timber harvests, and, once a County guy found out and showed up, usually multiple grading violations and a stop-work order. The tree harvests created some income, and left a network of quickie dirt roads and scattered clearings within the parcel. Then came a lot split and sale, breaking up the large property into 5- and 10-acre lots, each with an unpermitted, unpaved road dumping roadcut sediment into the creeks. After the lot split, a larger remainder lot, typically with the best home site, was retained for the trophy house, future modest timber harvests, and perhaps some high-grade marijuana horticulture. To be an effective government representative, the County guy had explained to Harper, you had to understand the local forest.

Harper slowed to cross a steel deck bridge over the gulch, with a glimpse of a stream far below. This bridge was in his directions. Goat's driveway was coming up on the left. And there it was, a steep driveway curving uphill and out of sight. The gateposts were covered in moss. There was no name or number on the posts, just a crude stick figure drawing of a southwestern Anasazi bent-twig figurine. Of a goat, naturally. He pulled in.

The driveway climbed, then leveled out near the top of a ridge. The deep gloom thinned out to let in some sky up here on the ridge. Rain intensified where the sky was visible. Harper came to a steel cable stretched across the road cut. Steel I–beams sunk in concrete anchored the cable, and a brass padlock hung at the clasp. Pretty good security for a hillbilly driveway, Harper thought. A reflector circle, and a *No Trespassing* sign swung from the cable. Harper got out with his rain hood on, and examined the padlock. It was heavy brass, with numbered wheels on the base to spin a 5-digit combination. Shaking his head, Harper thumbed the wheels to 5-24-69. It clicked open.

The numbers stood for May 24, 1869, the launch date for the first Colorado River Expedition, led by Major John Wesley Powell, from Green River, Wyoming. The legendary First Grand Canyon Put-in. Lots of boatmen on the Colorado River used these brass 5-number locks on their trucks, campers, footlockers and beer caches. Half of them used the Major's original launch date as the "secret" combo. It was a way of giving access to those in your fraternity, while keeping out the rest of the world.

Tracer had told him about that, and used the same lock on his truck.

The sadness and loss of entering Goat's private realm suddenly hit him. The lock, and the connection implied his lost, doomed river buddy. But, he knew Goat's van registration would lead police here eventually, and he better to be gone by then, so Harper got back into his truck and drove.

In another hundred yards, the cabin came into view. A surprisingly large clearing in the woods surrounded a neat cabin with a red metal roof. Several outbuildings of various size and age sat on the margin of the clearing. A compact solar panel on stilts was placed on the hillside above the house. For this single solar panel, Goat had created the biggest chunk of open sky Harper had seen since leaving the coast highway. There were signs of tree felling and wood cutting everywhere, with stumps before and behind the cabin, and ranging up the hillside. A muddy stack of limbed trunks was stacked in the clearing, waiting to be bucked down. A hydraulic log splitter sat in mud, surrounded by splits. A herd of homebuilt sawhorses, scarred with deep cuts, sat in the rain around the clearing. Wet sawdust and chips coated the ground. Clearly, a tree killer lived here.

But not anymore, Harper thought sadly. He parked and stood in the late afternoon rain. One entire wall outside the cabin was lined with cordwood, stacked dry under an overhanging roof eave. Harper went directly to the back corner of the woodpile, and lifted a dirty tarp. It covered a metal ammo can. Popping the lid, he found a metal flashlight, and a keychain with half a dozen keys. The second key he tried opened the cabin door.

The Goat's Lair

Inside, the cabin was a single large room, dimly light by

bare windows. A stone fireplace dominated the space, with a sleeping loft built over the back third. Except for a large kitchen worktable strewn with books, the cabin was neat as a cell. The bachelor kitchen had a set of cast iron pans, a rack of good knives, and no ornamentation. A Bighorn ram skull with full-curl horn sheaths sat above the fireplace. Now there's a fine protected species artifact, Harper thought to himself. Goat must have been proud of that sucker, since it was a serious Federal offense to possess one. Heavy-duty goggles and logger's gloves lay with a disassembled chainsaw on folded newspaper next to the fireplace. A rat-tail file, the old chain, and small wrenches were carefully aligned nearby. There were bookshelves along every wall. Harper smiled at the black and white photograph of Georgie White, the First Woman of the Colorado River, in a hardhat and leopard skin unitard. Another black and white photo of John Muir, leaning on his walking stick, sat on the mantle. Twin icons and iconoclasts, they were Goat's kind of people.

The kitchen table looked like a research project. Books, and stapled pages of printed text spilled across the table centered in the kitchen. It was an odd collection. Harper pawed through the titles: *The Cold Water Aquarium Keeper's Bible, Becham's Guide to North American Endangered Species, National Audubon Society Guide to Amphibians and Reptiles, Have Fun and Make Money Raising Trout!, The Tide Water Goby Endangered Species Listing Decision, Stokes Guide to Animal Tracks*, a laminated card with color photos of a fat frog titled **Rana Aurora Draytonii**, *The Golden Book of Endangered Species, Comprehensive Salmon Hatchery Management Plan, by U.S. Fish* and *Wildlife, The North American Mammals Field Guide*.

Harper picked up a research paper on Scripps Oceanographic

Institute letterhead, titled *"An Evaluation of Success Rates in Hatchery–Raised Steelhead Rainbow Trout (Salmon Gairdnerii) in the Sacramento River System"*. Underneath it was a well- thumbed copy of *"Baja Homesteaders Guide: The Real Deal on Buying and Living in Mexico's Coastal Paradise."*

Goat had been doing his homework. Based on the bulging sacks of red-legged frogs found at the quarry scene, his frog hatchery success rate was pretty good. Harper wondered how many projects Goat had transported endangered frogs onto. How many protected habitat designations in California could be under suspicion? Developers and their attorneys would milk this for every possible inch of judicial relief, if word got out. Legitimate populations of endangered species would be suspected of not existing, and real habitat would loose protection. Every finding of Potential Impact on Species of Special Significance for the past couple of years would be revisited and maybe reversed. All in all, it would provide lots of fodder for fat talk-radio hosts and lawyers. Abruptly, Harper swept all the books and papers together into a pile and carried the armload to the fireplace. He was not sure why it mattered, since Goat was dead and had been found with sacks of frogs, but he knew he did not want to leave the story of Goat's illegal enterprise out for anyone to find. He lit a corner of the pile with matches from the mantle and it quickly grew into a warm blaze. The sudden light brightened the cabin and brought a cozy feeling, as rain continued to hammer the roof.

Harper really felt like a criminal now. Not because he was destroying evidence, but because he was burning books. Only Nazis or Christian Fundamentalists did that. He felt a surge of anger at his dead friend, getting killed and making him into a book-burner. Just because Goat wanted to get rich and move to Mexico. And then got his head smashed in. Why couldn't he just grow dope like everyone else in these mountains?

He poked a fallen volume back into the blaze with his boot, and began scanning the bookshelf and worktable for other fire candidates. There was a small desk at the end of the table. A file labeled Tax Relief was full of nasty letters from the Internal Revenue Service. They were addressed to a Mr. Alvin McManus, at a Boulder Creek Post Office box. Harper recognized the PO Box as Goat's mailing address. Alvin McManus had not paid any income tax in over a decade, one IRS letter said. So, Alvin McManus, eh? Well, no wonder he was always just Goat.

Under the tax file was spiral bound notebook marked with Goat's Anasazi bent twig symbol on the cover. Harper opened it in the firelight. The words *Operation Johnny Appleseed* were written atop a column of numbers and dates. On the left, under the word Species ran a list: rana, rana, rana, steelhead, puma (Christ, was he raising mountain lions?), goby, rana, rana. The next column was unlabeled, but must be the money. It was doubtful that Goat had been releasing 5,000 frogs per event, and that was the most common column entry, though several were for 1000 and two said *gratis.* A final column was dates. The income totaled over 24 thousand bucks, with dates ranging from mid- 1999 to April 2000. The latest entry was last month and said rana, steelhead, 6000. Harper shook his head ruefully. Looked like Goat had been hired to work on the Lagunitas Quarry at about the same time as Harper.

Business looked good. There were three entries from the last month. The going rate to have convincing evidence of endangered species appear on your site was apparently one to five thousand bucks. Hopefully a good deal to derail somebody's development plans.

Harper shook his head in wonder. What a brilliant niche Goat had found. The consulting industry was specialized, but it was hard to think of a more a promising combination of low overhead and growing demand. There were no names of specific projects or record of who had made payments. No record of where the money went, either. The notebook went into the fireplace, landing in the burning pile.

Harper recognized several thick copies of completed Environmental Impact Statements for big local projects; a timber harvest that including several stream crossings, and there was Rancho Ojo, a residential and golf development in Monterey County. Both had highlighted sections on Species of Special Significance, indicating red-legged frogs were present. Harper chucked them into the fire with the notebook. He picked up a stack of Cabela's catalogs lying at the end of the bookshelf and added them to the base of the blaze, just to burn more stuff. Flames rose and filled the fireplace. The rest of the bookshelf and desk contents looked OK. Now, where was the hatchery?

Back outside in the rain, Harper sized up the outbuildings. One key opened the woodshed, where gloves, ear protection, hand tools, cables, straps and a neat row of various size chainsaws were lined up. Harper grabbed an axe from the corner just in case, and moved on to the largest building, a windowless steel shell with twin roll-up doors. It looked promising for illicit activities. A steady plume of smoke was rising from the cabin chimney, giving it a cheerful aspect as Harper fumbled with keys in the rain.

The steel door of the warehouse swung open into darkness and admitted uncertain light. Harper flicked on overhead fluorescent lights powered by a deep cycle marine battery. He found himself looking at two bays; one empty parking space, presumably reserved for the new van last seen in the bushes at the Arena Quarry. The second parking bay held a large wooden rowboat with a graceful swell and curve, hidden under a tattered canvas cover. It sat on a metal trailer. The tires looked good and the safety chains were in place at the hitch. No frogs. No fish tanks, no dope bales, no tall rows of fragrant green bud growing in pots. Just a big old wooden boat that looked like it had not been wet in years. In the rafters were some sets of wooden oars, and a metal raft frame hanging from brackets. A pile of dry bags and life jackets lay in the back corner, along a wall of several racked mountain bikes. At the back, he found a stack of long fluorescent grow lights, sacks of potting soil, and two empty, dry glass aquariums, one with cracked glass. Both aquariums were free of endangered species. Beside one of the dry aquariums, he found caster plasts, positive and negatives, of a large paw. The positive cast had a wooden grip handle mounted in the plaster. He lifted it and turned it in his hand. It was a big footprint stamp, with a hint of recessed claws. This must be for *Puma Concolor*, the elusive mountain lion, rumored to exist here in the Coast Ranges, in the Gabilan Mountain peaks and down in the Big Sur barrancas. Oh, Goat, you clever bastard. This cast was for leaving big cat tracks on the ridges above proposed housing developments, for field biologists to find and photograph. Think of the excitement. As long as it wasn't those biologists from Less Than Significant Consultants, Harper thought. Those guys probably never found a wildcat track in their careers. They never got out of their truck long enough.

"Damn it, Goat where are the frogs?" Harper cried, tapping the axe head on the slab in frustration. He stood on the garage threshold thinking. A thin foot track led away from the cabin and entered redwoods, following the drainage. Harper stared at it, then started down it at a trot, holding the ax and a flashlight. He remembered Goat telling him that his cabin was on ten acres which backed up against the vast Big Basin State Park Property, with a stream on the boundary. Dope growers up here often used the State property for their plots, to avoid losing their land to law enforcement by growing at home. Why not use it for frog growing?

The rain was steady and the trail was muddy, running through ferns and mossy ground. There were signs of steady foot traffic along it. Briefly, Harper wondered if his footprints could be traced to him. Of course they could. Have to loose these sneakers on the way home. If he got out of here before the cops arrived and cuffed him to the car, that is. Serve him right after burning those books. He almost giggled, getting silly from the strain.

The path dropped steeply down to a small creek, swollen to knee-deep by the rain. It was the end of Goat's property. Standing on the creek shore in the failing light, rain dripping down his neck, Harper reluctantly got ready to cross the steam. How could he explore thousands of acres of State forest for a hidden frog farm? Then, one foot in the creek, he realized he was looking at a hidden water tank on the far side. Two black tanks actually, now that his eyes adjusted to the gloom. He splashed across. Two large plastic cattle troughs were also pinned against the stream bank with wooden stakes, covered with camouflage tarps and layered with brush. They would be invisible from above. A pile of empty burlap sacks lay under the tarp.

The first tank was half full of running water, but empty of life. Creek water flowed into the tank from a black hose, and then escaped from a vent halfway up the tank side. This supplied well-aerated, clean water to the cattle troughs without using electricity. He lifted the tarp on the second trough and shone his flashlight in. Dozens of large reflective eyes shone back at him. Croaking, movement, and splashing broke out. A rich musky smell emerged. Frogville. He had found the amphibious inventory of Operation Johnny Appleseed.

21

Santa Frog

The secret of a long life is knowing when it's time to go. Forty-five minutes after finding the frogs, Harper got the hell out of Goat's cabin, leaving in full dark and steady rain. His truck rattled down the dirt driveway, with the dory and boat trailer hitched behind him. Like a guilty pirate slipping out under cover of darkness, he crossed his fingers and spit out the window for good luck, subconsciously waiting for cannon fire to start. He had taken several milk crates full of Goat's Grand Canyon library, river lore that he simply could not burn or leave behind. It included water beaten Belknap and Larry Stevens guide books, a complete set of the Harvey hiking books, and 10 years of back issues of Boatman's Quarterly Review, the gossipy journal of working river guides in Grand Canyon. He also had a full bottle of Jameson's Irish Whiskey, grabbed off the kitchen shelf on his way out of the cabin. With his knees against the steering wheel, he twisted off the cap and drank a slug that burned his throat. The truck filled with the aroma of good Irish whiskey. He poured a splash out the window as he rolled away, spilling it onto the ground in a toast to Goat and his place, to the hideout he had ridden out from on his last run. May he find peace and clean runs on great rivers of dreams somewhere.

Lots of booty had been left behind; chainsaws, paddling gear, and other goodies. Harper was no thief. This was a mission, and taking Goat's boat was vital. The books and river journals would be respected and honored, rather than donated to some Salvation Army bin. And on the passenger side floor of his truck, damp and respirating, in violation of Federal and State laws regarding endangered species, were two burlap sacks bulging with live Red-Legged Frogs and on the seat, the Bighorn ram skull with full curl horn sheaths.

Christ, what was he thinking? There must be sixty frogs in there. He had no idea why he had taken them all, pouring them into the sacks at the trough, working like a madman, dragging them across the stream in the rain. But the frogs were Goat's slender legacy. Harper had no plan. He was driving way out in front of his headlights. Tracer had sent him to get the boat and get rid of the frogs. He was on a mission and the outcome was still uncertain.

Harper stopped and locked the driveway cable behind him. No need to make it easy for cops when they arrived. He looked back up the drive towards the hidden cabin. The sad vision of Goat fallen, sprawled dead in wet sand, returned to him. A wave of sadness and anger took him. He took a slow breath and changed his mental image, to Goat rowing into Lava Falls the last time, in the lead raft, calm and at home at the oars as he plunged on the perfect line. The sadness was still there, but the anger faded. Whoever killed Goat, whether it was that bastard Hitch or some one else, had only been competing the arc that Goat had been on since he was arrested by rangers on the Arkansas River a decade ago. Since then, he had hardly ever made good moves off the river, while he rarely made bad ones on the river.

Harper stood at the cable in the driveway and had another sip of the Irish. A strong rush animal spirits began rising in him. It felt like he was standing on a scouting rock above a big drop. Now he was headed back to Grand Canyon, towing an unregistered, uninsured trailer with no brake lights, whiskey on his breath, carrying a couple of sacks fulls of endangered frogs, after destroying evidence at a scene linked to a recent murder. His friend was dead, the bad guys were winning, and he had to get almost a thousand miles to Flagstaff, Arizona to do a speed run in big water. This was not a time for caution. It was time for balls and luck, not moderation. Might as well try and visualize a positive outcome, while he was at it. Once he thought of one, that is.

Too late for Goat on that score, he thought bleakly, tasting the whiskey again. But that was not yet the final word. The storm was on, raining steadily and blotting out the stars. The black night was to his advantage, making him invisible. A good night for frogs, Harper thought as he rattled downhill with trailer and boat.

The winding blacktop ran downhill through redwoods until it emerged at the coast. The straightaway of Highway One led twenty miles back to town, and he turned onto it. The storm was fresh down here at the ocean, howling, beating down the grasslands and drumming rain on his truck. His headlights made tunnels of light in the night rain. Harper saw no other cars. The trailer rocked behind him in the wind as he crept south, wondering about the straps that held the boat to the trailer. The sacks of frogs croaked in the cab, like a question about his plans.

He imagined Goat out a night like this, collecting breeding stock with a net and headlamp from creeks along this coast. Harper knew that despite the state-wide scarcity and loss of habitat of the Red-Legged frog, they were still relatively common in some ponds around here, if you knew where to look. Goat must have worked on this since last year, gathering wild frogs, raising breeding pairs for eggs, nurturing tadpoles, maybe using his network of dope buyers to carefully spread the word of his new service. The convergence of his frog harvest business and the hatch of dozens of development battles in coastal California was no coincidence, but a natural co-evolution, with environmental opportunity and market demand calling forth supply.

Highway One crossed a bridge over Molina Creek, the first coastal stream on the way south into Santa Cruz. Harper stopped in the gravel pullout along the highway without knowing exactly why. Every stream along this coast made a sand bar, and then a wave where it hit the ocean. And every decent surf wave had a scouting pullout, so he had been pulling off the freeway at these spots for surf checks for years. Humming Jimmy Cliff's "Many Rivers To Cross" softly to himself, he put his rain suit hood up and got out. He looked down at the dark water of Molina Creek. Be a shame if someone built a golf course up that creek. And, likely, someone would try to before long, the way things were going. He reached for the burlap sack.

Working quickly in the dark, he scampered down the side of the highway bridge, and stood at the edge of the Molina Creek lagoon with one sack of frogs. He could hear the frogs croaking steadily from his sack, as if they could smell the rain and freedom coming.

Harper hesitated a moment before untying the knot in the throat of the sack, considering how to optimize the survival of releasees. Coastal streams emerging from the redwoods made small lagoons where they hit the beach sand. In winter storms, the rivers swell, cut through the sand bars and spill to the ocean. They pond back up in spring and summer as lagoons behind a sand bar. The lagoons acted as brackish nurseries for amphibians and young-of-the-year steelhead, as well as hunting grounds for herons, raccoons, and whatever else was looking for a meal. But frogs liked their water fresh, not salty. Also, this storm might breach the lagoon and wash them all out to sea. Then again, this storm runoff was filling the lagoon with fresh water, dropping the salinity. It might be good timing for frogs. He had heard that the coastal lagoon of the Wilder State Park were a population center of the frogs (probably the collection area for Goats' breeding stock, Harper mused) so these frogs were probably coastal stock to begin with. They might like it here fine. Besides, he was in a hurry to leave for Flagstaff, it was pouring rain, and this was highly illegal. If he got caught, he was screwed big time, and would never get to Flagstaff with the dory. Better release some frogs.

He shook a dozen fine healthy specimens out of the sack and into the lagoon, trying to spill some smaller males along with the larger females. The frogs hit the water and disappeared, as he cinched the sack off to stop the cascade. Clambering back up the slope, rain dripping down his neck, Harper started giggling. Behind the wheel, he started singing, "Jeremiah was a Red Frog! Boo, boo, boom, Was a Good Friend o' Mine!"

Now he knew what to do. On his way south, Harper stopped

at every swollen stream and released frogs. He put handfuls of *Rana Aurora Draytoni* into the San Vincente and Liddell Creek lagoons, then drove on south. At the Arena Lagunitas quarry, fearful of possible security guards and the crime scene tape waiting on the quarry road, he stopped right out in the middle of the Highway One bridge over the Lagunitas Creek, and shook a dozen frogs out his truck window to the lagoon, airmailing them into the water ten feet below. They fell into darkness like commandos infiltrating enemy territory. Harper remembering his meeting with Tony and Hitch here a month before, when they had talked about the frogs that already existing at the quarry. He smiled bitterly at the irony of Goat getting killed planting red-legged frogs at the Lagunitas Lagoon ponds, where they were still abundant.

"Go forth and multiply, you frog fuckers! Make old Goat proud!" he cried out to the rain as he rolled the window up. He was loving his crazy distribution mission now, talking to himself and to Goat, sipping from the Jameson bottle occasionally and making stops to scramble down to Majors Creek, Wilder Creek and several unnamed agricultural ponds along the freeway. He imagined he was casting a protective spell on these places, placing a potent charm against future development made by the Goat Boatman, a Frog Wizard fallen in battle. He was drunk on the whiskey and on mourning, full of loss and self-righteousness. He felt dangerously invulnerable.

Finally, he came into the lights of town. Inside city limits, conscious of his conspicuous boat-and-trailer profile, he left the main drag and drove slowly through residential streets just below the University campus. There he released the last ten frogs, males and females, into the Bay Street Spring. It was a lovely spring-fed creek that flowed out of the campus limestone and through a riparian corridor, into a fancy residential neighborhood favored by old town money and tenured professors. No harm starting a little resident breeding population in a protected spot, after all. Who knows when a fellow might need to find a few healthy frogs to change the balance of a wetlands proposal?

Finally, Harper he stuffed the empty burlap sacks into a dumpster outside a convenience store and tossed his soggy sneakers in after them to hide his tracks. He walked barefoot back to his wet truck cab, as rain made the lights of the parking lot shiver. He dialed Tracer's phone. The recording answered. He spoke.

"Tracer, buddy. This is me. I got the boat and I'm rolling. Gotta sleep a few hours right now, or I'll keel over, but I'm on my way in the morning. See you in Flagstaff at the raft warehouse, say tomorrow by midnight."

Next he dialed Shira. As it was ringing, he checked his watch. Pretty late, but not too late. He still felt giddy, wrapped with tendrils of fatigue and loss. She answered sleepily. He held the phone close and spoke.

"Hello sweetheart, it's me, Santa Frog. The Mad Herpetologist. The Johnny Appleseed of Endangered Amphibians." A pause. "Yes, of course, I've been drinking." he sighed. He listened again.

"Yes, I found them. I found it all. They're free now. Released into their former historic range. Maybe a few new ponds, too. Oh, honey, I broke so many sections of the Endangered Species Act. I could be in jail forever. But it is the right thing I'm doing." He listened again.

"Well, now I have to leave for Flagstaff. Well, first thing in the morning. A week. I have to meet Tracer for a special plan. There's something we have to do." He waited while she said something.

"Yes, the same guy I paddled Cherry Creek with. I know, yeah, again with the plan. But I gotta go. Well, if that road is closed from the storm, I'll drive around. My friends need me to bring them a boat I got at Goat's. Maybe, some trouble, and well, pretty high water, but if I don't go, I'll never know. Can I come see you before I leave? I'll tell you all about it. Um, now?" He waited breathless.

"Thank you. OK, See you in five minutes." He whispered and hung up. Driving carefully now, not wanting to be stopped and asked to recite the alphabet by a local cop, he left the lot and drove through wet empty streets to Shira's house.

22

One Last Call

Sometimes, you just have to keep on marching. So, at dawn, Harper patted Homer the dog's head as he slipped quietly out the door of Shira's house and headed for Flagstaff. The neighborhood was still sleeping, and the rain had paused. Grey clouds hung low. Broken tree branches lay across the sidewalk, still wet from the storm the night before.

He hated to leave Shira. She was still dozing upstairs, enjoying a few hours of sleep to offset her chronically sleep-deprived schedule, the fate of the working midwife. Harper had 14 hours of driving to do to reach Flagstaff, and he wanted to stop at his office first.

Last night before they had slept, she had lifted a tiny leather bag out of her purse and handed it to him. "Take this with you for the speed run. It's good luck".

He took the bag with an expression of wonder.

" But, I don't have anything for you" he said lamely. She laughed and tossed her head.

"Of course you don't. That would require you planning ahead. But I am still allowed to give you something. Open it."

He tugged opened the neck of the tiny bag and spilled it out in his palm. It was a small bone carving, a stylized white fishhook complete with point and barb, strung on a heavy waxed thread. He lifted it up. She took it and slipped it over his neck. He fingered the necklace and looked at her quizzically. " Is this a Jewish thing?"

"No, It's Maori, silly. I got it in New Zealand. The Kiwis wear them when they leave home to go on voyages. One version of the story is that the hook is to pull you back home, safe from danger when your voyage is done. This is so I get you back."

Now he smiled and touched the necklace against his chest, remembering slipping into her room last night. The cloud of scent, fresh sheets, and piles of pillows in her feminine nest, with a curvaceous tigress within. Shira had cried with him over Goat, and had held him while he told her about the cabin and the discovery of Goat's endangered species operation. She had gasped and giggled with delight as he described the coastal frog release into the storm. Finally she had responded to his caresses with a fierce and loving embrace. She was a healer.

The forlorn loss and anger he had carried from Goat's cabin was gone, replaced by a yearning for the road. The dory sat on the trailer behind his truck like an exclamation point behind a sentence. It was calling for redemption, and release. Everything was changing, and everything he wanted before seemed empty now. Except Shira. Whatever else was coming or going, whatever storm was building, he wanted to come back to be with Shira. He could get through it with her. After the speed run. But now, to his office to make a few fast calls before driving.

He parked downtown in the newspaper lot, blatantly occupying several spaces with the truck and trailer. He jogged to his office through the rain-washed streets. The shops and coffee houses were not yet open, and only a few bedraggled homeless folks and a Public Works repair crew were on the street. At his office, he climbed the stairs and pawed through his desk papers, looking for phone numbers. He picked up his Arena Corp Lagunitas Quarry Water Study Proposal. Was it just two days ago he was so involved in this? Was it just two weeks ago he was revising his proposal, angling for the big time payoff, imagining being the local water champion and still getting a deal on a building lot as part of his legitimate payoff? All that was before he saw Goat lying in the quarry pond with his head crushed. But what had really changed? And the irony was, there were Red-Legged frogs in the ponds at the Lagunitas Quarry all along. Well, he was leaving town again, and he better leave a few messages for clients if he wanted to still be in business when he came back. He called his driller and cancelled a drilling date, traffic control, and cement delivery for a well installation later that week, leaving a message asking to reschedule. He heard the landscape architect come into his office downstairs and turn on the copy machine. It was eight AM. Time to start for Flagstaff. But, there was one more call to make. He dialed the office number and extension for Tony Armstrong's desk at Arena headquarters, hoping for the recording. Instead, Tony's salesman voice answered, industrious and eager.

"Arena Environmental Compliance, Tony speaking. "

"Tony! Good morning, it's Harper Purcell. I wanted to speak

to you before I left town. I'm leaving for a week for … for a memorial. I guess you know, my friend was killed out at the Lagunitas Quarry yesterday." His voice sounded wary and distant.

"Good lord, Harper. The police would like to talk to you about that, you know. I spent all day there yesterday. I understand you were at the scene and left. Your friend, you say? What was his name? They are having a devil of a time getting a proper I.D. What a dreadful tragedy. Our former plant manager, Hitch Owens, was released on bail, and is in the hospital you know. He's apparently had some sort of breakdown. I can't say anything more, attorneys working on it now. Terrible, of course, but it shouldn't affect the quarry permit. The new plant manager, Gary Covington is charge of all that now. Still, a dreadful thing. "

"Tony, I don't know if I can still work on the quarry water project. A lot has happened. Sorry. Maybe we can talk about it when I get back. "

There was a pause.

"Well, certainly, let's speak when you return Harper. It is not clear if the company is going to need a water study. Actually, I've just heard from our attorneys on that topic, too. It's why I'm in here so early today. The Quarry habitat study is moot now, since an intruder with sackfuls of frogs has been discovered. And, our corporate office attorneys told me to cancel your work order for now, and halt all work on the traffic and habitat assessment studies, too. But, not to worry, there's always another study somewhere, I suppose. Lucky for you consultant chaps, eh?"

"What do you mean?" Harper spit out incredulously. " How can you stop an impact assessment for water and habitat? What do you mean, the habitat study is moot?'

"Well, aside from this body at the quarry, we've just learned that our appeal was successful and our Lagunitas permit renewal will be re-considered at the County commissioners meeting, this Friday. We're quite hopeful for a positive outcome. Our attorneys appealed the last vote, and asked the Commissioners to approve our permit renewal without new environmental study, since it is a grandfathered existing use. They voted no two months ago, of course, but have agreed to discuss it again this Friday. We will agree to maintain the same sand mining basal depths and same water demand with no increases, so they can renew and grandfather us in, as a pre-existing and ongoing use. Environmental Assessment for sand mining is only mandatory for new projects, you know, at the discretion of the Commission. They can approve renewal with no traffic study, no endangered species studies, no water study. The environmentalists will scream of course, but that is to be expected. And this fatality, this trespasser carrying in endangered species, throws a lot of doubt on the validity of any environmental claims. According to the attorneys, you understand, of course."

Harper heard the hesitation in Tony's voice, and was it embarrassment? Shame? Still he was incredulous.

"But Tony, the Planning Commission would never do that. The quarry project wasn't even on their agenda for this month. And I thought there are at least three commissioners on that board dead set against you." Harper's voice trailed off in a dawning realization. Ed Larson was the commissioner who was the leader of the quarry opposition, and he was in the bottom of the Grand Canyon. On a river trip with special invite from Dukie.

Tony's voice was formal now and fading. "Possibly. The Chairman agreed to our request to place the item on the agenda for this meeting, and it has been publically noticed. All quite legal, I assure you. There have been some personnel changes on the board. One of the commissioners is out having back surgery this month, and of course Professor Larson, the most vocal opponent to the quarry, is on vacation. The substitute members of the Commission have authority to vote in their place. Our attorneys are optimistic for a favorable outcome. We have a relationship with the remaining commission members and…"

Harper couldn't take it anymore. His eyes misted with tears and he cut in savagely.

"You fucking wanker, Armstrong! You got Dukie to take Ed Larson away so you could bring this back for a vote! Didn't you? You never even meant to do a water study! And you bastards killed Goat!"

Silence. Harper was breathing heavily into the phone, his nostrils flaring. He wanted to drive to the Arena office and strangle Tony, and punch out every corporate attorney. Quietly, in a flat voice, Tony offered, "I am very sorry about the death of your friend. That was completely unnecessary and unintentional. Hitch is a violent idiot and completely unreliable. He was only supposed to have him arrested. As for the rest, please do not speak to me again in such an unprofessional manner." There was a click, and the call was over. Harper stared glumly at the phone. There goes that prize client. Goat was dead, and now the quarry was trying to get a green light from their toadies on the planning commission. Scape up that lovely clean sand, and plant reclamation bushes, pump that aquifer right down to the bottom, sell off the sand, and then build some McMansion houses out there. But, why was Dukie enabling it, taking Ed Larson into the Grand Canyon for 16 days, just before the quarry permit approval came back up for a vote? That smelled rotten. A Commission meeting this Friday? Today was Sunday. He counted off six remaining days. He better get to Flagstaff. They had a Speed Run to launch, and a commissioner to bring back.

23

Dory Warehouse

Western mountain towns have been partitioned by freeways and blurred by sprawl, but they still show their old frontier habitat zones, as distinct as a coral reef. Flagstaff is no exception. The original downtown has fine stone buildings, good shade trees, and the banks, and is bounded by the railroad tracks which separate the shabbier district of warehouses, row houses, and dingy motels. Both are approached nowadays through a flashy outer road of chain stores and fast food drive-throughs. Near the core, there is a good residential district with blocks of old homes with yards and more shade trees. Farther out on the newer side of town, there is the scary Mall Zone, giant box stores and vast lots of cars, devoid of pedestrians. Then, one reaches residential neighborhoods of small homes with stunted cottonwoods, mixed with newer patches of big homes, skinny trees, curvilinear streets, and no sidewalks. Keep driving, and trailer parks appear, next to bare spots planted with "Will Build to Suit" sale signs, and heavy equipment rental places. Finally on the town outskirts, moving away from Grand Canyon National Park traffic and going towards the Peaks, a string of muffler shops, liquor stores, and motels with Katchina signs gradually diminish and give way to scattered mini-storage buildings, hillsides of Ponderosa pines, and a large steel warehouse where the Redwall Rafting Company was based.

Harper was headed there to the raft warehouse to meet Tracer and Billie. The heavy rain of the last several days had broken and the air had the sparkling clarity of high mountains, fresh with rain and sweet with pine. The colors of sunset were gone from the snow on the San Francisco Peaks and the first stars were out when Harper pulled into the gravel parking lot towing the dory trailer. The office of the river outfitter's warehouse was dark.

Harper's truck was littered with fast food debris and empty coffee cups, and his eyes were red. He had made good time, driving hard for twelve hours on the "reverse Oakie" route: from the Monterey Bay coast southeast into the Salinas Valley, across and down the Central Valley to Bakersfield, through the Mohave desert along old Route 66, past the rows of mothballed airliners at Edwards Air Force Base, a glimpse of the tamed Colorado River at Needles, then the Arizona mountains and high plateau, past the famous fault offset revealed in the Kingman roadcut, and finally into view of Humphreys Peak, the ancient strato-volcano that was Flagstaff's guardian and the highest point in Arizona. The Navajo name it their sacred mountain of the West, a female-gendered mountain, said to be lined with abalone and attached to earth with a sunbeam. Harper named it the end of the drive, and he finally arrived at the Redwall Rafting Warehouse.

Harper pulled slowly around back, where the fenced equipment yard was hidden from the highway. Tracer's truck was there, a familiar shape among the shuttle buses and flatbed trucks with winches. Harper climbed out and stretched his back. He stared at the stars and enjoyed lungfuls of the delicious high altitude air. It tasted like wine after his day in the truck.

The roll-up door to the warehouse lifted with a rattling chain, and let out a gradually rising wall of light. Backlit by the bright interior, two dark shapes ducked under the door and emerged from the warehouse. It was Tracer, and a young woman with her blond hair in long braids. They strode to him without speaking, their body language welcoming.

Harper turned and began to reach out somewhat stiffly to shake hands, but instead accepted a bear hug from Tracer.

" Thanks for doing it, man." Tracer said into his ear. "Goat would want us to go." They broke and stood together, not sure what to say next. The woman next to them stepped forward and Tracer managed, " Oh, hey, this is Billie Thorsvik, from Moab. She's a guide in Cataract Canyon. She's done, like, twelve private trips down the Grand. She never met Goat, but I told her a lot about him."

Billie stepped forward and gave Harper a quick hug. "I'm sorry for your loss. Trace told me about your friend." she said simply. She had the knack of looking directly into your eyes when she spoke, and Harper felt kindness coming from her blue eyes. Her pretty face had the freckled skin of a sunburned Viking, with blond eyelashes and braids. Her powerful shoulders and arms looked like she would be a natural in a helmet with horns swinging a battle-axe, or rowing a boat in big water. She was one of those Mormon gals gone wild, the ones that refuse to wear a floral print dress, big hair, and have eight babies. Tracer said she came from big family in a little hardscrabble central Utah town, and had fallen hard for the joy of running rivers and playing in canyons. Harper liked Billie already. They stood quietly for a moment, under the night with warehouse light at their feet. Their thoughts ran back and forth, and they all waited a moment to speak. They could feel a coming together of their small group. The dory sat silently ready.

"Well, then Billie got our permit!" Tracer stated finally, as if concluding a line of thought. "She is Trip Leader Thorsvik now. She went to the South Rim office and picked up a cancellation permit yesterday. A private from Sacramento backed out at the last minute because of the high water. We are launching tomorrow, if you can believe that. A one-boat trip. You better sleep, my friend. We did the food shop today, set up a Groover, a fire pit, hand wash system, everything the Park Service requires. We just needed the boat. And another crew member, of course. God, I wish Goat were here!" Tracer walked over to touch the dory. He continued, gaining excitement.

"Oh, that Goat. Wouldn't he just love this? Well, we're gonna' row his dory, at least. That's something. And we have big water, brother. 60,000 cfs release today, and the Bureau of Wreck-The-Nation could increase it tomorrow. They can afford to now. Their reservoir is almost full and the Upper Basin snowmelt is on. The storm that just came through here is melting snow right now."

Billie looked up excitedly. "This is a perfect chance for the record. If we wait and launch tomorrow after dark, we can hit Crystal early the next day, sleep somewhere way down below Lava, and come out in under 30 hours. It's possible. I talked to some guides from Canyoneers that just took out at Diamond

Creek. They did two extra layovers, and their trip still finished seven days early. The current is moving 10-12 miles an hour, even in Marble Canyon. We heard that National and Kanab Canyons both flashed earlier this week, and there is a lot of logs and sediment. A lot of the rapids are washed out, but a S- rig flipped in Crystal, went into the left side wall upside down and was trashed. The people swam all the way to Lower Tuna before they got out. The Crystal Monster Hole is back, and trips are walking people around it, running boats through empty with just guides. Granite Narrows is a bad place for motor rigs, but we should be OK in a dory. Things are just getting crazy in there."

Harper looked at them in the dark. "60 grand! I have never seen half that water. And in a dory…" He said quietly. He had not been thinking much about the run. He was still stunned from the drive, from the chain of changes that had overtaken him in Santa Cruz, from the monologue of loss and anger he had carried on while driving all day over the death of Goat, the injustice of losing the quarry job, of the quarry skipping environmental review, of.. suddenly he remembered about Dukie and Ed Larson.

"Holy Shit!" he exclaimed. "Tracer! I didn't even tell you yet! We have to find Dukie and the Comish down there. Ed Larson has been taken on vacation on purpose. And we have to get Ed out and bring him back to Santa Cruz by Friday. He is a County Commissioner. He has got to be back by Friday. He can stop the assholes that killed Goat from getting their permit!"

Tracer and Billie looked at him and back at each other.

"What? Who is Ed? What permit?" Billie asked.

"How can he stop the quarry?" Tracer asked.

Harper sighed. "It's my turn to have a plan! Kind of. Let's get this dory inside. I'll explain everything".

They started walking into the lights together. Tracer and Billie held hands, and Harper slung his arm comfortably over Billie's shoulders from the other side. As they approached the roll-up door, he said,

"I almost forgot to make my formal request to join. Oh, mighty Trip Leader Thorsvik, please give me a place and let me accompany you on your historic river trip! Although I am not worthy, I will be helpful, and promise to highside, bail, and respect your mission. And hey, do we have any coffee for the trip?"

She patted his hand and smiled back at him. "Thank you for asking so nicely, Harper, you kayaker scum. You must have received some proper training. Yes, you are invited on my permit to join the Speed Run. Tracer says you are OK. You can be the second swamper on my boat. There will be good coffee." Their shadows made them twenty feet tall as they walked into the warehouse.

24

A Noble Craft

While they moved raft frames to make a space for the dory trailer, Harper explained the plan to rescue the Commissioner, return him to Santa Cruz for the vote, and stop the quarry. Billie and Tracer were quiet, listening. This was serious. Harper said, "It's your permit and your trip, Billie. But getting the Comish back to Santa Cruz to change the quarry vote is all we can do for Goat now."

She looked back and forth from Harper and Tracer, her eyes steady and engaged. "I want to honor your friend. If the research group is stationed at the Little Colorado River doing fish survey work, they won't be hard to find. If the high flows haven't chased them off, I mean. Research trips all camp upriver from the confluence on river right. We can stop in and add this Comish guy to our trip. We just can't stay too long. We are on a speed

217

run, baby." Tracer didn't have to say anything. Harper gave Billie a long hug and there were tears in both their eyes.

Harper and Tracer pushed the dory and trailer in under the lights of the cavernous warehouse, then unlashed and pulled back the tattered cover. Billie stood at the bow in anticipation as the wooden craft emerged, and she clapped her hands together in glee. An elegant, even dashing, wooden dory was revealed. She was 18 feet from stem to stern, with dramatic upward rake at bow and stern. She had a flaring center section, white decks, sharp chines on the sides leading down to a flat bottom, and a small tombstone-shaped transom at the back. The faded white paint and a thick layer of dust and grime on the deck hatches spoke of a long period of inactivity, but she looked agile and sound as a nut. They paced in excited triumph around the dory, touching her sides, and noticing details and old wounds. Billie clambered up and sat in the oarsman's seat, a neat gap in the center of the covered deck that commanded clean view lines fore and aft. The plywood decks sloped inward towards the oarsman's footwell, where a simple self-bailing drain emptied any collected water.

She pulled on imaginary oars, took a stroke and feathered them, and then skootched her buns in the seat to settle in. She clapped her hands again and hugged herself delightedly.

"Oh, I love this boat!" she declared, eyes shining.

"I hope it floats.' Harper said from the stern. He was examining a small wooden plaque screwed into the transom that read, *Built by Willy L., Grants Pass, Oregon, 1972.* "I never knew Goat even had a dory. Why didn't he bring it on trips, Tracer? Did he row dories?"

Tracer was examining an old repair near the bow, where a cracked section of wooden panel had been glued and covered with fiberglass resin. He stood up slowly.

"Goat could have rowed a truck tire down the Colorado if he wanted. He did row dories, up on the Rogue in Oregon for fly fishermen for a couple of seasons. Then the owner died, and the outfit went broke still owing the guides pay. I think he grabbed the boat for back pay and took off. I don't think he ever actually got the title for it. The rumor was, this was built in Oregon off the old Briggs dory lines, using the original strongback jig and details board borrowed from Joe Briggs, the guy that built dories for Martin Litton. I helped Goat deck it over and reframe in the hatches in ten years ago, and we did an 8-day Main Fork Salmon river trip in it together. We hit a rock and flipped in Big Mallard on that trip, and did this fiberglass on a layover day. It looks like its holding up OK."

"It is a beauty," said Harper, stroking the sides." Built in 1972, makes it 27 years old.

"Same as me! " said Billie gleefully. Harper and Tracer looked at other wryly.

"I was 6 then," said Harper.

" I was playing center field in Little League already then" said Tracer. "Hey, that makes two knarly old guys and two 27-year old beauties. This is gonna' be a great river trip. "

Harper peered at the old repair. "Seriously, do you thing this old boat is strong enough for a high water trip? What if it leaks?"

Billie was busily opening hatches and peering into them on top now. "Dry in here" she called down. Tracer looked at Harper with pride.

"This old boat is a treasure chest of wood. She was built in the 70's when you could still get the old-growth Doug Fir marine plywood, the vertical grain sheets from grandfather trees. You can't get that stuff any more. The stern and stem posts and frames are Oregon ash, strong as hell and also mostly gone now. We built the deck out of marine grade plywood and sealed the hatches with surfboard resin. She is heavy for the three of us to lift, but plenty strong. We'll rig flip lines, of course. And if she leaks, or if we touch a rock by chance, we will have duct tape, clamps and epoxy to fix what we ding. "

"Hey, what's her name?" Billie's voice came from inside the boat, where her head was investigating a watertight compartment.

The guys looked at each other, shrugged and walked to the stern. The transom was not labeled.

"No Name" said Harper.

"Didn't Major Powell's party have a No Name boat? The one they smashed in Disaster Falls?"

"Sounds like bad mojo. We need a better name. We could pick a special place lost to man's stupidity, like Martin does for his dories."

"Well, plenty of place to chose from, I guess. The Reventazon River? They dammed my favorite section of that river in Costa Rica. It was the perfect Class IV kayak run."

"The Hetch Hetchy?" Harper suggested. " Is that taken?"

"I don't know. But, lost places is Martin's thing. Our dory is not his. We need our own boat name. And we have a mission, too, remember. How about The Goat Boat?"

"Boats are female gender, like the Navajo mountain of the west. She should have a female name. What do you think, Trip Leader?"

"I got it!" Billie stood at the helmsman's seat on top of the boat and raised both arms in inspiration. Her blond braids framed her triumphant face. "I name her Freyja! Freyja, Valkyrie Queen, the Raven Goddess, Shield Maiden and Protector of the Fallen

Warriors!"

The guys looked at her in admiration and nodded. Tracer smiled up. "Wow! Great name! But that won't all fit on the transom, honey. Can we just use Freyja?" She smirked down at him.

"Yes. Just Freyja is perfect. My Grandma was from Norway, and told us all the Norse myths. Freyja was the lead Valkyrie, a goddess who selects fallen warriors from the battlefield to go to Valhalla, where they revel, drink everlasting cups of mead and tell tales of glory."

"Sounds like a spring Grand Canyon guides training seminar. " muttered Tracer.

"That is a great name, Billie." Harper smiled. " Freyja will ride wings of glory to rescue the honor of our fallen buddy." Billie smiled back and bowed ceremoniously.

"So let it be written, so let it be done!" cried Tracer. "Now, we need to pack. This boat need flip lines. We need sleeping gear, food, water. A repair kit, duct tape, C-clamps, epoxy, resin, catalyst, maybe a cordless skil-saw, what about a 12-volt battery and floodlight?"

As Tracer began making lists and collecting gear from around the warehouse, a wave of exhaustion came over Harper. He had been on the road since 9:00 AM that morning. He was coming down from the anger at Goat's death and at Arena's plans.

"Um, guys, where am I crashing tonight? I think I better find it soon. Tomorrow we shop, pack, rig and drive out to Lee's Ferry, right?"

Billie hopped down from the boat. "C'mon Harper, you can sleep back in the boy's dorm room. No guides are here until the next trip comes back in two days. Get a big rest, 'cause we won't be sleeping much on the trip. Tomorrow we want to be out of here by noon, and be out at Lee's by 5 pm. Then we get rigged, and launch after dark, so we run all night and be at Crystal the next morning. "

"Better I shouldn't think about big Crystal right now," said Harper, following her down a hallway to a crowded room of bunk beds. He felt fatigue coming down like a curtain. He sat on a bed and took his shoes off. Billie stood in the doorway.

"Hey, Harper?" she said softly. He looked up at her through heavy eyelids.

"Hmmm?" he replied.

"Tracer was in a lot of pain when he found out about Goat. He thought he should have saved him somehow. Got him out of California before it happened. So, thanks for bringing the boat out. I think this trip is going to help him heal."

Harper considered for a moment. "A one-boat trip, super high water, launching at night, in a freaking dory! That is to heal? Can't we just have a group hug or something?" He smiled weakly and lay down in feigned collapse. From the bed he said, "I know what you mean, Billie. I'm feeling better already. And you're welcome, Trip Leader Freyja."

"See you in the morning," she said and shut the door. He was snoring in moments.

25

Back to Lees Ferry

It was launch day, sundown already, and they were late to the Put-in. The Vermilion Cliffs were dark when the group of three reached the Colorado River and crossed Navajo Bridge. The dory rattled on its trailer behind the truck. Harper and Tracer were nervous as cats. Billie had been a sunshine beam all day, but was quiet now. They had scurried and packed gear into hatches on the boat while watching TV reports of storms hitting California, of rain moving across the Mojave, of flash flood warnings across the southwest. They checked flow releases (still 60,000 cfs!) on the BuRec Glen Canyon Dam hotline. Tracer and Billie had ransacked the Redwall Rafting warehouse for spare oars, flip lines, and throw bags. Harper had tried to reach the U.S. Geological Survey office in charge of the research trip Dukie was on, to find if they were still camped at the Little Colorado.

No information on the trip had been received since they had launched a week before, he was told. Their official take-out was still 10 days off, three days too late for the Lagunitas vote back at the Santa Carla Planning Commission Board meeting. Harper fumed, then gave up and went back to packing.

Tracer had been on the phone too, getting high-water beta, talking to old-timers about runs in the 1960's, about the 1983 high water. Guys who had run it in the days before the dam, when spring flows of 60,000 cfs were normal, were scarce, but anyone who was there in 1983 said, Holy Cow! When you see Crystal, you going to want a pistol. So different at that water, they said. No place to stop for miles. A lot of stuff just disappears; no rapids at high flows. Watch out for Granite Narrows, they said. The river is just 80 feet wide there. Always a tight spot, and a bitch of a sideways current, smashing you into a wall strike. Plenty of paint on the wall there in the old days, they told him. You gonna' have a backup motor and fuel tank, I hope, they asked him. What, a dory? Just oars? One dory? Like those crazy fellas' in 1983? Oh, Christ. You a good swimmer?

Billie had selected oars, loaded the food, checked permit requirements twice, packed a kitchen strainer and a handwash system to satisfy the Put- in Ranger, lashed extra oars to the decks of the dory, and called Lee's Ferry to say they would arrive late for their launch today. Somewhere in there, she found time to paint a stencil of a large black raven, and the name, FREYJA, in lovely script on the dory transom and bow. There was no answer at Lee's Ferry, so she called the Park Service Headquarters at the South Rim. A helpful lady there told her if it was urgent, they could reach the Put-In Ranger on his belt radio. He would return to his trailer at Lee's Ferry and call the South Rim for the message.

"Can I just leave a message for him?" Billie had asked sweetly. "The Thorsvik Private Launch Permit for today has been delayed, but is en route to Lees Ferry from Flagstaff now. We regret the delay, would appreciate a late check out and will launch one dory, with three people, including two licensed Grand Canyon Guides." She frowned as she nodded at the response, and hung up looking unhappy for the first time all day.

Finally, they crammed into Harper's truck as the day was closing out, and drove out of town on Highway 89. Rain began falling again. It started soft, a female chipi-chipi rain, not the hard, drumming male rain. As they drove, it built to a steady drizzle, wetting and brightening the bare red land of the Navajo. On the radio, there was a report of a helicopter evacuation underway in Grand Canyon, but they could not tell if the victims were hikers, or members of a river trip. Halfway to Lee's, they crossed the Little Colorado River on Highway 89. Harper was shocked to look down and see the canyon flowing full of red mud and water. Usually, the Little Colorado river bed was a dry rocky grazing ground for tough tribal sheep, with sparse vegetation and lots of rock. Now the water looked bigger than the Colorado River had on his first trip, in 1993.

As they passed over Navajo Bridge, and began turning down the stretch to the Lee's Ferry ramp. Tracer and Harper were talking about scouting strategy.

"We'll definitely scout a couple drops. Hance, for sure, and maybe Hermit. The Hermit wave train will be intense. Crystal is going to be the crux, then maybe Upset and Dubendorf, and then Lava Falls…"

" I always heard Lava Falls washes out at 60,000."

"Well, it did in 1983, but what if this is different? Everything moves at big flows."

Billie broke in. "Guys, I think maybe the Put-in is the real crux. The river might be closed. They're gonna' try to stop us."

There was an unhappy silence. Harper stepped on the brakes, and the truck stopped in the rain. The river would come into view downhill and around the next bend, then the campground, ranger trailer and ramp.

"But we have a damn permit." Tracer growled.

"Well, when *I* called the South Rim office today, the lady said she had heard that the river was now closed to launches."

"Maybe she meant commercial launches?"

"She sounded like it was not clear. "

"We gotta launch. The Comish is down there" said Harper.

"Well" said Tracer " we're here. Our gear is all on the dory. This is a speed run, so we might as well do a speed launch. Let's stop and get loaded up now. Drive right on past the campground and Ranger Trailer to the launch ramp. Then we just back up, float the boat, and get in. Harper get the truck and trailer, park it in the lot, and run down the rocks to the Paria riffle and jump in as we go by."

"We have to note the time we launch. And we should have a witness to make the Speed Run official." pointed out Billie. "We should get a fisherman or a hiker at the ramp for a witness if we can." Everyone got out of the truck into the rain, stood in the road and put on their pfds. They crammed back into the truck cab. The truck was above the final descent. With life jackets on, they were packed in like sardines, with their hearts suddenly racing. Harper extended his hand out, palm down, into the center of the crowded truck. Tracer piled his hands onto it, with Billie clasping the top and bottom of the pile with both hands.

"Alright, my friends. Always Above Lava! This launch is for

The Goat."

"Always Above Lava". Three voices breathed it together. It was a hopeful whisper, not a shout, and the truck rolled down to the river.

No Way, Jose

The Lees Ferry campground was empty in the rain. It was too dark to see the river. Tracer, Harper and Billie held their breath as they rolled past the long-term parking lot and the Ranger office trailer. Lights were on inside the trailer, with a single patrol car parked outside and the government-issue blinds drawn. The ramp was 100 yards away. Harper turned off the truck lights and crept past with just parking lights.

"Any of you guys ever launch at night before?" Harper whispered. They both shushed him. The truck crept ahead in the near dark.

At the ramp, their stealth plan fell apart. A barricade of portable fence segments had been placed across the concrete ramp, blocking access. A large diamond-shaped highway sign, *ROAD CLOSED*, was erected at the top of the ramp. The river appeared calm, but it was halfway up the ramp, licking at the base of the interpretive signposts and flowing over the electrical outlets boxes.

Harper attempted to squeeze the truck and trailer past the barricade and onto the ramp. The gap was too small, and the trailer caught the fence and began to drag. Tracer jumped out to free it. Racing back along the truck, he almost ran right into a stern, unsmiling Ranger walking down from the bathrooms. The ranger was swinging a six cell Magnum flashlight like a nightstick and wearing full regalia: Smoky the Bear Hat with plastic rain net, green khakis with NPS shoulder patch, Sam Brown belt with gun, mace, radio, and handcuffs, badge on his chest and a little brass nameplate, Ranger Harshberger. He pointed the flashlight at the truck.

"Stop that vehicle! This river is closed to all launches, effective immediately!"

Billie peaked out of the cab. "Shit! Joe Harshberger!! They call him No-Way Jose!" she hissed to Harper. "This guy can be a total tool!"

Tracer's voice out on the ramp was his best imitation of respectful behavior. "Oh, Hello, Ranger Harshberger! Remember me? Charlie Trace? You did our put-ins the last three years in a row. Good to see you! We thought just the road was closed. This is the Thorsvik trip launch. Did you get our message? Our launch permit is for today. We're one boat, a very experienced group, and we have vital information to relay to a USGS research trip camped at the LCR..."

The Ranger ignored Tracer and came to the driver's window. He tapped on the glass with his flashlight. Harper began to open the door slowly, and the Ranger pushed it shut, hard. Harper rolled down the window, sadly and looked at the Ranger.

"Yes, Ranger?"

"Stay in the vehicle, sir. Nobody is launching. License and vehicle registration, please."

The Ranger 's face was grim and devoid of personality. Rain was dripping off his hat. He ignored Harper's feeble pleasantries as he took the wallet and kept it. He walked to the front of the car and wrote down the truck license plate. He walked to the back, and went slowly around the trailer, scanning the dory with his flashlight. Harper slumped at the wheel. He felt it all slipping away. No dory trip, the speed run record attempt shot down, Dukie and Comish sitting in the rain in the bottom canyon while Arena ramrodded the quarry approval through, bad guys winning, Goat dead, his first big money water project gone, all of it.

"Run him over when he walks back in front of the truck" Billie whispered to Harper and then she giggled brightly. Harper snorted sadly despite himself. He heard Tracer outside still talking to the Ranger, explaining about the plans, their experience, the permit. He was keeping his voice low, soothing and a little desperate, like a cornered man trying to coax a dog not to bite him.

"We're fucked" he said quietly. Billie raised her eyebrows, tilted her head sideways at him, and said nothing. Her cheerful nature had flagged, but seemed to have returned now that everything was lost.

The Ranger returned to Harper's window and handed him back the wallet, soaking wet now from the rain. His gaze flicked to Billie in the truck cab. A trace of satisfaction flickered across his face. Tracer returned to the passenger side door, got in and slumped in the truck. He was mute.

"Are you Ms. Thorsvik?" He asked. Billie nodded owlishly, and handed him the folded launch permit. He took it disdainfully, and did not glance at it.

"You folks always wear your pfds while driving? " he asked nastily. When they did not reply, he said briskly, "This river is closed to all launches, pending further notice from the Park Administrator. Canceled private trips will receive priority in rescheduling, so Ms. Thorsvik can contact the river permit office for a new permit."

He paused with a gleam in his eye and said maliciously. "I'm afraid your boat trailer has a five year old registration sticker. I am going to have to impound it, and turn it over to the Arizona Highway Patrol. You can claim it at their Flagstaff yard after you present the title and proper registration for renewal."

This brought Tracer out of his gloom. He looked up alarmed. "Aw, c'mon Harshie! Don't take the dory! We might not get it back." A wild gleam came into his eyes.

The Ranger stuck his face into the truck cab and glared across them at Tracer. "It's Ranger Harshberger! And if you want to fuck with me, I'll be glad to write you a ticket right now for attempting to pass the barricade here at the ramp. That's a $250 fine, for starters. I can impound this truck too, for pulling the unregistered vehicle. You two are working guides, aren't you? So you think that means you can show up here at night on your launch date and do whatever you want? You think that I didn't check if any of you already been on a private river trip in the last 12 months? Two of you guys have! You're ineligible! If you want to' complain, how about if I make sure every trip you're on, commercial or private, from now until forever, gets tore apart here at the ramp, every item checked, every piece of your paperwork checked, every enforcement action carried out?"

He withdrew his head and his mask of grim indifference returned. He reached in, shut off the car and took the keys from the ignition.

"Now, your trailer is impounded, and your river trip is cancelled. Wait here." He turned and marched off into the rainy gloom.

Harper wanted to cry. Tracer was mumbling obscenities and looked violent. Billie slid over on the bench seat and kissed Tracer on the cheek. She spoke calmly. "Don't worry, Trace. The Grand Canyon will outlast all this petty bullshit. It will all be fine, even things that are not fine. Now let me out, I gotta make a call. "

She ran across the ramp towards the old pay phone on a stand, the loneliest pay phone in America, then stood under the plastic canopy in the rain and dialed the old rotary. Harper and Tracer got out of the truck cab and walked down to the river. It was strangely close to them on the ramp. Neither of them had ever seen it so high. The steady rain made a pleasant hiss on the surface of the moving river. It was somehow comforting to be close to the river, out in the rain. They hunkered down and touched the water.

"We'll never get Goat's boat back without a legal title." Tracer said glumly.

"Well, we probably just would have gotten killed in it anyway," said Harper.

Tracer grinned ruefully "Be careful what you wish for, eh? A fella could do worse than that, though, I guess. Man, look at Billie. Who is she calling with that grin on? That girl is just a permasmile sunshine beam. I do like being around her. Good karma from my previous life or something." They watched Billie talking on the phone. She seemed fine, and as she hung up and walked towards them, almost jaunty.

"You are right. She is a keeper. Treat her good, brother, and knock wood that she likes you back." Harper said quietly. Tracer put him a gentle headlock and knocked on Harper's scalp with his knuckles, and Harper hugged him back.

Billie reached them and joined the awkward hug. Just then, the Ranger pulled up at the wooden barricade, back in his NPS patrol car. As the forlorn group walked up the ramp, he stepped out with a chain and padlock, and walked to the dory. He slid the chain through the ringbolt in the dory bow, around the trailer frame, and clicked the padlock in place, chaining the boat to the trailer.

"This will keep your property secure until you claim it" he said to them with satisfaction.

Tracer was quietly reciting a string of obscenities. Billie looked alarmed, and put her hand on his arm to stop it. The radio on the Ranger's belt came to life in a crackle of static. Ranger Harshberger adjusted the squelch and reached to the microphone attached at his shoulder to respond. The voice was broken at first, but then a clear transmission came through.

"South Rim Central Station to Lee's Ferry Duty Ranger, your family requests an immediate phone call".

Ranger Harshberger thumbed his mic and replied, "South Rim, this is Lee's Ferry ranger, please say again?" There was nothing for a moment.

"Miserable reception down here" said Ranger Harshie to himself, and he moved 10 feet farther up the ramp, twiddled the knobs on his radio, and he repeated his call. A burst of static, then a distant voice came back.

"South Rim Central to Lee's Ferry Duty Ranger, I say again, your Mother called and wants you to call her immediately". More static bust out.

"My mother? In Scottsdale?" The Ranger looked at his radio with annoyance, and then at the group on the ramp. Harper and Tracer were noncommittal and hostile. Billie was staring hard at her river sandals. The ranger rattled the trailer lock and then walked towards his patrol car.

"Just don't move! " He said over his shoulder. " I have to make a call. I'll be right back with your truck keys and we'll put that trailer in the impound lot". He slammed the door and the patrol car made a U-turn off the ramp into the night.

As soon as he was rolling, Billie started squirming in excitement. They looked at her with suspicion, then dawning amazement. She jumped and squealed as the patrol car disappeared, and began pushing Tracer toward the truck.

"Let's go, let's go, let's go, let's go! " she blurted as the car lights disappeared. "Launch it!" If they craned their necks, they could just see it's lights pull into the Park Service trailer lot, just a pistol shot down the road. "We only have a few minutes!"

"You called the South Rim! Billie, you are a genius!"

"Even Ranger Harshie has a mommy! But he locked us! Can we break the ring?"

Harper dove into the truck, and he emerged with a huge grin, and lifted up a pair of red steel bolt cutters from behind his seat.

"The master key, for opening old well locks and ranch gates!" he cried. He lifted a magnetic box in his other hand "And a hide-a-key for surfing!" He tossed the bolt cutters to Tracer, then jumped in and started the truck with his hide-a- key. Billie tore the fence barricade away from the trailer and threw it down on the ramp. Tracer leaped onto the trailer frame, hung on and worked on the lock while Harper drove down almost into the river. He did a U-turn back up the ramp to put the dory in launch position. He backed up 10 feet, and the wheels of the dory trailer were in the river. The water piled over the tires, gurgled around the trailer frame and kissed the stern of the boat. The dory shifted on the trailer, held in place by straps, and by the chained ringbolt at the bow.

"She moves! She floats!"

"Let's go, let's go, let's go!" Billie was chanting, even as she reached for the straps.

"Harper, you are the greatest!"

"I love the Trip Leader!"

"Mr. Wizard! Get us out of here!"

The bolt cutters clamped and the lock shank parted. The chain fell to the ramp. All three of them were running around like chickens with their heads cut off, grabbing things from the truck, pulling straps off the dory and tossing them into the truck cab. Harper gave the bow a shove back towards the welcoming water. Tracer jumped up on the dory as it lurched off on the trailer. He took the oarsman's seat and started slamming oars into the oarlocks. Billie came running from the cab pulling on her pfd back on, tossed three water bottles up to Tracer and reached for his hand. Harper stood on the trailer holding the dory nose and looked at his truck. The engine was running, all doors were flung open, the cab light was on, the headlights shone in the rain. Leave it? No choice. The stern of the dory was touching the river, and beginning to be pulled sideways.

"Oh, God! Here comes Harshie! And he is pissed!" Billie cried from up on the dory. Gravel crunched as the headlights pulled out from the Ranger trailer, moving fast towards them. Harper pushed hard on the bow of the dory, and the boat slid back off the trailer, settled into the water and pivoted bow upstream, easy as kiss my hand. He chased it down the trailer, dancing along the steel trailer frame while reaching up for a handhold on the retreating, high bow. Harper's hand found the bow rail just as he ran out of trailer. He pulled himself up, hooked a foot, and flopped aboard as the dory bobbed free eagerly. Tracer had the oars in and took two soft strokes back. The dory moved away as the patrol car screeched to a halt on the ramp. The Ranger jumped out and stared in disbelief. He had his sidearm out, so Harper resisted the urge to give him the finger. Instead, he waved peacefully, like a beauty queen on a parade float.

Harper watched with disbelief as his truck and the ramp scene shrank away. The dory accelerated gently into darkness. Billie was next to him in the forward compartment. "Fastest put-in I ever did " said Tracer over his shoulder with a grunt, pulling at the oars. Billie was leaning forward, waving eagerly back at the Ranger. "We love you, Harshie!" she yelled. "Don't worry, we'll be careful! This is a Speed Run. Check our time!" To Harper's amazement, the Ranger slowly straightened and waved back at them, with his gun in his hand. As they disappeared into the dark, they saw him check his watch.

26

Speed Run is On

Their dory passed under the Lee's Ferry cable and swept down the Colorado River towards Marble Canyon. The rain and darkness enveloped them. The shoreline was a dim suggestion. Back at the ramp, Harper's truck lights were still visible in the rain, gradually dimming like departing freightliners on the highway. After some euphoria, and then adjusting their pfds, and then some self-justification on their bolt-cutting departure, the crew settled into place. Face the river now, face the consequences later. Billie claimed the first shift at the oars, and Tracer and Harper shared the forward passenger compartment. Tracer found the 12-volt floodlight, switched it on, and began testing the light on the riverbanks. The sound of the river had changed as they moved over the delta where the Paria River joined the Colorado, but there was no visible change in flow at the confluence. It was just big water, moving fast in the rainy dark. Already, they were adjusting to boat and water noises, and to the night sensations of the dory moving.

"This river is closed, effective immediately" Harper repeated softly, imitating Ranger Harshburger, then a kind of nervous chipmunk voice, then switching to a space alien, and a drunken French Count Dracula voice. He was close to giggling, high on the reckless silliness and desperation of their put-in. He was trying not to think about what would happen to his truck, or to them at their takeout. Finally Tracer elbowed him sharply in the ribs.

"Earth to Harper, please come in. "

In his best Three Stooges voice, Harper replied, "Hey, Moe! I try to think, but nothing happens".

Tracer elbowed him again. Harper looked at his buddy next to him, playing the beam of light downstream and on the rising canyon walls. They were already around the first bend, and Navajo Bridge was coming up somewhere downstream. Harper tried an obsequious Peter Lorre, whining to Bogart in Casablanca.

"But, Rick, dees reever, she is close-ed, eefective eemediately, Rick".

Another elbow. "You're going to be swimming if you don't stop it. "

Harper was quiet and let the water slide by for a moment.

"Do you think Goat would have done it that way, Tracer?"

Tracer nodded, "Goat would be proud".

"Boy howdy. It wasn't the easy way, but it was definitely the Cowboy Way. "

Billie did some experimenting at the oars, spinning, pushing and pulling, then pausing to feel the dory track. The boat wanted to gallop. Because of the high flow, there was a broad swath of current down the center, with boils and whirls, but no eddy lines along this shore. The boat ran with the water in a clean line. Billie sat alert amidships, working easily to keep the dory pointed downstream in the dark. She dipped and touched the water repeatedly with the oars, listening to the river through them, through her seat, and with her whole body. The arching waterline and pure curves of the dory captured and were guided by the flow.

"We're so light!" she said to herself. "Maybe we should have taken some ballast. But it goes like it's ready to fly!" The dory bobbed happily, aligning naturally with current, and turning readily when asked. Billie kept the dory with the moving water, and the walls grew up around them as they sank into Marble Canyon. Tracer switched off the floodlight after a while, switching it on only when the voice of the current changed. He opened and closed every hatch he could reach from the front compartment, and found no water coming in.

Down through the darkness they ran, calming, gaining confidence, and speaking little. They moved into an alert trance, floating and listening for signals of acceleration or change in the current. They were past Badger Creek before they realized it, glimpsing Jackass Canyon receding in the dark. There was no sign of the rapid or the central hole in the fast current of the river. It was spooky, like Badger Rapid had never existed.

They were not tired, not sleepy. The darkness and rain contributed to a suspended feeling, without a sense of time passing. The canyon moved past like speeded-up film. Soap Creek, Sheer Wall, even House Rock Rapid had no surface expression, just more fast current in the night.

"We are moving like a freaking cannonball!" said Harper quietly as he realized they were moving along the wall past House Rock. It had taken a day and a half to reach here on his first kayak trip. He remembered that day, staring from the scouting rock at the snarling hole called Adolf in the center of the rapid, then pulling out from shore to run, his kayak the last boat, his group waiting in the eddy and holding their breath, his heart in his mouth, and angels spinning in the clouds. There was no sign of that hole there now, just a river-wide flushing jet of current.

Billie sat at the oars facing downstream, pushing calmly left and right, her face a study in relaxed concentration. They entered the Roaring Twenties and found more washed out rapids, some with big eddies below them and tighter turns. Tracer shone their flood beam on the river licking at the ancient driftwood atop Boulder Narrows, normally fifteen feet or more above the water. Seriously squirrelly water became normal, with boils and whirlpools as large as their boat. The dory was captured and spun by one of these whirlpools, spiraling down until the rest of the river surface was at eye level, with the boat on the whirling center of two converging currents. Billie was helpless, with the oars in the water on both sides, seeking a brace and waiting for release. They all tensed, balancing in their seats like tightrope walkers. The dory fluttered as it spun, suddenly feeling as rootless as a blown leaf. Then the whirlpool closed, the surface of the river healed, and they rose up with the water surface, springing back into linear flow in clean current. Billie dug hard to gain speed and they were moving again, with uncertain grins on their faces, looking back into the dark at nothing. It was already like no river trip any of them had ever done.

The night moved on. The rain stopped and the moon came through broken clouds. They swept around the graceful bend in canyon walls at South Canyon. Tracer had taken the oars now and Billie and Harper talked quietly in the front to the boat, floodlight at the ready. He was telling her about Shira. It was past midnight and the adrenaline from their Ranger escape was gone. The whole Lee's Ferry launch episode already seemed like distant past, and the consequences were too far ahead to consider.

There was only this night, the sound of the water, and the high dark walls going past. The three of them and the dory were a single floating organism, with a shared desire to move. They were alive to nuances, focused on river current, balance, avoiding hazards and maintaining their wits. The crew's body core temperatures were fine and they peeled off and stowed rain gear. More than ever before in life, they had a consuming, immediate, and dreamlike task at hand. They raced on. Their unusual pace seemed normal after a while, as they moved through the glory of Marble Canyon, with stone cathedrals stretching downriver ahead of them, echoing river music in their ears. A thin slice of clearing night sky and a few stars visible between the rims above. They marveled at the high water filling Redwall Cavern to the back, but they did not stop. Harper checked a river guidebook with his headlamp and looked up. He spoke quietly to Billie.

"We're at Redwall Cavern, Mile 33, Nankoweap is 52 and then the Little Colorado River is at Mile 61. Say thirty miles. At 10 knots per hour, say three more hours to the LCR. We'll be there before first light. If Dukie and the Comish are still there, that is. We'll have to wake 'em up."

"I never did a trip that didn't stop at Redwall before," mused

Billie.

"Me neither. But, I never was a river outlaw before. Ranger Harshburger is very, very, upset with us right now. "

"Well, we do have a permit. Plenty of people did trips with no permit back in the old days. Bill Beer and Daggett didn't have a permit when they swam it in 1955."

"The Major didn't have a permit when he ran it in the 1800's, strapped to his chair and waving his good arm."

"Yeah, the first Lefty to run the canyon".

Harper turned and spoke back to the rowing station.

"Hey, you think we'll be arrested at the take-out, Tracer?"

"Arrested? Sure. Fined? Sure. But, will we be imprisoned? That is the question." Tracer spit in the water and adjusted the dory with the oars delicately.

I can't live in prison," continued Tracer thoughtfully. " I read about Masai warriors, how the British would put them in jail for a week for stealing cattle and they would just wither up in the cell and die on day Five. Finally, the British had to come up with new punishment. They took away their cattle instead."

"We'll be persecuted heroes. Martyrs. But first, we have to survive to make it to prison. We still have to run Crystal. And Lava Falls. And, remember, never worry about the future when you're still above Lava." said Billie.

"But, we're always above Lava" Tracer protested.

"Ah, very wise, Young Master Tracer" said Harper in a mock oriental accent, then added, "Confucius say, This riva is crowsed, effectively immediately."

"Exactly."

"My outlaw redneck zen philosopher boyfriend." said Billie with a smile.

"Thanks, Ma'am, and mighty fine of you." drawled Tracer.

"But Rick, dees reever, she is close-ed, by de Nazi High Command" Harper said after a soft pause.

"Shut up, Harper." Tracer and Billie said together.

"Hey Billie, how much do Tracer's parents pay you to get you to call him your boyfriend?

"Shut up, Harper." Billie said with a smile.

Harper grinned like a fool. He touched the fishhook necklace Shira had given him. He wished this night would never end. There was a roar building ahead. They all tensed. What rapid was this?

"Yeah, I hear it," said Tracer, standing up in the footwell and peering downstream. Billie switched on the spotlight and pointed it at the noise. They floated closer; there was no eddy and it was not clear if they could stop. Harper looked up from the guidebook with his headlamp shining.

"Could we be at President Harding already?" he asked himself, craning his neck to check the walls and sky.

They were. The Colorado River wraps around Point Hansbrough here, and emerges from the tight Marble Canyon cliffs into an open amphitheater caused by the Eminence Break Fault. There is a central rock at President Harding rapid, roughly the size and shape of a large Airstream trailer, usually splitting the river and making a famous surfing wave on river left. Recent rock fall on the right constricted that channel and closed off the right side. Tonight, the rock was completely underwater, and it was forming a loud surging hole in the center of the river. All current seemed to be flowing into it, and through it. It was hard to tell how bad the hole was. It was coming up fast, though.

"The safe run or the sporty run?" Billie called back to Tracer.

"Highside and hold on!" cried Tracer, pushing forward on the oars. "I am trying to miss it!" The dory bow accelerated, dipped, plunged and then went into the hole. Tracer had shifted the dory left for his entry line to hit the weaker side of the hydraulic, and then turned straight into a small gap for the moment of contact. The dory stood up and exploded through the top of the big wave, with Harper and Billie standing in the forward passenger compartment high above the oars, both of them holding the handrail, straining forward. Solid water poured over their heads. The dory felt like a rocket ship for a moment, never hesitating or wallowing, going up instead of forward. The front third of the boat went into the air. Then the dory was through, splashing and rocking into the tail waves, slicing cleanly past the hydraulic like a salmon.

"Yee-hah!" cried Tracer from the oars, already pushing the dory into the next bend for the straightaway towards Saddle Canyon. "Big air! This Freyja boat, she can fly!"

"She's a Valkyrie!" answered Billie proudly, bailing out the forward foot well with the plastic scoop.

"Christ," muttered Harper with a wet grin, looking back at the fading noise in the dark, as the dory re-entered an alley of limestone walls, " If that was President Harding, what is Crystal going to be like?"

27

Little Colorado River

The research camp was asleep when the dory arrived. It was still long before dawn. The dory team had dodged another unexpected huge hydraulic at the top of Nankoweap Rapid, and then raced down to the confluence with the Little Colorado River. Now, their floodlight beam found the rubber tail ends of two snout rigs, 20-foot motor rafts tied up on river right, just upstream of the confluence.

The Little Colorado River is the longest tributary to the main Colorado, flowing out of an enormous drainage in eastern Arizona and the Navajo Nation. It has its own seldom-seen canyon of narrow sections, dozens of unnamed waterfalls, blind drops, bare stone and mud. The ancestral Sipapu of the Hopi people is located upstream from the confluence, at a mysterious salt dome and mineral spring of abundant azure blue water.

The Hopi believe this dome is a portal to the underworld. Their creation myth teaches that from this door, mankind first emerged blinking and naked, into the present world. After rains, the Little Colorado carried a dark red stream of liquid mud. But in the dry season, when only the Sipapu spring fed the river, the Little Colorado flows electric blue, which seems to confirm it's otherworldly origin.

The last few years, it seemed like there were always research trips camped at the confluence, as stream and fish guys from the US Geological Survey, the Arizona Game and Fish Department, the Department of Interior Park Service, and even the Glen Canyon Dam Adaptive Management Plan office all competed to schedule some user-days, get a grant, round up some cute young interns, and do research in Grand Canyon. The few remaining humpbacked chub around the confluence had been trapped, tagged, weighed, and released so many times they had calluses on their dorsal fins. The working guide community generally grinned at the research trip scam, and loved these gigs. Research trips, called "government checks" by guides, combined salaried river days, abundant free time in camp, no tourists to feed, and a fair share of the interns that each research trip seemed to stock. At least Dukie's group was measuring stream sediment load, not shocking fish.

Most of the recent Little Colorado research work was related to trout removal. Only the non-native trout suffered, as they were relentlessly electroshocked by the biologists, netted, killed by the thousands, and mulched into fertilizer, all in the name non-native species removal. This fishy research was sort of like Japanese whaling industry "research", only focused on trout, justified by the Endangered Species Act, funded by creative grant writing, and carried out in a National Park.

None of the trout removal researchers talked much about the fact that the endangered humpback chub had evolved in a warm, silty, pre-dam river, and now the trout were thriving in the cold, clear water the Glen Canyon dam had caused. Easier to spend their days in Grand Canyon, zapping fish with electricity from runabouts, and trapping, weighing and tagging any chubs that wandered down from the warm waters of the still undammed Little Colorado River drainage. These Arizona Game and Fish biologists had become a lot like lawyers, willing to do any dubious professional assignment as long as it provided decent pay, health benefits and in this case, some Grand Canyon river time.

Tracer had to pull hard on the oars to get the dory into the tiny eddy next to the snout rafts. Billie jumped ashore with a bowline, and Harper clipped the dory line to the nearest raft with a carabiner. A para-wing tarp was rigged on shore over a substantial camp kitchen area with a propane stove, tables and a pile of folding chairs. Tents were scattered like mushrooms among the tamarisk bushes. The full river was strangely close to the camp, well above the regular beach and terrace levels.

Stiff from hours on the boat, Harper, Tracer and Billie moved tentatively into the camp, speaking in whispers and poking around for matches. Harper clanged a pot lid off the stove, cringed, and then touched it to stop the noise. They were like a gang of marauding raccoons wearing headlamps.

"Let's heat up some water. Coffee will be required here pretty soon. "

"Coffee gooood!"

Billie spoke. "The clock is running on our record, my friends. Let's get this Commissioner guy and get on down the river. "

"He doesn't even know we're coming. "

"Well, I'm going to use their Groover. You find him and tell him he's coming". Billie disappeared downstream towards the river.

Tracer had attached the propane hose, and the stove flame came to life with a pleasing hiss. He set a pot of water on it.

"Five minutes to coffee" he said quietly. Harper nodded.

"Let's find Dukie. He got some 'splainin' to do."

That was Not the Plan

Ten minutes later, the kitchen lantern was lit and an emergency meeting was in session. Under the tarp sat a circle of figures in an odd collection of long underwear, raincoats, paddle jackets, and puzzled expressions. Tracer and Harper had roused Dukie from in his tent with twin headlamps and minimal explanation, and now he sat blinking in his fleece jacket, sniffing the steam off his mug of coffee, and looking every day of his sixty-five years. Ed Larson was next to him, with his steel framed glasses in place, and wisps of white hair straight up in an eruption of suspended surprise. Their guide, a young Flagstaff motor boatman named Floyd, had also appeared and accepted a coffee mug from Billie graciously. He sat calmly considering the night visitors in his kitchen and awaiting an explanation.

Ed was excited to see them, telling Billie how wonderful the research trip had been so far, the thrill of the storms and high water, radio reports of wreckage downstream and flash floods, and the difficulty they had had completing their research objectives. She nodded distractedly, and then put her hand on his arm, stilling him in mid-sentence and said, "You must be the Commissioner we are here to grab. Have you ever been on a dory?" He stopped talking abruptly, with his mouth forming an O, tilted his head and looked at her through his spectacles. He resembled a startled snowy owl. There was a moment of silence, then Tracer and Harper both started talking at once.

"Listen, Dukie, you fuck, everybody, we have bad news." Tracer said. "Goat is dead. He was clubbed to death out at the quarry. "

"And if you had anything to do with it, Dukie, your ass is grass."

"They killed him over his frog business. I think they were waiting for him'

"He was planting endangered species for hire. We found the operation at his cabin".

"I was there with Shira when they found him, Dukie. Crushed his head with a goddamn water meter. And did you know about this new vote on the quarry while Ed is gone? Is that why he's here?"

"Ed, we need to get you back to Santa Cruz as soon as possible, to stop the County from giving Arena a free pass on the quarry."

"They put Lagunitas mining approval back on the agenda for the Board meeting this Friday. They're gonna' waive all environmental review and give those bastards their mining permit.'

Billie spoke up "Also, we're doing a Speed Run right now, for a record, so we really have to get going. Because, once they can get a helicopter up, we might all get arrested. We had to launch, um, illegally," Billie stopped and looked around the startled row of faces. Ed burst out the first questions, followed with free association, explanations, and hostility from the dory crew.

"Who killed Goat? Did they catch him? What vote? And what do you mean, launch illegally?"

"Dukie, did you know about this vote bullshit or not?

"We still have to stop to scout at Crystal, don't we, Billie?"

"Oh, god, we are so fucked with the NPS. Ranger Harshburger

tried to impound our dory at Lee's. They have my truck."

"Billie called the South Rim and said she was his Mom".

"Yeah, I guess that does it for my Grand Canyon Guide license."

"God, remember his face when he came back and we were in the water. I thought he was going to shoot us."

"No, he waved at me. He's OK. I think he kind of understood. But still, we are fucked. I am trip leader, so it is on my head. That's why we have to set the speed run record. This is our last trip for a while. So lets get the hell out of here."

"Ed, you can ride with us, cause Harper says they need you to stop this thing, but you know you might be in some trouble at the end. Can you get your stuff please?"

They all stopped talking at once. Billie was addressing Ed. Harper and Tracer were glaring at Dukie. Floyd was watching them in consternation, alarm, then growing amazement, his head swiveling among the speakers. Dukie let out a groan.

"Goat was only supposed to get arrested!" he cried. He set his coffee down and put his face into his hands. His bald head shone in the lantern light as they all stared. Harper glared fiercely at him.

"My God, I never dreamed Goat could be killed." said Ed in a shocked voice. "That is awful. It's our fault for hiring him. We should have never tried to play dirty." He looked over at Dukie, "What do you mean, supposed to be arrested? Goat assured us he would never get caught?"

Dukie's face remained hidden in his hands. He was cursing softly.

"What is going on with you and Arena, Dukie?" Harper said hotly. "Tony Armstrong told me you knew about the plan to put in houses after the mining is done, and you were in on it. Yeah, he offered me a building site, too, to approve boatloads of water use. And what were you two guys talking to Goat about at the Landing that morning? Huh, Ed? And how come you're conveniently down here when there is suddenly a second vote on the quarry approval?"

Ed looked surprised. "I don't know anything about a vote. That must be the Board Chairman's idea; he's a weasel, and must have smelled the opportunity. But, I may have gotten your friend killed." He looked over at Dukie. "I had heard about Goat's, um, Johnny Appleseed Special Species business from some renegade friends at Earth First. I got Dukie to introduce me. We, well, I mean not Wetlands Watch, paid him to enhance the red-legged frog and steelhead populations, to insure the biological assessment would find them. He was going to do Tidewater Gobies in the lagoon, too. The coastal wetland habitat was just too special to take a chance with, we thought. So many times, the process gets abused and we were just tired of being on the losing end. We tried to play dirty to save the place. I am so sorry."

"Its not your fault, Ed.' came Dukie's tired voice. "It was a set-up. Goat knew he was supposed to be arrested. He got another five grand from Arena for that end of it. He was using it to buy his Baja place. Most of the money actually came from them. I was their bagman. They knew about Goat after his last job. They got his plates at the quarry he did in Gonzales. Arena brass wanted to arrest him, put him in jail, but Tony Armstrong wanted to use him. I was trying to protect him, and get him out of a jam. Wetlands Watch were just supposed to think they hired him. Arena wanted their security to catch him, and then publically invalidate the biologic opinion. Goat was OK with it. Otherwise, he was looking at jail time for the Gonzales offense. He wanted more money and he knew the fix was in, and he expected to get arrested. He got rid of all his dope plants so they couldn't add charges. That was the deal".

Dukie looked up, his face a mask of fatigue and sadness. Everyone in the circle, including Floyd was staring at him in varying degrees of anger, amazement and pain.

"I fucked it all up. Arena hired me to help get them the quarry approval, which I told them had not a snowball's chance in hell. So, they were gonna' arrest Goat. Then, I told Tony we could do a deal, and I got Ed to hire Goat to stop the quarry. It was a front for Arena, and they were supposed to catch him. But he kept getting away. Then, I got Arena to hire Harper to get him some income for water study work, figuring Harper would still make them do the right thing on water. And then I brought Ed down on this trip to get out of town while the whole arrest went down. I didn't think about another vote while we were gone." He looked up helplessly. "They thought they could make you say whatever they wanted on the water, Harper, but I knew you would stick to your guns".

Harper glared back at him, remembering how close he had been to doing exactly what Armstrong wanted. Until Goat got killed.

"Goat figured even with an arrest, he would be out in a month, and then he could afford his Baja place. Armstrong said Arena would even cover his fine and attorney's cost if Goat said nothing. Oh, shit, Goat just wanted that desert cabin. I knew even with no biologic assessment, Harper could do a water study that would stop the quarry cold. Then Wetland Watch would be happy and we could all make some money. Everybody wins. The Big Rock Candy Quarry. And, hell, I needed money to pay off my ranch. My last divorce cleaned me out." Dukie blew out a shuddering breath and stared at his hands, avoiding the ring of eyes glaring at him. Billie had moved over to sit with Floyd in a neutral corner, taking it in.

Tracer was nodding his head slowly. "I get it. I get it, Duke. That would have been a good payoff for Goat. It could have worked. What a play that would have been. Paid once to plant the frogs and paid again to get caught. You know, I might have to kill this Armstrong guy when we go back. "

"No way!" said Billie from the sideline. "Then you would be the one in jail."

Harper spoke. "Don't bother Trace. Armstrong didn't kill Goat. Everyone was just playing their own game. That nasty Oakie quarry boss might have killed him, but he probably didn't know a thing about the plan. They never would have trusted him with it. Meanwhile, we were all chasing the dollars, including me. Goat is just the one who got slammed. And, well, Dukie, thanks for thinking of me with the quarry job, anyway. I guess you were just trying to go big on Arena's money, and bring your friends along."

Ed stood up stiffly and ran his hand through his shock of white hair. "Well, that didn't work out too well, did it Dukie? Now, Goat's dead. And you got me out of the way while they engineered a vote on the Planning Commission to get the damn permit!"

"That was never my idea!" Dukie protested forlornly.

"Nobody is doing a water study, either." Harper added. "It's the final nail. They're not gonna study anything if they get this approval. They just keep pumping rates the same, not change anything, and keep on grading, and run the sand mine for another twenty years as an ongoing operation."

Ed stepped into the center of the circle and looked fiercely around "But you said the vote is not until Friday! I can get two more votes on that commission, easy, as soon as I get to a phone. And I can vote if I get there. We can shut it down. What day is today?"

Everyone looked at everyone. Glances flew around the kitchen and to the flapping tarp roof seeking help. Floyd had been following the story with rare interest. Now he looked around and glanced at his fingers trying to count back. Calendars are notoriously absent on Grand Canyon river trips.

"Um, Sunday?" ventured Tracer.

"No, Tuesday, right? " tried Ed.

"Have we been down here eleven days or twelve?" Dukie said, mostly to himself.

"Wait, our permit was for a Monday launch," said Tracer.

"I've been traveling since Saturday", muttered Harper, counting fingers on his hand.

Billie stepped into the circle and set her coffee down. Her blond braids were wrapped like a helmet around her head and her blue eyes shone wildly.

"It is fucking Tuesday morning, gentlemen, three hours before dawn. Friday is still a lifetime away. We have a dory in the eddy, the Colorado River in flood, Crystal and Lava Falls to face, an illegal Speed Run to finish, Park Service helicopters to avoid, and a Commissioner to deliver. The Grand Canyon speed run record is 37 hours, and I want to beat it by 5 hours. Now, get your thumbs out of your assholes and load up the boats!"

The men looked at her with awe and something like worship. The mood shifted from recrimination to hope. Everyone stood up, except Dukie. He remained slumped guiltily in his chair. There was an awkward pause, and then Tracer and Harper surrounded him. Without a word, they linked arms and squeezed him between them, together with his camp chair, in a mix of punishment and embrace. They squeezed harder, crushing him and each other, pushing inward until the chair folded up and they all fell over into the sand together. Someone was crying there in the pile, but by the time they all stood up and brushed the sand off, their manly composure was regained, they thumped each other on the back, and a sense of purpose was established.

Dukie began to rub his bald head wildly, and look around the kitchen. "Ok, let's load up! Shit, we need another boat. Floyd! We need you, come with us! We need to take your snout boat to follow the dory. Then, if something happens to either boat, we can still get Ed out. Can you keep up with them?"

"Well, sure, we have a motor." Floyd stirred, looking pleased to be joining the party.

"Leave the kitchen, leave the camp, and leave the tents. The other boat can deal with that crap. They've got another week. Grab your sleeping bags and personal gear. I'll go wake up Mount and tell him we're bailing out. He'll be OK with it. Everybody get their poop in a group. Harper, how about you make more coffee, a pile of bacon and a dozen toasted bagels! Ed, show him where the food is. Everyone meet back here pronto. We launch in 10 minutes!"

When you see Crystal, You gonna want a pistol

It is a fair bit of canyon from the Little Colorado River to Crystal Rapid; 36 river miles as the raven flies. But, that distance is in the Inner Gorge, the least accessible part of the Canyon, where the river cuts a narrow V into ancient Vishnu Schist. Mostly, just mountain goat trails reach the river. Major rapids include Hance, Sockdolager, Horn, Granite, and Hermit Creek. Then, Crystal! Most rowing rips take two days to cover the stretch. The dory and snout raft covered it in the three hours of darkness before dawn, ripping along on current and boils and whirlpools. Tracer estimated the river was moving at least 12 knots per hour, and faster where there was a constriction.

Billie was back at the oars on Freyja, with Dukie, Ed, and Floyd purring along behind them on the 20-foot snout raft. Most of the major rapids were underwater. The Picket Fence of large rocks atop Hance Rapid was underwater, making fearsome new holes at the top left. But the normal holes down the right at Hance were washed out, so the boats took a straight line down the river right, rocking away on enormous rhythmic waves.

They raced under the pedestrian bridges before and after Bright Angel Creek as the stars faded and indistinct grey light spread. The sky took on the color of polished steel. Harper thought of the old guitar hanging on the wall up at the Phantom Ranch canteen, up Bright Angel Creek. He nodded in its direction as the dory moved past. Not this trip, old friend. Bright Angel Creek was running high and had cut a new path through the sand beach. It looked like part of the hiking path up to Phantom might be washed out.

They flashed past Horn Creek in a steep drop and a rush of waves, then through Granite, Harper's old nemesis, and on to Hermit Creek. The standing river waves at Hermit Creek are famous as the largest and most symmetrical series of upsie downsie water in Grand Canyon (or North America for that matter). They form a large example of the classic hydraulic laboratory flume converging-diverging wave pattern, and would probably be cited as proof of intelligent design if more religious creeps were hydrologists or rafters. The Fifth Wave was often two stories high at 20,000 cfs, with an exploding, backcurling summit. Everyone wondered what the Hermit waves would look like at this water level.

Tracer and Billie discussed scouting Hermit, but agreed that since, no matter what, the only run was right down the middle, there was no point in stopping. As dawn reached the rim, Billie tied a red bandanna around her flaxen braids, so she looked like a crazed Viking biker chick at the oars. They had fed on hot bacon and toasted bagels before leaving the research camp, and felt uncommonly awake and strong as the day came on. Billie was rowing with confidence, with judgment, and a mad gleam in her eye. The long night of travel down huge water, the excitement and urgency of their mission, the speed and the new conditions at every rapid, all had pulled them into a heightened state of experience. No matter where life took them, they all knew that there would never be another dawn like this.

Harper was looking up at the first slice of sun to hit the canyon rim and trying to remember the Navajo Beauty Way prayer. He turned to Tracer in the forward compartment as dory lined up above Hermit Rapid, speaking quietly.

"What will we do with our lives after this, brother?

Tracer considered the sky, and the slice of new color where sunlight touched the rimrock.

"The art of living my life fully and free, as a creative act I renew each day, is my chosen quest. Don't ever tell anyone I told you that, brother. "

"On a trail of Beauty, lively may I walk.'

"With Beauty before me, happy may I walk" smiled Tracer back.

"With Beauty before me, singing may I walk." Harper slipped into chanting.

"With big humongous waves before me, holding on tightly may I walk!"

The dory entered the chute, and rose up the first wave, and the sequence of the Hermit wave train was lain out before them, a range of ascending downriver liquid peaks.

"Dropping in like a big dog, and holy shit, look at the size of that thing, may I walk!" Harper sang out from the bow.

"Finished in beauty, finished in beauty, it is finished in beauty!"

they chanted together as the dory accelerated down the backside of the wave.

With Billie pushing on both oars and keeping the boat straight, they ran right down the centerline, soaring up and over the tops of the Hermit waves, and blasting a spray field out of the top of each. The dory never hesitated, and never shuddered under an impact as a heavy raft would do. Instead, it dipped and bucked powerfully in the trough, then rode smoothly up, up, up, and sliced cleanly through the tops, the graceful bow dashing a path for the stern to follow through the wave.

Billie cheered a battle cry at each summit, reloaded her arms, corrected the dory slightly between each wave, and pushed hard into the next mountain.

"I love Freyja, and she loves me!" she cried to herself in bliss as they settled into the tail waves. She spun the boat so they could watch the snout boat, which followed the same line with motor on full throttle, and plowed over the giant wave tops they had sliced through. Thick water cascaded back over the snout and over Dukie, Ed and Floyd in the back each time. The motor on the snout skipped and halted after being dunked five times, then caught again and ran smoothly. Both boats swept past Schist Camp and on down towards Crystal Rapid, around the bend.

Lake Crystal

Eddies were scarce on the river, as high water had washed out coves, beaches and backwaters. But the Lake Crystal eddy was huge; a vast spiral with logs circling in it, a backwater above the bend into Crystal Rapid. Two large commercial rafts and a smaller snout raft were tied up at the shore. The snout was a ranger boat, with the National Park Service logo on the bow. Fifty yards back and high on a knoll above Crystal

Creek, a cluster of several figures were visible in morning sun, presumably boatmen making plans for safe passage.

A ranger in green NPS uniform was down on the shore, glassing them with binoculars. He stood on the beach, next to a large fluorescent orange "CLOSED" sign, set on a folding pedestal and facing upstream. It looked like an incongruous prank, something stolen from a Flagstaff road construction site and brought down canyon by rowdy rafters.

"Effective Immediately" said Billie quietly. They exchanged anxious looks as the dory approached the eddy. The snout was just behind them, motoring up and beginning a turn to make the eddy. The dory stopped outside the eddy line, drifting, not yet committed. They could hear the noise of Crystal from around the bend. Every Crystal horror story from the High Water of 1983 came rushing back, including the deaths and wreckage from boats that had been caught in the hole. The pit of their stomachs felt a common icy knot.

"Don't pull in, they'll arrest us" Tracer hissed. "They can have a helicopter here in 40 minutes."

"We have to scout!" Billie said.

"I don't want to see it " said Harper flatly.

Tracer shook his head. "We know it's a giant center hole! Just hit the right side sneak as hard as possible, miss everything, and pray."

As the snout raft pulled up gently alongside and bumped the dory, Floyd cut the engine throttle and went to neutral to talk. Dukie and Ed looked scared and alert, their pfds cinched down and their eyes large. "What next, TL?" said Floyd to Billie. Already, the roar from around the bend was huge. The ranger was waving them in firmly, pointing to shore. Dukie waved back.

"OK, we're gonna scout it" Billie said, pushing the oars forward toward shore. "That's my call. They won't arrest us here. Somebody would have to row the dory out. Anyway, they might arrest me, but they won't arrest Dukie and the Commish."

As she spoke, the snout motor made a funny noise. It sputtered once, and went from idling to dead. Floyd look startled and leapt to the gas tank like a puma. He began pumping the bulb in the fuel line and pulling the starter cord. Nothing. He swore, glanced at the eddy line location, lifted and slammed down the motor, tried it, and then pulled the starter cord on a second mounted outboard. No joy. Floyd grabbed another small red gas tank and hoisted it into place beside the motors. He bent over the motor well and began working on the gas lines quietly and desperately. The snout was still in current. Immediately, the space between the dory and snout widened. The snout drifted away from the dory and from eddy line, as a seam of flowing water took it. The ranger on shore was within hailing distance, but across the huge eddy. He stood watching silently. Now, he pulled a radio from his belt and spoke urgently into it, looking downstream. Everybody on both boats made quick calculations of drift and velocity. The dory was carefully holding just outside of the eddy. Floyd yanked hard on the starter cable again and again and no engine noise came.

"Water in the fuel" he said grimly, and jumped up from the motor well to the steel deck where the spare oars were lashed. The snout was still in flat water, but it was accelerating away, towards the long tongue and the invisible roar.

"Oh, sweet Jesus!" breathed Harper. Billie pulled smoothly on her oars, backpaddling to hold the dory just on the eddy line, but they lost ground, slowly following the snout downstream. The eddy and the beach moved gradually past them, like a choice not taken. It was a dream sequence, inevitable and unstoppable.

Dukie had a rope throw bag in his hands now on the snout deck. He stood transfixed, looking for a target, but saw that he could not reach the ranger on shore. As the snout began to drift towards the bend, he turned and fired it like a quarterback to Tracer, in the bow of the dory. Tracer caught the line in the forward compartment, and took a quick dally with the rope around the handrail in the dory bow. Dukie braced holding the line, as Billie pulled back hard on the dory oars. The line came tight. Instead of bringing the snout back to the eddy or at least swinging it towards shore, the dory nose spun hard downriver towards the snout and was pulled out after it. Tracer released the dally and the rope dropped into the river. It was too loud to talk. The ranger on shore started at a run down the trail towards the scouting rock, shouting into his radio. The river was taking them.

The two boats floated effortlessly around the bend on the beautiful long tongue above Crystal. There was no eddy left. Floyd had freed two oars from their lashings on the high center deck of the snout and was back paddling with them to buy some time. The snout was not really an effective oar boat, and he stopped rowing and stood to look downstream. Ed and Dukie stood looking also, then nodded to Floyd, shook hands solemnly, snuggled in low in front of the rowing station and sought handholds. They were seated behind the snout tubes, one on either side. The dory followed them around the bend, fifty yards behind. Everything was slowed down. There was plenty of time now, vast seconds to look as they floated in. The Crystal Hole at 70,000 cfs was a hypnotic wonder, a hydraulic mystery heightened and laid bare.

It was a monster in the middle of the river. It was perfection in water chaos, an enormous pile, focused, snarling, backwards curling. The demonic hydraulic feature was tall enough to throw a shadow onto the shore in the morning sun. There were steep lateral waves emerging on both sides, stretched from the shorelines to converge into the center hole. All flowlines led to the churning liquid core, where a singularity of gravity and space-time existed in the mountain of force, so dark and strange that it could link to another dimension. It was scary to look at. Floating into it on a silent raft, drunk on the surrounding noise, was surreal.

Floyd pulled like a champion for the right side shore, but he never got there. The cumbersome 20-foot snout raft did not move well without a motor. The lateral waves caught them and carried them straight towards the center. Floyd had a moment to straighten the raft as it met the hole, then they were in it. At first, the motor rig rode up onto the back of huge reversal, and it hung there upright, chattering. The monster toyed with them. The motor raft was dwarfed by the breaking water under and all around it. All the figures were visible, frozen at their places. After an eternity surfing, the raft began to rotate in place, spinning sideways. Then a sickening, inevitable angle developed, and the whole boat was violently slapped over, like a pancake flipped by an angry logging camp cook. Later, Dukie would say he was chanting "Keep it together, keep it together", as they sat there shaking, and he bit his tongue on the last syllable when they flipped. The entire raft disappeared, was glimpsed twenty feet beyond, being folded and mashed, then appeared again downstream in an unidentifiable tangle. There was no sign of swimmers. The raft swept away downstream.

The dory was just upstream, no hope of stopping now, with Billie pulling both oars to slow them and try not to crash into the raft. They accelerated into the chute, bow first, with a ferry angle moving from left to right on the tongue, shooting hard for the right side lateral waves.

The flying dory bow hit the right lateral wave just a few feet from shore, stabbing to miss the hole and reach the shoreline flow moving through trees that normally shaded the scouting point. But the lateral waves were ten feet tall and thick as bank vaults. Instead of breaking through, the dory rose up onto the wave, caught the sideways force with its curving chine lines, and was surfed gracefully down the wave, back to the center. The lateral delivered them right to the churning hole, skating in with increased speed and a great view of what was coming.

Billie cried a Viking scream and turned the dory with one oar to hit it face on. Harper and Tracer clung to their handrail and stared enthralled into the oncoming portal of water wall. There was no hope, realistically, of the dory making it. But as the situation was unprecedented, no one could be sure, and they all felt completely hopeful and truly alive. Together they leapt to their feet in the forward compartment and at the oars as the impact came. The nose went straight up. The force of the reversal struck the bottom of the racing dory as their momentum peaked. Instead of skating or surfing as the snout had done, the dory was shot straight up, launching like a moon shot. It left the river, an air gap opened, the dory trailing spray and soaring for a dozen yards. It was the world's first dory Endo, an enormous aerial move stolen from the playbook of tiny kayaks. The flight took them over the meat of the hole, traveling across clean air for an eternal second. The ranger on shore caught that airborne moment in a photo that became a famous poster, Freyja the Flying Raven, with the dory suspended above Crystal Hole, Billie at the oars, blond braids streaming, and Harper and Tracer buried in spray at the bow.

They landed transom first on the backside of the reversal in an enormous splash, almost dumping the boat on the landing. Tracer and Harper threw themselves down in the front of the boat, high-siding wildly to control the bucking, amazed to be not upside down. The dory dipped and wiggled, and continued hurtling downstream. They all stared at each other in amazement, eyes bulging, and brains struggling to comprehend. A quick glance confirmed all crew were still present and accounted for, so Billie pulled hard left to miss the turbulent Rock Garden water of Lower Crystal, and they started chasing the snout boat wreckage. As they left, the distant figures onshore on top of the scouting knoll could be seen jumping up and down, slapping each other on the back.

They chased the snout a long way, right through Tuna Creek Rapid, past the stripped wreckage of a flipped 35-foot J-rig, deflated rubber like a beached whale on river left. Ed Larson was visible first, swimming in current. They focused on him. He saw them coming after him, patted the top of his head valiantly in the "All Well" signal, and started struggling towards them. They got him alongside after a half a mile. Before they could get him in, violent whirlpools below Tuna Rapid spun the dory and pushed them towards the rocky cliff. Billie stood up in her seat pulling hard on both oars, as Ed went under water next to the boat, then reappeared out of reach. Harper hit him in the head with a throw bag, he grabbed the line, and they began to haul him in. Billie pulled away from the cliff and after the floating raft wreckage. Tracer reached over and got hands on Ed's pfd and hauled him in.

Once Ed was in the dory, they caught the raft. It was a twisted, half-inflated, corpse of a boat, and they got it to shore at Mile

104. Floyd the boatman was clinging gamely to the D-rings, laying on the bottom like a castaway. He was conscious, but non-responsive, remaining prone on the rubber and shivering while they called to him, tied the boat off, and searched the river for signs of Dukie. Floyd stayed stuck like a tick, unable to let go or break the spell of what he had just experienced.

Billie was desperately scanning the river for Dukie from the rowing station while Tracer and Harper tied the raft to shore. Ed had lost his glasses in his swim, and was sitting alertly in the bow, holding the handrail and asking if anyone could see Dukie.

Harper jumped out in shallow water holding the raft bow line. There was a muted sound of familiar steady profanity, mixed with the background river noise, but he could not locate the source. He was still dazed from the run, and he shook his head to stop the sound, staggering a step in the eddy. He noticed a pink cloud of blood in the water beside the raft. He checked his nose with his hand for blood, and bent down closer, puzzled.

"Am I hurt? The raft is bleeding. " he said quizzically to Tracer.

From underneath the rubber floor of the flipped raft, the buzzing became a louder disembodied voice; "Not the fucking raft, you numb nuts! My face is bleeding!"

Everyone stared at the raft and broke into a broad grin. Harper leaned down addressed the raft floor.

"Professor Gerhart, I presume?"

"Get me out of here! I'm caught in a strap and can't move!"

That brought Floyd back to them. His post-traumatic shock was ended by a problem involving his client and his boat. Floyd sat up on the raft tube, looked around in wonder, called down reassuringly to Dukie, and found a sharp knife in his pfd. On his knees atop the flipped boat, he probed, then carefully cut a slice through the rubber raft floor near the voice. Dukie's head emerged from the slice, like the birth of Caesar. His mouth was a mask of blood, which made his cheerful smile ghastly with red teeth. He lay in a tangle of webbing, his head wedged in a large air pocket between the raft snout tubes and frame. In the thrashing flip, his life jacket webbing had slid into a normally non-existent space between the frame and tubes and been firmly clamped. He had been carried in the airspace under the raft all the way downriver. Floyd reached in and cut the strap that was pinned, freeing him. As they surrounded the raft, professing amazement and asking medical questions, Dukie wriggled free, forced his head and shoulders through the cut in the raft floor, and flopped out. He stood dripping water and spitting blood, grinning at them all. The blood was from a bite wound in his tongue and mouth. Although he had ridden far trapped in the dark under the raft floor, he was otherwise unhurt. He looked around at the raft wreckage, the pleasant sunlight just clearing the rim, the giant river and he grinned bigger. He seemed very pleased with himself, as if the whole thing was wonderful and proof of their good judgment.

"Oh, yes, By God, it is the right thing we are doing!" He lisped. "Hey, Ed, don't you just love this? I told you to hold on!"

"You crazy fucker. I forgive you for everything." Harper said in amazement and led him to the side of the dory. They helped him up onto the dory and Floyd gave him a quick professional medical evaluation. Other than his bloody mouth, he was intact.

"We didn't get to see your run, Billie! How did you do back there?" he grinned his bloody teeth at her and waved upstream.

Billie fluttered her hands together like doves, smiled beatifically and said nothing. The sun was just hitting the river, and the warmth of the rays were filling her. Everyone was accounted for and OK. She closed her eyes, to see again the sight of the dory going into and then over the Crystal Hole. Freyja had flown, and she was reluctant to think of anything else yet.

"Maybe its better we didn't scout, eh?" Tracer suggested to Billie. She opened her eyes at his grinning, tired face, and sweetly gave him the finger from her place at the oars.

Floyd shook his head slowly, looking at the wreckage of his boat. His laconic, accepting style was already coming back. "Well, if a motor failure can happen at a bad time, that's when, I guess. We must have got water in the gas when we got doused at Hermit. The spare tank was no good either".

Tracer contemplated the dead raft and offered some professional consolation.

"Well, you got the oars out and made a run of it anyway, Floyd. And with a pack of guides and rangers as witnesses. That surf session and flip will live in infamy. Floyd's Big Dance at Crystal. "

"Speaking of which, um, we better get going," said Billie looking upstream. "They could still try to stop us."

Everyone looked upstream, as if expecting storm troopers. There were only rocks, and the Colorado River flowing huge, but they felt the unseen presence of authorities.

Floyd nodded. "Guess I'll stay here with this boat and do some salvage. I can slow down any pursuit boats when they check on me. The other research raft will come down in a few days, if the water drops. We can take the frame and engines down in their boat. Probably can roll up the rubber and patch the tubes later. Hey, I'm gonna make that cut in the floor raft famous, Dr. Dukie. We'll draw some pussy lips and pubic hair around it, and paint your face there at the seam. The River Re-Birth of Dr. Dukie."

Harper was already climbing back in the dory. Dukie saluted

Floyd and shook his hand.

"Sir, it has always been my wish to have a raft vagina named after me. I feel like I spent nine months in there, too. I am reborn, a new man. Thank you for everything, Floyd. When this is over, I will return to Flagstaff, and we will have a beer or twelve, and tell our story."

"Sorry we can't stay to help you de-rig the boat, pard" Harper called with a wave. "The secret to a long life is knowing when its time to go." Tracer shook hands with Floyd and climbed on the dory.

"God, I love working these research trips." Floyd said with a grin looking at the deflated tangle at his feet. "Such easy days. Y'all go stop that stinkin' dam now or whatever it is. See you downstream some time."

They left him standing on top of his wrecked boat in the eddy holding his river knife, waving as the dory pulled into the current. Billie stayed at the oars, with Tracer and Harper up front. Dukie was seated with the Comish in the rear passenger compartment. Dukie pulled on a spare pfd from one of the dory's watertight compartments, and called out to Billie in his lisp.

"Got any beer on this boat? How about snacks? Hey, can I row Lava?"

"Sit down, shut up, and hold on!" she said firmly. "We got a speed run to finish. Somebody treat Dukie for shock. And sew his mouth shut. He's delirious."

Lava Falls for Breakfast

The dory crew pulled over at National Canyon that night, too tired to continue. Lava Falls was just downstream, but Billie was dropping the oars carelessly into the water for each stroke, arms spent. They were 166 miles below Lee's Ferry. The sun was below the rim, the air was cooling and the night was coming on. They had made roughly 105 river miles since leaving the Little Colorado before dawn that day. They had been on the river for 20 hours since Lee's Ferry, with only two stops, at the Little Colorado research camp and to cut Dukie out of the flipped raft below Crystal. Park Service helicopters had buzzed them twice since Crystal, flying low along the river corridor. They felt exhausted from facing the constant threats of high water and unexpected conditions, and they resented the unseen pressure of an angry Park Service administration laying in wait downstream. They were cranky. Ed was almost blind without his glasses, Duke's mouth was too swollen to talk (finally), and Harper, Billie and Tracer had the thousand-yard stare of zombies. They staked the dory to shore, made mugs of tea, ate meat and cheese sandwiches, and laid down in a row to sleep on the sand in their bags.

They lay there exhausted, looking up at the first bright stars overhead. The weather was turning clear and fine. Billie was sore from rowing and busy calculating the remaining miles to the Diamond Creek take-out (60), Ed was worrying about rounding up other Planning Commissioners to vote against the sand quarry, Harper was wondering what happened to his truck, and what the fines would be. Tracer felt bad about leaving Floyd alone with a wrecked boat. Dukie was snoring softly.

Everyone left awake was sinking into a deep lonesome funk, when Billie started to hum a lullaby. Starting quietly and building, she sang,

"Oh, your sweet and shining eyes, are like the stars above Laredo.

Like meat and potatoes ...to meeeee!"

Everyone smiled involuntarily and nestled a bit deeper in their bags. She took a breath and paused, and several male voices joined her for the next line.

"In my sweet dreams we are...in a bar, and it's my birthday.

We're drinking salty margaritas with Fernando! "

Billie carried on, sang the other verse, and they all repeated the chorus. They held the last O of Fernando like coyotes, and finished with soft giggling. Everyone drifted off into the profound sleep of the honestly exhausted.

Billie woke them all after five hours sleep, and they were back on the river again before first light. They were 60 miles from the take out, moving fast under starlight and a descending moon, with Lava Falls and the wider miles of the lower canyon to go. Billie had wanted to set a resounding new record of 30 hours. They were at 25 hours and counting. But, Lava Falls was waiting just downstream, and old patterns of fear and respect for that place left every outcome still possible. Tracer had convinced the trip leader that running Lava Falls at night, at record water, with a dory full of passengers and no chase boats, was a foolish move. They were going to scout it and run it at first light.

They passed Vulcan's Anvil with the glow of dawn showing along the rim, stars beginning to fade. It would be a perfect day. The air was sweet and scented with sage after a week of rain. All their habits of Lava Falls superstition, their personal histories with the place, and the big water anxiety swirled around with them. They pulled the dory over way above Prospect Canyon, river left. The Prospect Canyon beach, like all others, was underwater. They made the short hike down to scout Lava Falls with their headlamps on, and stood on boulders peering at the river. It was almost too dark to know. It looked OK, but totally different. The central ledge hole, the V-waves, the black rock, all the standard Lava landmarks were gone, buried under water, erased into a beautiful central tongue and a series of huge converging waves. Fighting their disbelief that it was possible, even wise, to do a center run at Lava Falls, they waited for a little more light.

It became lighter by imperceptible degrees, until Billie realized they were seeing all they were going to see. They switched their headlamps off, and marched back to the dory. Everyone took a final pee to release internal tension, and they loaded up. Nostrils flared, faces set and eyes bright, they said little. With Billie at the oars and Tracer coiling the bowline, they pushed off, spun the bow downstream, and faced their fate.

Everyone on board felt wrong floating in on the centerline at Lava Falls. All their experience said that certain destruction in the Ledge Hole would be the result. Instead, the dory made a glorious accelerating drop over the lip, down the center on a ribbon of fast water, an exhilarating break through the waiting waves, and a racing turn with Billie pulling away from the cliff on the left below. It seems impossible that so much water can move so fast, drop so far, and be so beautiful without becoming destructive. But they were past it in a flash, and racing down the miles below Lava before it registered that they were almost done. Ed let out a whoop from the stern, cheering his first time through Lava Falls, wishing that he could have seen it better.

They had a floating breakfast of meat and cheese sandwiches with Oreos, laughing with black cookie teeth and talking about old trips through Lava Falls, about flips, swims, and trips down there with Goat. Harper was telling about the time he started celebrating too early and got a raft stuck in flatwater on the rocks 200 yards below Lava, before he even got to Tequila Beach. Suddenly a black helicopter appeared from upstream, moving two hundred feet above the river, roaring down the river corridor, then banking around a turn and disappearing downstream. They fell silent, realizing the take out would probably be a well-attended affair. Some classic end-of-trip melancholy seeped into their mood, as amplified as every other aspect of the Speed Run had been. They were tired and almost out of food, and all realized, there was no stopping now. They might be Always Above Lava, but this time they were in hot water, too.

30

Takeouts are a Bummer

The unmistakable shape of Diamond Peak stabbing up from river left signaled the end. Diamond Creek take-out, mile 225. The Diamond Creek road descends the creek bed here through the Hualapai Indian Reservation to reach the Colorado River, giving river runners a way out without having to motor or be towed across Lake Mead.

When no river trip is there, the ramp at Diamond Creek can be a forlorn little piece of third-world concrete, somehow washed up at the Colorado River. There is a cluster of sun-faded wind shelters, a few horror show Porta-Pottys, perhaps a couple of lazy reservation dogs, and a discarded disposable diaper alongside the ramp from some family outing down to the river.

But today, there were two patrol cars (a white Hualapai Nation

Police Services and a green National Park Service cruiser), a black van with an empty trailer, and a cluster of somber uniformed men standing on the ramp. A government helicopter sat at rest in the sun on a terrace above the river, complicated and gleaming like a giant insect.

"Jeez, I feel like a criminal."

"That is because you are one, Harper."

"We could cruise on by and go on down to Grand Wash Cliffs. Row across the reservoir and slip away over the flats at night. Or hike out at Separation Canyon and disappear mysteriously, like the Howland brothers and William Dunn on the first Powell expedition?"

"Nope. We got the dory to consider. This is it. And hopefully that whirlybird is gonna' be Ed's ride back to stop the quarry."

"But this is Escape from Grand Canyon, the outlaw movie! It can't end with us in custody."

"They can put my body in prison, but not my mind".

"When rivers are outlawed, only outlaws will run rivers."

"Look, I think that is Goat's old trailer behind the van. No registration. Now that is illegal of them, to drive that here."

"Hey, isn't that Harshie?"

It was Ranger Harshberger. He stood apart from the other authority figures, waiting in the sun on the ramp as Billie pulled hard to make the eddy. The dory came in fast and spun as it crossed the eddy line, then came to a halt just off the ramp, responsive as a quarter horse to the end. Tracer and Harper splashed off from the bow compartment and held the boat as Billie shipped the oars. She climbed down and walked proudly up the ramp to the waiting Ranger Harshberger. The others hung back uncertainly. She was as tall as the ranger, proud as an Indian princess, and she did not hesitate with formalities, but immediately gave him a full bear hug, squeezing him tight like a comrade. She buried a sunburned nose against his uniform, squeezed even more irresistibly, and spoke gently into his neck.

"Sorry for burning you at Lee's, Harshie. We had to go. We were on a mission".

Ranger Harshberger stood stiffly at first, aware of the eyes of his superior officers on him, but he relaxed into her hug after a moment, and finally patted her back.

"I know, I know. I'm glad you're OK, Billie. I got your time. You're all under arrest." he said kindly. "I heard about your run at Crystal. Sorry I missed it. How was your trip?"

Billie paused and released the hug. "Unforgettable." She breathed out and stepped back. "Fantastic".

"Congratulations' he said quietly.

She nodded, said nothing, stood beside him as if receiving a medal. She gave a shy wave to the crowd of uniforms waiting in the sun.

"What's our time? " She said, offhand, still eye to eye with the Ranger.

He checked his watch. "31 hours, 45 minutes. Fifty seconds. That's good. The record is 37 hours, of course, but the 1983 crew went all the way to the Grand Wash Cliffs for a full run. Your trip ends here. " He paused and looked at the dory. "And you stopped for hitchhikers?"

Billie sighed. "We don't want to take their record away. We are the record in a new category, Lee's to Diamond. 31 hours, 46 minutes is our time. Let someone beat it if they can. " A pause. "And we could have made it to Temple Bar in under five hours, easy." She glanced back at the dory. "Oh, yeah, we got two passengers from a wrecked raft below Crystal. They never rowed on the trip, so they are not a Factor in the record. No pun intended."

Harper and Tracer were coming up the ramp slowly now, eyes down and feet dragging like truant schoolboys. "Hello, Ranger Harshberger," they said, dragging out each syllable together in doomed voices.

The Ranger nodded curtly and spoke in his official voice, loud enough for the waiting crowd of officialdom to hear. "Fellas. You are both under arrest. You too, Billie. I will allow you to load up the boat on the trailer and get into the van yourselves, but I'm taking you all into custody. You're going to the South Rim office for processing and detention".

"Yes, sir, Ranger Harshberger" they said together, wearily and turned to trudge back down to the dory.

"Well, that went pretty good, considering.' muttered Harper.

"I hate take-outs." said Tracer.

Dukie charged past them, marching up towards the officers like General MacArthur coming ashore at Manila. His rooster walk was full of purpose, his bald head was gleaming, and he thrust out his hand energetically.

"Hello, Officer!" he boomed to the surprised Ranger in a voice roughly loud enough to be heard at the rim. "I'm Professor Werner Gerhart, Earth Sciences Department, University of California, Emeritus. " He pumped the tentative hand of Ranger Harshberger and did not release it. "I just want to tell you, these marvelous young people saved our lives!" A sweeping arm gesture. His swollen tongue still gave every word a slight lisp. A hint of blood was visible on his bite-wounded mouth when he spoke. He resembled a sunburned Elmer Fudd doing an inspirational speech after getting a beating.

"They saved me and my colleague, Dr. Edward Larson down there. We're with the Grand Canyon Monitoring and Research

Program. We were working at the Little Colorado research station. (Dukie gestured to Ed, now looking quite elderly and blind as Harper helped him down from the dory).

"They deserve a commendation, I tell you," he repeated cheerfully in his triumphant deafening Fudd voice. He discreetly turned and spit out a little blood. " Yes, they charged into Crystal Rapid after us, when our motor failed. They ran the hole! I didn't see it, I was trapped under the raft at the time, but they saved us both, and our boatman and raft as well. God, you should see Crystal now, Ranger. It's enormous!" Ranger Harshberger opened his mouth to explain that he had seen Crystal from the helicopter, that very morning in fact, but Dukie was on a roll and cut him off before could speak. Dukie began to describe the wreck, and was soon waving both arms. Tracer looked over from unloading the water tight compartments on the dory and tossing bags down to Harper, both of them fighting back grins.

"You come back here, you kwazie wabbit" whispered Tracer under his breath.

"Maybe they'll release us if we promise to keep Dukie away from them" Harper replied, giggling.

Now Dukie was advancing up the ramp on the main body of officialdom, a bantamweight tide of personality. He burst among them in a friendly whirl, shaking hands indiscriminately, mispronouncing names off their metal nameplates, effusing about the power and the glory of the Grand Canyon, the wonder of the river, and going on again about the miraculous rescue at Crystal. Smiles gradually spread among the serious faces, against their will. He complemented the Hualapai Tribal officer on the state of his ramp, on his patrol truck, and on the Diamond Creek road, finally working his way over to greet the helicopter pilots standing in the sparse shade, grinning at the whole performance.

"I tell you, I'm going to make sure everyone at the Park Service knows of their brave actions!" he assured the pilots, waving back towards the ramp. "A fine example of swift action, a great human interest story. Say, fellas, we're kinda stranded here, Dr. Larson and myself. Is there room in that helicopter for two old professors?" Harper and Tracer couldn't contain a giggle at that point, and both hid it by swallowing, hawking and spitting as innocently as possible.

Fifteen minutes later, Ranger Harshberger backed the van and trailer down the ramp and the dory was loaded and lashed in place. There was a quick group hug among the boat crew on the ramp, and promises to meet up at the Planning Commission meeting in Santa Cruz in two days, "Si Dios Quiere".

Harper, Tracer and Billie were led into the van, while Dukie and Ed were escorted up to the helicopter with the Park Service senior officers. Ranger Harshberger had produced three sets of handcuffs, but with a glance toward Dukie, declined to use them on his van passengers. Instead, they all seat belted themselves in and started the rattling drive up Diamond Creek, with Freyja the dory sitting proudly on the trailer behind them. Billie opened the provisions bag, and the prisoners shared leftover cookies with the Ranger. The van followed the patrol cars up the Diamond Creek Road in morning sun, driving in the creek and on the gravel bars. They talked with subdued exhaustion and shared professional interest about the high water. About Crystal now, versus Crystal 1983, about Lava Falls, what about Granite Narrows, and about the Peace that Passes All Understanding that sometimes comes over one the river. When the helicopter clattered off into the distance, the dory crew followed it with their eyes until it went out of sight over the rim.

31

One Man, One Vote

"Quiet! Quiet down, please!" Up on the dais, the short, portly Chairman of the Santa Cruz County Planning Commission banged the gavel. His face was red, and veins stood out in his forehead.

It was the Santa Cruz County Planning Commission monthly meeting, Friday afternoon, on the top floor of Santa Cruz County Building. The graceless room was concrete walled, industrial-carpet covered, and currently a sea of noise. The crowded hearing room swirled with cheers, comments, angry side conversations, and gradually fading waves of applause. Commissioners up and down the row had their hands covering the microphones in front of them as primitive mutes, and were talking animatedly to one another. Ed Larson sat behind his nameplate in the middle of the row of Commissioners, quietly beaming out at the audience. The Commission had just voted 5 to 1, with the Chairman abstaining, to require a full Environmental Impact Report prior to any renewal of the County permit for sand mining at the Arena Corporation Lagunitas Sand Quarry. They had named the County Planning Commission as Lead Agency, and had voted to notify the State Coastal Commission and a dozen other agencies of a Coordinated Review Period to determine the scope and thresholds of significance for the mandatory EIR.

The drab meeting room was packed. There had been a parade of lawyers, Arena Corporation representatives, (including Gary Covington, the new Quarry Manager, nervously reading statistics of proposed mining operation in his suit and tie), community groups, outraged Wetlands Watch members, and even the State Representative, an outgunned San Jose Republican pleading respect for property rights and an end to burdensome government regulation. Standing in the back of the room, there were 15 people dressed as steelhead, wearing cardboard fin hats, swaying back and forth together and singing "We Shall Swim Upstream". A small knot of middle-aged men and women carried surfboards and signs reading "No Private Waves" and "Give us Access to Our Ocean" were celebrating. A smaller, disheveled, angrier group from up in the Santa Cruz Mountains had been ejected before the vote for chanting "No Blood For Sand" and "Arena Kills for Money". Those were Goat's friends from Lompico and Boulder Creek.

The silver-haired attorney for Arena Corporation emerged from a huddle in the front row and stood at the microphone. He was seething, but spoke soothingly to the Commissioners. He had realized early on in the meeting that the unexpected return of Ed Larson for the vote, combined with hard and effective lobbying for more votes by Ed behind the scenes, had probably doomed Arena's chances for a permit renewal today. To make it more galling, he had to sit through a series of forceful technical statements on wetlands degradation, aquifer interconnection with the coastal stream, and potential occurrence of steelhead, red-legged frogs, tidewater gobies, and snowy plovers read by the Wetlands Watch. Then, some eager conspiracy nuts and gadflies made unsubstantiated murder charges related to the death of a trespasser at the quarry. Finally, the local TV news had captured the appearance of dozens of vocal protestors, including the Fishheads, to put the final nail in the coffin of his scripted outcome, ensuring more cost, delay and trouble ahead.

But, this was not his first environmental rodeo. The attorney smoothed his tie and assured the Commissioners that Arena Corporation was committed to responsible development, and in fact had already conducted preliminary studies on the potential for interconnection between the aquifer and the stream, and how to shield existing habitat from damage. He mentioned potential development of a deeper well that would not impact the surface water, and careful biological mapping and monitoring of any species of special concern. A preliminary hearing was scheduled for two months later, when Arena's technical experts would present a scope of work for the environmental review. The quarry agreed to study a plan for public coastal access, but refused to allow any trespassers yet, due to potential harm to sensitive habitats. And of course, Arena Corporation would reserve the right to review the implications of the Commission's decision and could still appeal for judicial relief within 30 days. Blah, blah, blah.

As the mood shifted from celebration, to legalistic accommodation and bureaucratic wrangling, the energy faded from the crowd. They knew they had won for now, and they began to file out in droves. The steelhead hat people and the surfers migrated up the street to the Wandering Poet Pub for a pint and a rare celebration of sticking it to the corporate machine. The die-hard environmental activists and Mom and Pop public attendees left politely as soon as the discussion closed, helping each other with their coats and with the door, then stood outside swapping emails and organizing strategies for the next step.

Finally, the Chairman gaveled the meeting closed and the commissioners left the stage, as the phalanx of Arena Corporation flunkies, attorneys and hirelings filed out the door. Tony Armstrong, impeccable in a tan suit, excused himself from the group and walked back to a small group in the last aisle.

Harper and Dukie sat side by side in folding chairs, flanked by their gals, Shira and Colleen. Harper had arrived only hours before, after being processed, held overnight, and released from custody by the National Park Service. He was wearing his Kiwi fishhook necklace and was holding hands with Shira. Dukie had received three neat stitches in his mouth and had a white bandage on his cheek. They looked up as Tony approached. They waited for him to speak, their faces formal. Tony did not offer his hand, but nodded to them both. He seemed sheepish, but determined. He glanced at both Shira and Colleen, automatically scanning their figures approvingly, then clasped his hands behind his back, and rocked on his heels.

"I never got to tell you how sorry we are, or I am rather, about the death of your friend. A tragic outcome."

Harper and Dukie both nodded. "You are right." Harper said levelly. Dukie growled low in his throat, and Colleen put a warning arm through his.

"I had nothing to do with it, I assure you." Tony said earnestly, glancing towards the door where the Arena gang had departed, then giving a searching glance at both Harper and Dukie. "You know that jackass Hitch. He has not made any statement of course, and Arena is providing him with legal counsel. Now that he has had a seizure and stroke while in custody, why, he may never even be charged, but, well, I wanted you to know. Play hard, but play fair and all that. "

Harper nodded quietly. "I know Tony. No hard feelings". Dukie said nothing, but he nodded, too.

Ed Larson joined them, waking quietly up behind Tony on the carpeted aisle. He poked Tony in the ribs and made him start.

"Almost pulled it off, didn't you Armstrong?"

Tony shifted uncomfortably and turned to address him. "Ah, Commissioner! Good work today, great outcome for you and your supporters. Sorry you had to cut your vacation short. No doubt you created a wealth of more work for our consultants, and increased the price of sand by a dollar a ton as well. Of course, we will do the studies and we will drill the new well, and in six months we will again mine the sand. And we still own the land, so we can't really lose. With all the Internet stocks suddenly tanking, California real estate is the last best investment, what?'

Tony glanced at Harper and Dukie. "I'm sorry that you two won't be getting any assignments from this new work. Corporate office directive. Too much conflict of interest. Your friendship with this Goat fellow, who was running an illegal business stopping developments at all costs. Sorry about that, actually. Enjoyed discussing the project with you both. "

Dukie smiled a fierce grin and spoke through his bandage. "Fuck you very much, Armstrong. We don't need your work. And we'll see you at the next hearing, too. You don't have any permit yet. I think that quarry parcel would make a great addition to the State Park next door. We're working pro bono for Wetlands Watch. Actually, I've been thinking of writing a book about this all. Something fun, about the sleaze balls I have met in California development projects."

Tony smiled back at Dukie, shameless and blameless, a gap-toothed tiger. "Good luck with that writing project, Professor Gerhart. Onward and upward. Let me know if you need any quotes." He turned his smile to Harper. It seemed remarkably genuine. Harper was still holding hands with Shira. He released one to shake with Tony.

"Thank you, Tony. You actually helped me a lot. May you live in interesting times".

"Ouch!' Tony took that one on the chin. He released Harper's hand, and left, soundless on the industrial carpet. They watched the door close behind him.

"I'll give him an onward and upward" Dukie muttered as Colleen nuzzled him. Shira grinned, hugged Harper, and kissed his cheek.

"C'mon, my river renegades! Let's all go to the Poet and have a pint for Goat! You guys did it! You won!" With one arm, she drew Ed Larson into the hug, and pulled Harper closer with the other.

"And I'm blackballed from getting a Grand Canyon permit for five years, and waiting to find out what my fine is, and I'll never work for a big developer in this county again" said Harper glumly.

"Even more reason to celebrate!" said Shira, squeezing him and shaking. He could not resist grinning back a little. Shira was a lot of fun to be near when she was celebrating.

Dukie and Colleen joined the hugging. "I wish Billie and

Tracer were here" said Dukie, hiding a sniffle and a tear.

"At least the Park Service agreed to release the dory, and didn't revoke their guide licenses," said Colleen. "Those two are heroes on the river. Tracer told me Billie is already getting a job offer to row dory trips on the Green River next season."

"Tell me more about the Speed Run!" demanded Shira. "I don't understand, what did you get arrested for anyway?"

They all started talking at once. Arm in arm, they moved towards the door, a wounded, elated and merry band of five musketeers. Squeezed between Shira and Colleen, riding down the elevator, Harper realized he was happy. Nothing lives long but the earth and sky. But this was a good day. A geologist knows that nothing is forever, not even the Grand Canyon. For now, this was enough. Dayenu, as the old Hebrew river guides would say. They marched out the door of the County Building and turned as one towards the pub, with Ed and Dukie both trying to describe for Shira and Colleen just what the hole at Crystal had looked like.

32

Love in the Gunks

Harper and Shira sat outside gazing across pond, woods and open fields to a line of imposing white cliffs. The cliffs were the south end of the Shawangunks, the Gunks, the best rock climbing destination in the Northeast. There were in their new backyard, up the river, deep in the Hudson River watershed. Watching Catskill sunsets was their new twilight ritual for the last several months, since they had moved to New York together. The sun was dropping behind the cliff, ending the first week of November. Colors were peaking, and some bare trees had appeared. They had on colorful wool sweaters and long johns under their jeans. Harper's fingertips were getting cold as he idly picked a bluegrass tune on his guitar. The upstate air had a hint of coming winter, fulgent with notes of fallen leaves, apples, and wood smoke. The intangible sadness of autumn was present, carrying memories of a thousand cycles of seasons, of winter descending and the coming rebirth, of spinning around the old sun again.

"Should I pour you some wine, sweetheart?"

"Silly, I'm not drinking, remember?"

Shira put down a newspaper article about the coming election between Gore and Bush Junior. Out in California, internet businesses were closing fast, as stock values on dot-com companies plummeted back to earth. She let the newspaper drop and watched the sunset color grow. Her belly just hinted the start of her baby, three months now into pregnancy. Harper sat contented, watching a line of geese high against the cliff moving south and honking. The sound was loud and chatty, more a busload of gossipy tourists than a high lonesome lament.

"Those geese remind me of your Jewish aunts.' Harper mused.

"Jewish aunts is redundant, darling. All aunts are Jewish in my tribe. That reminds me, we have a bar mitzvah in Westchester next weekend. I will brief you on the family names again".

"Hmm, yes, please do." Harper filled his glass with wine and played a Beatles tune intro. "Will this be an ice sculpture bar mitzvah?"

"No, this one should be very tasteful. Lots of cute Jewish moms."

"Hmmm, very good. I can't wait. Shira, did you read the e-mail from Dukie?"

"Yes, can you believe it? After they found frogs up and down the coast? The State is going to buy the quarry and add it to the State Park System? A wetland reserve, no less. And a new surfing beach access? It's like a hippie dream."

"It is amazing. I can't wait to tell Tracer. I think he and Billie are down in Baja until spring. Of course, it will be a huge tax write-off for Arena. But still, Goat would be proud. The work Dukie did on faulting and seismicity up there was a big blow to the residential idea. No three hundred homes and a golf course this time. A victory for the surfers. And the frogs."

"Did Dukie ever start his book?"

No, he's too busy again with expert witness work."

Shira came over and sat on the arm of Harper's chair. He put the guitar down and rubbed the bump on her belly lovingly.

"You know, I gotta get back on the waiting list for a Grand Canyon private permit. This little guy will be ready for his first river trip in five years when my penalty restrictions run out. You happy?"

"So happy. Maybe you should write the book, honey. The Good Guys win one. You have some time before teaching your class, now that rock climbing season is ending."

"Well, I don't know. I'm kinda' busy, as a country squire with a wife and a baby on the way. Still settling in at the University and I have to make my lesson plans. Bow hunting season for deer starts soon, and I need to put up a tree stand behind the orchard. Gotta' get some firewood in before the snow. We're gonna' be snuggled up by the stove together all winter. And, there's a bluegrass jam in Kerhonkson I wanted to go to. I was thinking of starting a little string band. But, still, I guess I could outline a story. I could change the names around. Make it a cautionary tale. What should I call it?"

He paused and looked up her. They both smiled and spoke in unison.

"Always Above Lava!"

Photo Gallery

This is why Old Kayakers have tendonitis. *by Scott Knies*

Double Happiness Grease Bomb *by Scott Knies*

Stripes *by Scott Knies*

Bill Hayes Rows Lava with 3 stitches in his head 1995 by Scott Knies

Advanced Kayaking by Scott Knies

It takes a Village: below Upset Rapid, 1995 *by Scott Knies*

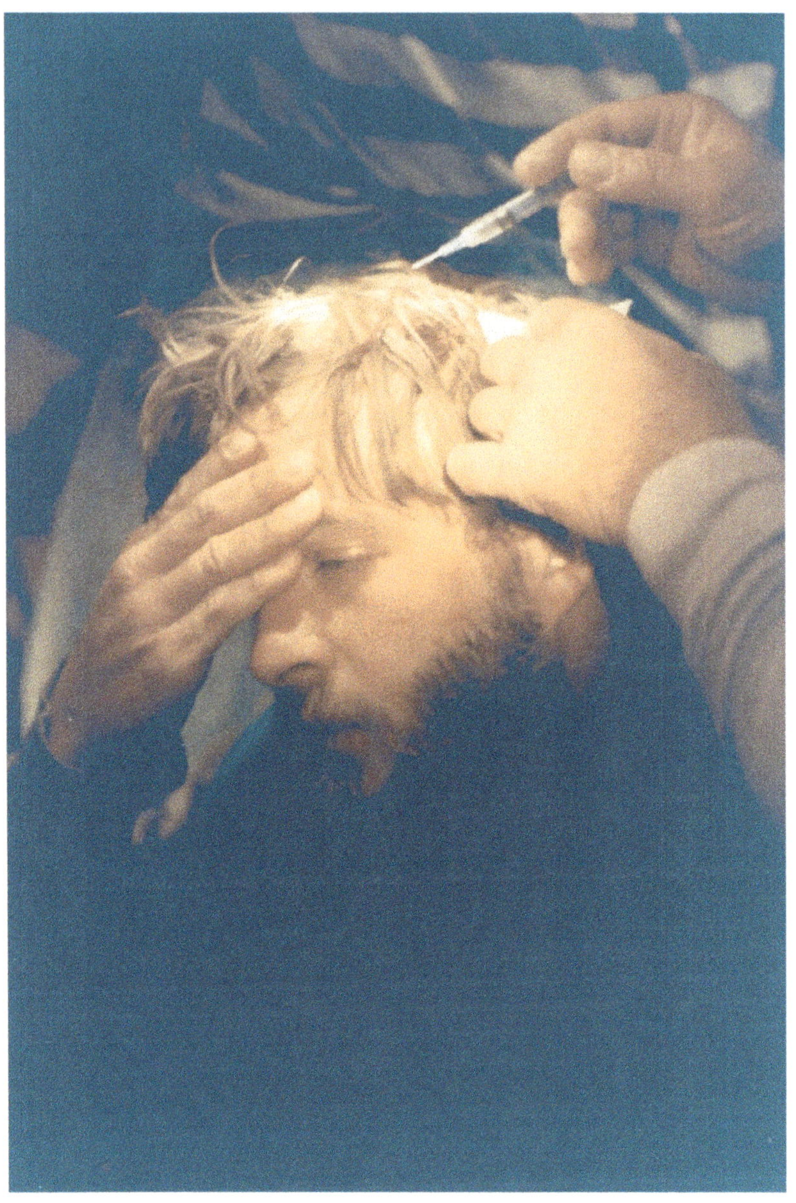

Dr. Joe to Surgery Training: Sutures at Ledges Camp *by Scott Knies*

Sutures and Budweiser, after Upset Flip *by Scott Knies*

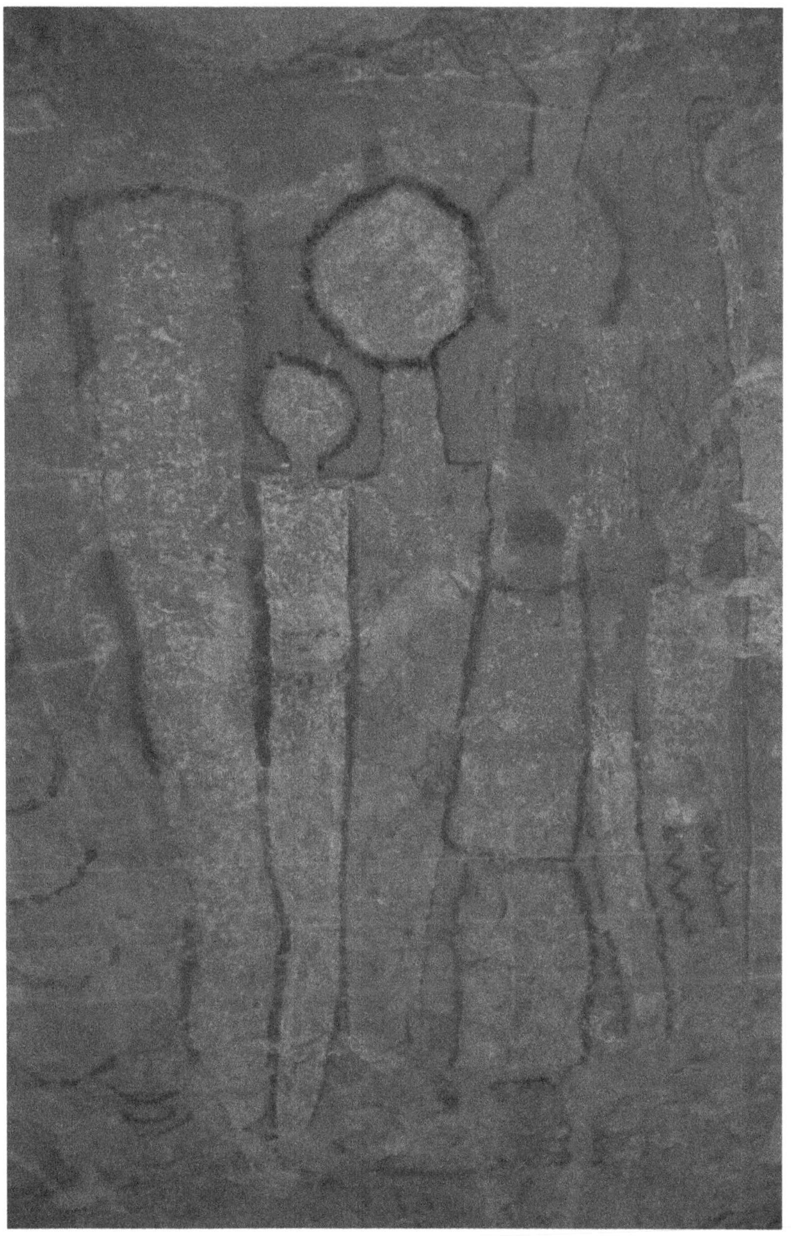

Shaman Vision by Scott Knies

High Water Hermit Wave by Dr. Gerald Weber

Big Hearted River Camp by Benjamin Hayes

I got Sunshine, and a Dry Suit; J Becker January 2016 *by Joe Hayes*

Marble Canyon Morning *by Miklos Benedek*

The Doryman Rows *by Paul Stevens*

Pretty Good Grease *by Miklos Benedek*

The Kitchen Eddy Band *by Scott Knies*

Dory in Hance Rapid, with Harper Kehn *by Miklos Benedek*

Blacktail Guitar *by Miklos Benedek*

Dr. Driftwood surfs Lava Falls *by Miklos Benedek*

Good Vibrations People, Day 18 *by Scott Knies*

Nooshie at the Patio *by Scott Knies*

Hance Guitar by Miklos Benedek

How Many Days? We live down here.

More Photo Gallery

Deer Creek Magic *by Joe Hayes*

Loneliest Phone in the West, Lee's Ferry, 1995 *by Joe Hayes*

Dr. Driftwood adds more Vodka *by Miklos Benedek*

The Safe Run, or the Sporty Run? *by Miklos Benedek*

First Cast of the Day *by Joe Hayes*

Tony Warman, the British Tiger. RIP. And, thanks for all the consulting jobs! by Joe Hayes

Visualize Positive Outcomes *by Scott Knies*

Chert Flakes at shady overhang *found by Joe Hayes*

He might still be there: Dr. Driftwood at peace in the Inner Gorge by Joe Hayes

Father and Sons by Benjamin Hayes

Eva, on a morning trail of Beauty by Joe Hayes

Peace that Passes all Understanding by Joe Hayes

Double Rainbow at Tapeats, Winter Trip 2000 *by Scott Knies*

Mike Hayes ascends to Upper Olo terrace. *by Scott Knies*

Johnny Colorado knows why it is called Tequila Beach. *by Scott Knies*

Ledges Camp Tie-Up *by Joe Hayes*

Dory Glory *by Miklos Benedek*

Diamond Peak at Dawn *by Joe Hayes*

Hooray for the Layover Day by Miklos Benedek

The End

316

About the Author

Joe Hayes is a recovering kayaker and California groundwater consultant, who is proud to have coffee hidden in ammo cans in various undisclosed Grand Canyon locations. This is his first novel. He lives "up the river" in NY, on his home river, the Mighty Hudson. He can be found there varnishing and sailing aboard Freyja, the 1964 Alden yawl that is his beloved, demanding, wind machine and work of art. A seven word biography is enough:

East Coast,
  then West,
  then East again.